Also by James Randall Chumbley

In the Arms of Adam: a diary of men (1997)

Before The Last Dance

Before The Last Dance

James Randall Chumbley

Lighted Tree Press / Atlanta

Lighted Tree Press
LightedTreePress@aol.com

Copyright © 2004 by James Randall Chumbley
All rights reserved

Library of Congress

ISBN 0-9767713-0-6

Cover design by Michael Erickson

For those who have walked this way before us, who we may have foolishly forgotten.

After all these years, I have the same mind, heart and soul with which I was born. They have learned great lessons and been tested many times. They have experienced joy and sorrow, and almost everything in between. They are ageless, but my body is not. I hope before it is unable to support them, I will have found a love greater than myself.

Before The Last Dance

Prologue

The night falls softly on the last hour of light. Quietly it descends from the heavens in a shower of cold rain, cascading over a picture of life, until it has washed away what is left of the color of day; like spilled clear liquid on a freshly painted watercolor, mindlessly streaking down until all that is left is a faint gray sky and a hint of dirty brown ground. Time's past is being erased, while time's future is uncertain. With this comes a sense of sadness, perhaps more of an anxiety, causing us to rush to finish the tasks which begin at the introduction of morning. Conceivably, what is not completed can be left for another day. Up until now, many were content with such a practice: to let that which was undone wait until tomorrow. But now, there is a sense of urgency to finish the things once envisioned and partly started; and realize the dreams, wrapped in passion, that have been cradled in the heart of many a young child. Hopefully, that passion has survived and will bring many to finish the work at hand before our tomorrow has diminished and that last hour of light has gone.

For Tom, the night had come and gone. Now morning, he sits at his computer, eyes red and tired, making a labored attempt to read the typed words on the screen.

"What else is there to write," he speaks, in a low whisper, as if talking to someone sitting next to him in a pubic library where one would be expected to speak in such a hushed voice.

Indeed for the moment, Tom is alone, as he had been through the night. Eight a. m. rings out into the room from an antique clock. He caresses the back of his stiff neck, while guiding his head in a circular movement. His eyes focus back to the computer screen. Tom repeats the question again in the same low whisper. Nothing comes. His mind is in a fog. His fingers remain still. Tom watches them, expecting each one to start typing individual letters, then words making sentences at any moment, expecting his fingers to have a brain separate from the one in his head.

He begins typing again with his right hand.

I miss you. Do you know what I am going through?

Tom's left arm is propped on the edge of the desk, its respective hand resting his chin. He pauses for a moment, shaking his head in dissatisfaction before repeatedly tapping the backspace key with one stiff finger until the two short sentences he typed

4

moments ago disappear from the white screen. In chorus, Tom sits up in the chair from his slumped posture as he removes his reading glasses, hastily tossing them aside. He rubs his eyes with his hands clenched in fists. Several seconds pass before the haze of snow caused by the resulting pressure disappears, enabling him to see once again.

He looks around the room in an ill attempt to find a source of inspiration. Tom's eyes scan tall mahogany bookshelves filled with hundreds and hundreds of books, covering two walls of the room from floor to ceiling. Scrupulously they move from shelf to shelf. An avid reader, he is usually never at a loss for words until now. From there, they move to the sitting area across from the desk. Elaborate pillows are scattered out of their usual order on the long Italian brown leather sofa where hours before he tried to embrace sleep. A rich pashmina throw, used for cover in the early hours before daylight invaded the city below, fell on the Persian rug sometime during the night.

Tom continues. His fingers feel heavy on the keypad as he types.

I miss you. Do you know how much I miss you?

Again, he stops, moving his hands to his knees, then slowly sliding them to the under part of his thighs. Like a little boy, Tom sits on his hands while attempting another stab at reading what he has written so far.

Andrew,

The whole time we were corresponding online last night I was waiting for you to write, "I'm coming back for good." After you signed off I tried to sleep, but my mind was tormented by the thought of losing you. I spent the dark hours thinking about our naked bodies touching with my arms wrapped around your torso, and my lips resting on the back of your neck. While the cold rain fell out of the night sky, our bodies would be warmed by each another. I miss you. Do you know how much I miss you?

At the other end of the hallway leading to Tom's office, a woman's voice in song begins to fill the morning silence, momentarily interrupting his nervous concentration from the words on the screen.

"Praise Jesus," Peggy, his housekeeper sings out greeting the day, as she does every morning. Her footsteps, marching like a soldier in formation, echo from the marble floors of the penthouse. Tom leans back in his chair far enough to catch a fuzzy distant glimpse of her ample frame making its way in the direction of the kitchen. She is carrying a large black tote and what appears to be an over-packed bag of groceries. Moments later, Tom faintly hears the rustling of the brown paper sack, as Peggy begins methodically removing its contents and putting them in their assigned places in the cabinets. As she often does, Peggy is singing one of her favorite religious hymns. There is no question she is a woman of God. In a few minutes, after starting the coffee, habitually she will make her way to see if Tom is alone, or if she needs to make breakfast for two; breakfast for him and "the boy."

His hands are turning numb from the weight of his thighs.

Tom feverishly shakes them in the air to bring the blood back to his fingertips before returning them to the sterile keypad.

As the feeling comes back, he finishes his typing.

As I love you, I love the feel of your sweet lips on my face in the mornings. I miss waking up next to you. My life feels empty without you.

Tom

He sighs, returning his hands to the underside of his upper legs before rereading the heartfelt E-mail in the familiar soft whisper.

"What else is there to write?" Tom asks himself one last time, searching his brain for the right combination of words to express the passion heavily beating in his heart. A minute passes before he nervously taps the send key, seemingly unsure of his decision.

"Mail sent," in a blue rectangular box, pops up on the screen. Frozen in a trance-like state, Tom remains seated in front of the computer. Peggy's voice continues to sweeten the air, slowly gaining in volume as she progresses inevitably closer, moving in and out of the rooms of the penthouse seeking what is in need of straightening like a hound smelling out a fox.

"Jesus loves me. Yes, he does," Peggy calls out, between verses of her hymn.

Her voice is unexpectedly serene for a woman of her robust size. The song continues to move throughout the penthouse, easing closer and closer, louder and louder, toward Tom's office, until it dismisses upon Peggy's arrival in the open doorway.

"How are you this beautiful God-given day, Mr. Tom?" she calls out in joy, as she walks toward the windows.

Without looking at him, Peggy reaches for a hold on the massive brown draperies trimmed in wide black piping. As she passes his desk, she can smell the faint odor of alcohol still riding on Tom's breath. Suddenly, without a second of hesitation, the morning light charges into the dim room, as the drapery rings make two separate quick scrapping sounds — one to the left and another to the right. The oversized black tassels hanging at both ends of the rod, swing back and forth, back and forth numerous times. Trapped dust breaks free as a result of Peggy's aggressive movement, scattering throughout the room like stars in a twenty foot by twenty foot universe. Tom's eyes squint with the introduction of the outside world. His hands, in reflex, shoot up protectively to his face in an attempt to block out the infusion of unwelcome light, as if he were a vampire.

"Peggy, why must you do that? Too much light," he scorns.

She purposely ignores Tom's comment.

"Are we having breakfast alone this morning, Mr. Tom?" Peggy asks.

She walks toward a library table to rearrange a stack of books and turn off a lamp, its light superfluous at this point. Peggy eases her eyes to catch a quick glimpse of him, while waiting for a response.

"Not hungry," Tom grumbles, his hands still partially shielding his eyes from the daylight.

With that, Peggy knows he is alone. She has not seen the boy for some time. A motherly concern registers on her face. She shakes her head in a bewildered manner while walking back over to where Tom is sitting at the desk. His shoulders are slumped, head low, his chin resting almost on his upper chest. Like a defeated man, Tom sits with his back to the world. It is a world he feels no longer a part of, a world he believes has no place for him. He is a man of great wealth, but in his eyes, he has no value, and as far as he is concerned, also none in the eyes of the world.

Peggy reaches for the empty glass sitting by the keyboard.

"I'll draw your bath, Mr. Tom. You'll feel better after you're all nice and clean and have some breakfast in your belly. It's a gift of a day. The rain has stopped and the sun is shining. You'll see. God has given us this beautiful day."

Peggy gives Tom a motherly pat on the shoulder, and then moves her hand to correct the thick cowlick of hair sprouting from his head. It is a fruitless gesture, but comforting to Tom. She unconsciously opens her mouth to speak, but after a moment of thought, forcibly holds her words in by quickly pursing her lips tightly together — cutting a word in half in the process — before any more sound can escape. Her lips remain tightly closed until the blood leaves them and they began to tingle. At this point, it is best not to say anything she thinks to herself; lips still pursed, imprisoning the thought, holding the words inside her mouth until reluctantly they melt and slide down her throat.

"You'll see, Mr. Tom," Peggy says instead, while turning toward the door.

He watches her leave the library carrying the empty glass before looking back at the computer screen.

I Just Came to Dance

Trey Bishop fidgets to get comfortable in his seat. His breathing has not settled to a normal rate since running the full length of Concourse A to catch the plane. The delay at security did not help matters, but thanks to a buxom female officer who took a liking to him, he was able to get moved ahead of the line allowing him to catch the fight just moments before they closed the door. It is a situation wherein he appreciates his good looks have come in handy. A flight attendant is checking that the overhead compartments are secure. She gives him a lingering smile as her associate stops to help an elderly gentlemen struggling to fit his carry-on into a tight space.

Trey pulls the cell from the inside pocket of his black leather jacket lying across his lap to see if Kyle has returned the call he made during the cab ride to Hartsfield-Jackson International Airport. He is sure the phone has not rung, but is hoping in all the commotion, it might have and he just did not hear it. He has been in a panic since getting the call from Nancy two hours ago that he needed to catch the next fight to New York City. Trey told the driver there was a twenty dollar tip if he could make it in record time. Traffic on Interstate 85 always sucked. This is his third plane ride in four days, having just gotten back in town from Dallas earlier that day.

He leans his head against the edge of the window mindlessly watching the baggage carriers outside load the belly of the plane. In the seat next to him a young girl, maybe seven years old, plays with two Barbie Dolls as her older brother intently concentrates on a computer game. Across the aisle, their mother digs through a bulky purse. The family resemblance is strong.

"God, why did Tom do it?" Trey speaks softly without realizing he is thinking out loud.

"Did you say something?" asks the girl next to him.

Trey turns his head in surprise.

"No sweetie, not really," he answers.

"You look afraid. Are you scared of flying?"

Trey is amazed at how astute his young traveling companion is. She is right, he is, but not of flying. Trey is afraid of what he will find when he gets to New York City.

"No. I'm fine," he answers the girl.

"Do you want to play with one of my dolls?" she asks, while pulling a strand of blonde hair from the corner of her mouth.

"Thanks," Trey smiles. "Maybe later. I think I'm going to try to take a catnap," he adds.

The girl goes back to her playing. Her brother has eyed him several times during the conversation with his sister. Now Trey can feel him looking his way with a more constant gaze. He thinks the boy, fair-haired like her, is fifteen. His head is down, but his eyes dart over in Trey's direction as he punches the keys on the computer without looking at them or the screen. Trey leans his head again next to the window. He thinks about being fifteen, anything to keep his mind off what is happening in New York City. Something tells him the young boy is gay, or will be, by the admiring stares and just his overall posture and exceptional attention to his hygiene and dress. Trey remembers having crushes on older men when he was his age, before he came to the edge of innocence and fell over.

Irregular rows of shoes line the gym floor in front of the bleachers. Many are scattered about by the traffic of kids migrating to and from the middle of the floor, to dance under scores of papier-mâché red, white and pink hearts of varying sizes hanging from the ceiling. Streamers of the same colors run the length of the gymnasium, connecting the basketball nets. Michelle Douglas, wearing a white dress with red polka dots, holds court on the bottom row. Trey has homeroom and third period English with her. She is the prettiest girl in school and does not lack attention because of this obvious fact. Surrounded by adoring classmates, her bright white teeth shine as she smiles with excitement. Trey sits high in the bleachers wearing a pair of white pants with red piping on the pockets. The day before, he asked his dad for the twelve dollars to buy them, especially in preparation for the event. A red long-sleeved shirt completes the outfit. His white Converses are lost among the mismatching of shoes below. It is Valentine's Day 1978!

The popular group: the cheerleaders, athletes and pretty kids are on the dance floor. The outsiders: the rebels, the nerds and the "wanna-bees" are scattered in different assemblies, mostly huddled on the bleachers and the sidelines, trying to feel just as important as they believe the other kids to be. They are the perimeter kids, living on the outside looking in on the rest of the world of junior high; their only connection to the others is their youth. Trey is somewhere in the middle, neither an outsider nor considered one of the popular. There is something about him that everyone likes, enabling him to maneuver through the halls of Griffin Junior High with little conflict or recognition.

As much as Trey wants to walk down to where Michelle is standing to ask her to dance, he cannot make himself. It is easier to wait until the next song to ask, but then as the next song plays, he tells himself to wait until the next. Before he knows it, the last song begins. Soon everyone will be trying to rematch their shoes. The gymnasium lights will flicker off as color streamers and papier-mâché broken hearts fall to the floor.

The sights, sounds and smells of small southern towns are distinctive. Obscure hamlets of life tucked behind thick tree-lined interstates, where kudzu encroaches on billboards while aggressively devouring the landscape, as cars race to bigger destinations, their occupants barely knowing of their existence. Junior high school dances fill little girls' hearts with joy. Fall Friday nights are for high school football games, where the whole town comes out to cheer on the local team, and young lovers experience their first kiss under the bleachers. The jasmine grows wild on old wooden fences, covering peeling paint from years of whitewashing. The summer sun bakes the air, intensifying the sweet aromas that cling to the mucous lining of your nostrils. The rich pungent dirt, mothering acres of cotton, soybeans and corn, rolls by as you are driving on a state road to nowhere. The rain falls clean from the heavens, filling the streams and rivers that will eventually run into the ocean. On Sunday mornings, religious songs awake the weary as Baptist choirs sing their praises to the Almighty from churches at the end of twisting dusty roads. The pace is slow, the air clearer and the summer days seem endless.

Growing up in such an environment has its advantages; it's the American way, even if you are born on the wrong side of the tracks. All you know is what you know. Anything else is foreign. Chances are, if you are born in a small town, you will grow old and die there, too. It protects you from the outside world, keeping you safe. Many may dream of the big city with all its allure of bright lights, fancy clothes, and big shiny cars, but few will leave to search them out. Those that do, will trade the clear star-filled nights for the artificial lights streaming out from mountainous buildings lining hurried, noise filled streets.

If you know you are different, you bide your time. You dance to their music, mimicking their steps pretending to fit in, when in truth you want to burst out dancing to music truer to yourself. So you sit on the bleachers, waiting for your song to play like a sign that tells you to get up and dance. Until then, if you are a good enough actor, you hide the secret thoughts and different revelations mounting inside — as life unfolds — that will soon disrupt a safe, small-town existence. You wait, as Trey did, to see what the interstate on the other side of the trees, connecting you to the outside world, brings forth.

Trey was a cute kid, almost a pretty boy with bright eyes and a fresh smile. He did not know it then, but he would grow to look even finer. Ultimately, Trey would spend most of his young life never knowing just how physically beautiful he would become. His early years would blind him to this truth, and every time he looked in the mirror, he would see a distorted version of what was real. He would never clearly see himself as the rest of the world would. In some ways, that would be a good thing, while in others it would cause him to overlook the potential of knowing what the beauty he possessed could bring. Underneath the last remaining layers of baby fat, the small town barber cut, and hand-me-down clothing, was a good-looking boy growing inside of him. One day, he would steal the hearts of many who gazed upon his face. Like the storybook ugly ducking, Trey would soon shed his gray, matted feathers to reveal the beauty which lay beneath.

As the late winter days began to thaw into spring, he found himself in the last year of junior high school. The barren trees awakened from a cold winter's sleep, to once again begin to show signs of life in the small green buds pushing out from the branches crisscrossing in the sun soaked sky. As with the changing of the seasons, Trey was also experiencing alterations and an awakening of his own. All of a sudden, after what seemed like endless years of waiting — waiting to grow bigger, stronger, and by all means older —his spring had arrived. Soon it would move fast into summer, which would prove to be a season that would change a little boy, and lead him into the first stages of becoming a man.

He was a smart boy — artistic and creative — always the teacher's pet. Trey had big dreams of becoming an artist. School was an escape from the blunt realities of rural day-to-day life. The son of a factory worker, it was a tough upbringing, which was left behind for a few hours of the day for a boy with dreams of romance and far off places while he studied in school. When the last afternoon bell rang, Trey returned to the realities of the life he shared with his parents in a gray-colored single-wide trailer, sitting at the end of a winding road, past a small pond and just around the bend from a weathered barn, in the trailer park called Hidden Woods, in Brighton, just a stone's throw from Birmingham, Alabama.

During the school year, the yellow bus dropped Trey off on State Route 17 at the beginning of the half-mile road leading to the trailer park. He walked it almost every day, longing to get away from the corn fields, the smell of cow manure, and the clouds of dust stirred up by the few passing cars and trucks of the neighbors dwelling further up the road. Sometimes, if he was lucky, Trey would catch a ride from one of them either going to town in the mornings or heading back down the road in the afternoons. Usually, he made the walk.

Finally another school year had come to an end and Trey found himself daydreaming the summer days away. June and July passed as viscidly as the pouring of a tall glass of warm buttermilk. Trey sat on the second step leading up to the front porch, which was badly in need of a fresh coat of paint. The mid-morning sunlight was wrapping itself around the trailer making it hot to the touch. Once midday arrived, the August heat would be almost too much to bear — the temperature of the air enough to scorch the nose hairs with each inhalation. By the time the sun climbed high in the sky, even Rex, their family mutt, panting incessantly, would seek refuge from the sun beating down on the earth under the trailer in one of the many holes he had dug in the cool dirt.

The small trailer community of Hidden Woods made for a quiet setting, especially when the temperature was well on its way above 90 degrees. On a Saturday, the good folk would be sitting inside cooling themselves by window fans, or if they were lucky, by one of those window air conditioners. The Bishop's single-wide had one, and as long as the electric bill was current, it was running.

The warmth feels good on his clean, fresh fifteen-year-old face, as Trey watches the street a few feet in front of him. He had been sitting on the wooden steps for the past hour, in the very spot he sat yesterday and the day before. Trey pulls at the overly-long shoe strings of his red sneakers, wondering if he should cut them shorter to keep from stepping on them — hence avoiding another potential tripping — which was happening often since replacing the old ones.

Across the black asphalt road, elderly Mrs. Weaver sits in a tall ladder-back chair on the front porch of her double-wide, fanning herself with a copy of *Life*. Her coarse gray hair flutters, as the tattered pages of the magazine brush just inches from her face.

"How ya doing son?" she calls out, while jaggedly waving her free hand.

Trey waves back, continuing to watch the street. A late model silver Cadillac races by flinging up road dust high into the summer day. It hangs in the windless air making a thick haze resembling gray talcum powder. By the time it settles, Mrs. Weaver is gone, the early heat sending her indoors.

Trey is patiently waiting for the mailman, who is almost

always on schedule, if not early. Without fail, by eleven-thirty each morning, the mail would be delivered. In anticipation, Trey pushes his brown hair out of the way of a pair of luminous sea green eyes, allowing his forehead to shine in the sunlight. He repeatedly checks his grandfather's old Timex that loosely fits on his wrist. Now, it is eleven-twenty-eight. Before Trey looks back to the street, sure enough, he hears the small dirty white truck turning the corner. Without hesitation, Trey jumps off the steps out onto the dried weed-infested path of lawn. Within seconds, he is standing by the road ready to retrieve the mail from Mr. Parker, the mailman.

The box shaped truck comes to a squeaky halt in front of Trey.

"Sorry, nothing for you today," Mr. Parker says, as he has for the past three days.

Mr. Parker hands him two letters for his father, most likely late bill notices.

"Are you sure, no package for me today?" Trey asks, with disappointment.

"Not today. Maybe Monday."

Trey heads toward the trailer, but briefly looks back at Mr. Parker just in case he has realized there is a package after all lost in the pile. As the mail truck pulls back on the asphalt, Trey pounces up the steps. Rex dashes from under the trailer in pursuit of his master, the screen door barely missing his tail as it slams shut. Trey drops the mail on a wobbly side table while making his way down the short hall leading to the back door. They run the back way to Jimmy Best's, where he is washing the August dust off his father's blue Dodge. A year older, Jimmy and his family moved to town at the beginning of June. The sun beats down on his shirtless tan back, as he makes big circles of soapy water over the car's windows.

"Grab the hose," Jimmy calls out.

Trey eagerly obliges and begins spraying the soap off the area of the car where Jimmy is pointing. He cannot help but notice how defined Jimmy's body is, making him feel a little strange. Trey finds it hard to keep his eyes on where the water is hitting the car. Instead, he keeps looking at Jimmy in the sun light, looking at the beads of sweat rolling down the sternum of his chest toward a tight stomach and the small patch of black hair trailing from his belly button to a hiding place in his shorts. It has been a bizarre summer for Trey anyway. He has shot up like a weed in an unkempt yard — three inches to be exact — since the beginning of spring. So much so, Trey is having growing pains in his legs, as his mother calls them. Some nights, she sits on the edge of his bed rubbing them to ease the pain until Trey falls asleep.

Four weeks earlier, he stumbled across an ad in the back of one of his mother's Hollywood magazines advertising men's underwear. A well toned good-looking man — reminding him a little of Jimmy — modeled a pair of briefs. Trey kept the magazine under his bed, usually viewing the ad before falling asleep, except for the nights his legs ached. Not long after finding the ad, he started having a recurring dream where he is in a secluded field wearing nothing but the briefs (from the ad) and Jimmy is walking toward him with a big smile on his face. A week later, Trey got a money order, in the amount of $15.00, plus

$2.50 for shipping and handling, from funds earned by doing odd jobs around the trailer park for some of the elderly residents. Trey enthusiastically sent off for three pairs of the Contour. The copy read, "Light, classic support styled in the finest cotton for a comfortable fit. Allow three weeks for delivery." That is why Trey has been waiting so eagerly for the mail each day; the three weeks are up. By all means, he does not want his mother to inquire about the package or open it by mistake. It is a secret, and to keep it requires a diligent watch for the mailman each day until the package arrives.

It was also strange that ever since Jimmy moved into the trailer behind him, Trey lost interest in Michelle. She was also in this recurring dream with her back to him in the field. In the dream, Trey screams out to Michelle, but she does not answer. Instead she keeps walking out of the field, never looking back as Jimmy gets closer and closer, still smiling. Now, all his romantic thoughts somehow have shifted to Jimmy. Any vow that Trey made to himself to get Michelle's attention at the beginning of the next school year was suppressed by Jimmy's arrival.

It is all he can do to keep his mind on washing the car and not Jimmy.

"Hey, watch where you're spraying that water, shit-head!" Jimmy yells out, as Trey's aim soaks his navy shorts.

"Sorry," Trey stutters out in embarrassment.

"I'll show you," Jimmy exclaims, as he grabs the hose turning it on him.

Trey makes an attempt to run to the other side of the car, not to avoid the water, which would be rather refreshing on such a hot day, but to hide the growth in his shorts. Rex barks at the stream of water, trying to bite it as Jimmy continues his pursuit. The summer's dried grass thirstily drinks up the water under their feet, as Trey stands there soaked and obviously excited. Now noticeable to anyone in eyeshot.

"Hey, man, is that a boner in your pants?" Jimmy laughs out, not understanding the mortification his observation has caused.

Trey's sight falls to the ground. The color of day changes to black and white, as he runs as fast as his feet will go with the water evaporating off his body into the hot air. Rex barks after him. Jimmy goes back to washing the Dodge.

Monday morning, Trey is back on the steps of the porch waiting for Mr. Parker. He has not seen Jimmy since Saturday afternoon, not sure what to do, and even more so, not sure what Jimmy is thinking, if anything, about the incident. Mrs. Weaver is on her porch again, like every morning, in the ladder-back chair fanning the early humidity from her face with the same tattered copy of *Life* magazine. This morning, she is taking advantage of the brief but welcome shower that occurred earlier, raining just long enough to take a bite out of the morning heat. As the August days grow in number, the morning temperatures increase giving little relief before the sun rolls high in the southern sky. Eventually, the sun will bake everything in its reach from sunup to sunset. Now, steam is beginning to rise from the asphalt.

Behind Mrs. Weaver's trailer, past a small dense forest of pine trees, lay an open field where Trey often plays ball with Rex. On the other side of the field is Interstate 20. From the porch, Trey can hear cars whizzing up and down the road into the far-off distance. He has spent many afternoons there, wondering what is at its beginning and what lies at its end. The only two things Trey knows about the interstate is it leads to a bigger place than Brighton, and it brought Jimmy to their small town. That summer, a lot of things were changing. His body was developing and Trey was feeling removed from the other boys at school, many of whom lived in the trailer park. They were beginning to talk about girls and going out on dates, but his mind was on other things. Sometimes, Trey was afraid things were changing too fast. First, it was the short-lived fondness for Michelle. Then the intense growing pains in his legs; Jimmy moving to town; the development of unexpected erections; wet dreams; and finally, that magazine with the ad. What did it all mean? Why was he so protective of the arrival of the package, and why did he want to make sure his mother did not get it first?

Trey hears an eighteen-wheeler's faint horn blow on the interstate. He is sitting with his knees bent at his chest, his arms wrapped loosely around them. Unexpectedly, he catches a glimpse of Jimmy's father's Dodge coming down the street, already blanketed in a thin coat of summer dust despite being washed two days ago. Jimmy had recently gotten his license, and it is Trey's reflex to duck his head between his knees to avoid Jimmy if he is behind the wheel. But it is too late. The temptation too great. Trey cannot help but look. Their eyes meet.

"Hey bud!" Jimmy yells out the driver's window, as the car slows and then speeds off around the corner. Trey feels a twinge in his gut, similar to the one he experienced on Saturday when Jimmy saw the bulge in his shorts. His face becomes red, but not from the late morning heat.

Like clockwork, the mail truck turns the corner. With its

squeaky brakes, it stops in front of the trailer. Trey's attention diverts from thoughts of Jimmy when he sees a small brown package hanging out of the window. Within seconds, he leaps from the porch and runs out to the street.

"Is this what you've been waiting for?" Mr. Parker asks, as Trey eagerly pulls it from his hand.

With a loud thanks, he does a 180 turn and runs toward the trailer, dropping the package as he trips on his shoelaces. Mr. Parker calls out that he has forgotten the rest of the mail, but in his haste, Trey does not hear him. Mr. Parker puts the orphaned letters in the mailbox and drives away scratching his head. After picking up the package, Trey races inside and into his bedroom. He shuts the door, and then takes a seat on the bed with the package in his lap. Trey is glad no one is home. His father left for the Brookston Enterprises Assembly Plant hours ago, and his mother just started a job in another factory after not being able to work the past few years. They both will not return until late afternoon.

Still feeling detached after seeing Jimmy drive by, and in long-awaited anticipation, Trey softly reads aloud his name and address as printed on the label, almost in awe that it has finally arrived after weeks of waiting. Carefully he pulls the tape from the package. Trey guardedly unwraps the brown covering, exposing three pairs of bright white cotton briefs wrapped in plastic, much different from the Hanes boxer shorts his mother always bought. In accompaniment, is a small catalog with another model adorning the cover wearing a black thong and a mesh tank top.

With unnecessary caution, Trey gets up to lock the door. Upon returning to his previous position on the bed, with great care, in a ceremonial fashion, he frees one pair of the briefs from its plastic confinement. Trey proceeds to pull the Hanes from around his hard penis; a tingle shoots through it, and now he is wet with pre-cum. After wiping himself with his old underwear, Trey carefully slips the new briefs on, not quite covering his excitement. They feel cool and silky smooth against his skin. Mindfully, he secures the other two pair in the plastic before placing them in the bottom of the closet under a messy pile consisting of comic books, shoes and a baseball mitt — where hopefully they will not be discovered.

Returning to the bed in his new briefs, Trey begins to play with himself while prudently examining each page of the catalog presenting more models in sexy underwear. His heart beats rapidly, unsure of what he is feeling, and in fear of someone finding out about his strange behavior. He eyes the door for a moment, and then returns his attention to the catalog. The summer day glides through the single window of the room like warm sticky honey, as more pre-cum flows steadily from the head of his penis. New thoughts race through his mind. Trey slowly runs his fingers over its mushroom head. The sensation is intense. His whole body tingles. His stomach feels like it is going to turn over in his abdomen. Now his hand moves up and down the full length of his shaft, becoming wetter and wetter, slicker and slicker.

A few minutes later, Trey reaches for the old pair of Hanes he tossed aside. He wipes off his chest and stomach, before stuffing them in a dark hiding place under the bed.

The next day, Jimmy calls him over from the back yard where he is doing chores. Trey's mother has taken Mrs. Weaver to a doctor's appointment in Clarksville, thirty miles away. It is a typical August day; the air carries the heated smells of summer. The weather report forecasts rain showers later in the afternoon. Trey is wearing a pair of his new briefs under washed out cut-off jeans. As usual, Jimmy has his shirt off. Halfheartedly, Trey responds, still embarrassed from the uncontrollable erection the weekend before.

"Want to play ball?" Jimmy asks, as Trey tries not to stare.

"Okay," he simply responds.

Jimmy throws the basketball he has been juggling in the air at his reluctant opponent.

"One on one. You go first," he instructs.

Trey makes his first attempt at the basket and misses. Jimmy reclaims the ball and scores. The sun evenly fills the air. After a few attempts to get the basketball, heated, Rex darts back under the trailer. Sweat runs down Jimmy's back forming a wet spot at the waist of his shorts. His next attempt at the basket hits the rim, sending the ball up for grabs. They both go for it, as it bounces on the ground. Now, a different kind of dance begins. Like boys will, they fight for ownership. They begin to wrestle. Forgotten, the ball rolls off to the side. Rex eyes it, but decides to stay put out of the heat. Trey's slightly smaller build falls under Jimmy, as he tries hard not to be excited by the horseplay. Now, Jimmy holds Trey's head against his chest in a friendly headlock. Trey's face is covered in his opponent's sweat; it tastes sweet and salty. In an effort to break free, Trey grabs for Jimmy's waist.

"Say uncle," Jimmy demands, as he flips him on his back still holding Trey in a tight confinement.

"Never," Trey responds, almost out of breath.

They laugh and yell while kicking up dry dirt and parched plugs of grass. Trey's hands fruitlessly search for a secure hold on Jimmy, but the sweat makes them slide in many directions. Their bodies squirm on the ground, their youthful flesh rubbing against each other. Trey continues to find a way to break free from the headlock. It seems futile, as his hands persistently continue to slide off Jimmy's slick body. It is even harder to concentrate on not getting excited. Trey grabs again for the waistband of Jimmy's shorts, as the boys roll and roll over the sun baked ground.

"Say uncle, say uncle," Jimmy demands again.

"Never, never," Trey protests, sticking to his guns.

Exhausted, Trey stops his struggle to catch a breath, one hand still tightly holding the waist band of Jimmy's shorts, the other grasping a patch of dried grass. His eyes look up to the sky at a large encroaching cloud hovering overhead. Within seconds, it releases raindrops of much needed relief, bathing the boys as they hold their ground. The dried dirt begins to turn into mud, as the August afternoon fills with an invigorating shower. The sprinkles multiply by the billions, turning into a downpour. Trey's excitement is growing, and he is too enamored to try to hide it anymore.

"Ready to give it up?" Jimmy yells out.

"Never."

In what he thinks will be a clever move, Trey tries to free himself from his captor. In retaliation, Jimmy quickly moves to regain his control, grabbing at his shorts. In the process, he gets a handful. Somehow, from fear and excitement, Trey manages to break free running toward Mrs. Weaver's yard. Jimmy follows.

The thunder cloud breaks wide open with a loud clap of lighting shooting at the earth somewhere on the other side of the interstate. Trey runs across the asphalt road, steam rising over it. His T-shirt and shorts soak up the rain. He bolts through the patch of pines behind Mrs. Weaver's trailer and out into the open field. As Trey reaches its middle ground, he stops and turns around. Jimmy is still chasing him smiling, just seconds on his tail. He catches up with him, pulling Trey to the ground.

"Uncle! Uncle!" Trey calls out, as Jimmy pins him down and pulls off his wet T-shirt.

The rain continues to burst out of the clouds. After another clap of thunder echoes through the sky, the rain slows to a gentle cascade.

That summer, Trey's dream extraordinarily became reality, and Michelle was nowhere in sight. But by September, summer loosened its vice grip on their small town, as the dust finally settled on its asphalt and dirt roads. Whatever happened between Jimmy and Trey, just past the small sparse forest of pine trees behind Mrs. Weaver's trailer, had apparently become a memory. That passion came and went — fast and furious — as did the overdue summer rain storm.

Once school started back, in a turn of events, Jimmy became preoccupied with Michelle Douglas. Sometimes, while Trey was sitting on the front steps of the trailer, listening to the cars and trucks whizzing by on Interstate 20 in the distance, Jimmy and Michelle would ride by in the blue Dodge, with her sitting close to him, Jimmy's right hand around her shoulder as he steered the car with the other. He would throw a glance to catch Trey's eyes before the Dodge disappeared down the road.

The few years that followed were uneventful ones. Trey's growing pains stopped. He grew two more inches after that summer. Soon, high school was over. Trey dreamed of going to college in a big town far away from the small world of Brighton. His grades were good enough to get him a scholarship to Jefferson State Community College, but that was not as far away as he wished. But it would have to be good enough for now. It was a small step closer to finding his music. Thank God, he thought, the interstate is close at hand.

A Place on the Floor

Usually the sight of Manhattan coming over the Triborough Bridge brings a rush of excitement to Trey; now it only brings dread. He has agonized during the flight and his stomach is still in knots from doing so much of it. He should have seen it coming, Trey thought over and over, especially since the late-night phone calls with Tom's well-liquored voice, slurring his words on the other end, had become more frequent. But then they stopped, and there was a week where Tom seemed calm, making Trey think he was going to be okay. Trey now figures he should have known it was the lull before the storm. He puts the cell back in his pocket, having just finished talking with Nancy, letting her know he has made it and will catch a cab to the hospital. Unlucky for him, he has arrived in the city at the height of rush hour. He still has not managed to reach Kyle. Trey listens to the cabby as he curses in a foreign language at a driver who has just cut him off. The street in front of them looks like it has been painted yellow. It is a parking lot of taxis as far and as wide as the eye can see. It will take some time to get to Tom; more than enough time to regret and mull over random thoughts of life and death, and a relationship passed.

◊

There is a time in our lives when we think we will never die, believing the arms of old age and death will never reach out to us. A time we believe we are forever young. We see older people – our parents, grandparents, their friends, teachers and others, but it does not resonate that we will become old like them one day. Such a realization is too far off in an unsure future, too far off to give more than a moment's thought, and any related thoughts of such are rapidly pushed out of our minds. But if the truth be told, life is but a moment lived. If we have the good fortune of a long life, we will indeed see an older version of ourselves looking back at us in the mirror of time. As a child, Tom, like Trey, could not wait to age — to a point — to become an adult. Even then, to him old age still seemed lifetimes away. As children, for both, it seemed aging was an extremely slow process. Almost agonizing, wanting to be old enough to drive a car; old enough to do as one pleased without a parent telling them what to do or not to do; and old enough to realize the dreams building inside of their little bodies. Those childhood desires would lead them down the road of life, full of struggles and successes, as the years advanced and their youth was left behind.

"When will I grow taller and bigger?" they both asked

themselves, time and time again. Inch by inch, pound by pound, they waited.

For different reasons, they impatiently anticipated adulthood. When times were better between Tom and his father, he would sit on the bathroom vanity watching Mr. Brookston shave. Similarly, Trey stood on the seat of a small wooden chair his mother always kept in a corner of the bathroom. His father would position it in front of the mirror. Excitedly, Trey stood on that chair next to him mimicking the act of shaving. His father would squirt lather in Trey's small palm, until it overflowed like a mound of soft Dairy Queen vanilla ice cream. With playful excitement, and in what he thought was a serious grown-up manner, he would cover his hairless face before running a bladeless razor through the white foam, longing to actually have stubble to shave.

At night, Tom lay in bed, his small hands wrapped around the rails connecting the imposing head posts, stretching his body, while pointing his toes toward the foot of the bed. He imagined himself growing taller, older, and bigger. Trey marked his height with a pencil on the inside jam of the bedroom closet door, checking it daily, and then weekly, always standing as tall as he could. Soon, his frustrations caused a loss of interest; the pencil marks of small gains in height were soon forgotten and eventually painted over years later.

They were both sons of the southland, but although Tom and Trey were born in close proximity, in fact in the same county of Jefferson, they may as well have lived in two different countries. Their births brought them into the world in predestined classes: one affluent and the other dirt poor. Right or wrong, they would be viewed and judged by that standing. For a time, the only thing they did have in common was the rain that fell out of the Alabama sky running over their flesh, wetting their lips, but not quenching their thirst. Almost from childhood, both longed for something different from what was given to – or expected of – them. Tom and Trey would want more than they were given, many things of varying degrees of desire and even need. Trey had always known some of what he wanted, but for Tom, it was unclear and harder to pinpoint. When you come from such wealth, what do you wish for? Those underlying desires and needs would send them on a path beginning with the entitlements of youth and eventually lead to the difficult realization of their own mortality. A path paved with emotions and ending in knowledge only few come to grasp.

There was a span of almost twenty years between them. By the time Trey was born, Tom was already starting college. There had been a generation of songs, fashion, politics, and television shows separating them. Before he was eighteen, Tom traveled a good part of the world; up until then, Trey had never crossed the state line. Those differences would be of little importance. Despite them, there was a common bond forming long before they would meet, and long before they would share a night together. They each had something to give the other, something lacking in their individual lives.

Their parents would never be friends, or even have an association other than that some of Trey's relatives had been employed by the Brookston family in menial jobs.

◊

The cabby yells something again as he slams the palms of his hands on the top of the steering wheel in annoyance. Trey leans his head back on the seat trying to fade out the sporadic horns blowing on the street. He closes his eyes as his memories take him back to how it all began.

◊

Trey's attention focuses on the cars coming toward him. One after another, a steady stream rushes over the eastbound lane of the interstate, as he steers his old yellow Ford Mustang south. To the west, the sun is setting on the canopy of a grove of pecan trees before its retreat begins pulling the remaining daylight from the sky. The wind rushes in the open windows, blowing his medium length brown hair in a thousand directions, and occasionally, in the way of his sight. The smell of warm honeysuckle fills his lungs, as the countryside dims, and the Mustang tears through the landscape. This is freedom. The road ahead is open, except for a few red taillights jumping in and out of sight in the winding, darkening distance. Scattered on the back seat are college texts, mixed with wired spiral notebooks filled with lessons and projects due before the end of the semester. But Trey has only one thing on his mind: getting out of town before nightfall.

Soon the night fills the open windows of the car. Checking his watch, Trey estimates his arrival in Atlanta in one hour. His body bulges with a combination of fear and excitement, as a smile of anticipation blisters on his face. Trey reaches over to search through a disarray of tapes on the passenger seat. He selects one of Donna Summer's, shaking it from its plexi holder. It bounces on the vinyl upholstery. Trey catches it and proceeds to insert it into the car stereo. Quickly, he scans to *Last Dance*, turning the volume up until the speakers almost begin to vibrate the car. It has become an anthem. Every time Trey plays it, something comes alive inside of him. He sings out, glancing at the road behind, reflected in the rear view mirror, as he brushes aside his unruly hair obscuring his vision again. Intuitively, he knows his past is in that rear view distance, as the car cuts through mating love bugs smashing onto the windshield, speeding to his future. Little does Trey know how important that music will be later on in his life. For now, it is a song that inspires him to become someone who will never have to return to that from which he came. Somehow he knows it is wonderful to be young with life unfolding in front of him. It is a realization he does not want to take for granted.

While attending junior college, Trey made weekend trips to the gay Mecca of the South, to dance the night away in the gay bars of Atlanta, Georgia. In doing so, he finally found his music. This was one of many road trips taken by a still shy, but determined young man to find his way to the dance floor. It is ironic how things do not change much, even some seven years later since junior high school. Sometimes, Trey feels like he is waiting to ask Michelle to dance, as he stands on the perimeter of another dance floor. Of course, he has no idea where Michelle is now, perhaps still with Jimmy. Even if she could remember who that almost timid, quiet, browned-haired boy was, who sat behind her in homeroom and three rows over to her left in third period English, he wonders if she even knows that he kissed Jimmy first?

It took years for him to realize he just wanted to dance more than he wanted to dance with Michelle. Trey spent many a school dance sitting on those bleachers — stuck as if he had been glued — trying to muster up the nerve to ask a girl to dance. Instead, he sat there until the last song played, barely having moved an inch, never asking a girl to dance. That awkward youthfulness had been left behind; the music changed, and so had the prospective dance partners. Now, in a pair of new Wranglers that fit tighter than they should, Trey is in a different world with new possibilities.

◊

The lights are blinding as they explode from somewhere in the dark ceiling of the warehouse onto the half nude bodies moving to the intoxicating music. A vast assortment of men, covered in sweat, are all partaking in a ritual dance, showing off their bodies like proud male peacocks trying to entice a mate. They are looking for takers — searching for someone to fuck or someone to fuck them — or just to be admired.

Trey nervously negotiates his way through the men, feeling the sweat sliding down his back and from under his arms. The bar is dark. It is jumping with energy. The air is searing, heat filling the confined space, radiating from the dancing men, circling their bodies like invisible flames of passion. His heart races from the exhilaration he is experiencing, as he walks the perimeter of the dance floor. There is a sense of oneness like he belongs here, with the men and the music.

Trey finds an open spot, giving him access to work his way onto the floor. Darting eyes watch him as he is swallowed up by the crowd. Convivial hands reach out to touch his body. They want him. Trey is the embodiment of all which is beautiful and desirable. He is a creation of magnificence, but strangely enough, he is oblivious. He does not see it, but the other dancers do. Trey is ripe for the taking. His flesh is smooth and sweet to the taste, his odor fresh and his loins are full of nectar. The men can smell it like a hungry lion can smell its next meal.

He is now in the center of the floor, where he begins to dance. His body moves to the music like no straight man ever could hope to. While the music plays, he is freer than he has ever been. Trey's arms reach up as if to touch the pulsating lights far above his head. He wants the music of the night to last forever. It is here that he can forget about his past and dream of a new future. But for now, he just wants the music to play and the morning to never come. Trey knows that it will eventually, but he pushes the thought back farther in his mind as the music funnels through his ears filling his head.

He dances like he has never danced before. Trey's movement is of a sexual nature – alluring and wanting. He is still at odds with an agonizing feeling of not wanting to leave when the music does indeed stop, but he will deal with that when the lights come on. For now, Trey has finally made it to the dance floor after so many years of sitting on the sidelines watching everyone else. Much of that time was spent trying to find his way to a place under the splattering lights, a place of his very own on the dance floor of life. This time, there are no paper-mâché streamers to dance under, and no Michelle Douglas to muster up the nerve to ask to dance. Now the floor is full of dance partners more to his liking.

His mind is full of questions. What is he doing here? Why must he be here? What makes him drive every possible weekend from school? What desires make him want to slide his body in with the rest of the men and boys? Why must he be a part of the music, and shirtless bodies dancing into the night? Part of the answer is that the music is like a drug. His body feeds on it, absorbing every pounding beat, every word being sung with which Trey can identify. It is much the same in life. Every soul is looking for its place on the dance floor, maneuvering its body through the crowd of strangers, finding a place to express itself. Some hang on the edge of life looking in, while others find their place deep in the crowd, dancing in the center: the heart of the floor and, perhaps, the center of life.

Some of the men return night after night, never able to get their fill. What once seemed to be a fantasy has become real, like the first time Trey opened the page of his mother's magazine to the ad for men's underwear, and the fulfillment of teenage desires that later followed. It took some time, but at long last, Trey made it to the middle of the floor. So, weekend after weekend, Trey continually made his way there. He did find the music addictive. Something he could make his own. It was an escape from his short past, a confusing present, and an unsure future. There, he left behind a false reality and found some truth about himself. Lucky for him, Atlanta was close. Interstate 20 was within running distance from his front door. As a young boy, he sat on the front steps of his parents' trailer wondering where it led to. Now he knows.

On those repeated drives, Trey came to terms with the truth of what he was becoming. Mile by mile, there was an innocence escaping out the windows of the car, and a new awareness unfolding, as the music was liberated from its speakers. Trey too was escaping, finding a sense of guarded freedom. At first he was afraid, so afraid of the feelings raging through him, like the music spilling out into the night. There were no lessons in the textbooks on the back seat of his car to find answers to the questions shooting off in his head, and no one to turn to in the secret world that began to change a young boy into a man.

On one of those nights, as Trey danced to the music, he met Tom. The music seemed to play louder this time, sucking him in like an industrial vacuum. Trey was on the inside now, no longer sitting in the bleachers. Unknowingly, he saw the future in the face of a stranger.

Years Later — Last moments of Truth

It has been two weeks since Trey flew to New York after getting the frantic call from Nancy that Tom had made a real attempt to end his life. The hospital room smells like a florist. Several fragrant elaborate arrangements mask the usual order of sterile alcohol and antiseptic. The beige and white room explodes with color: purple irises, red ginger stocks, orange birds of paradise, among others, offer a visual garden to the eye in a private room on the twelfth floor of New York-Presbyterian Hospital. Tom lays cocooned in extremely high thread-count sheets as Nancy instructed the orderly to dress the bed. Instead of a standard green hospital gown, he resides in a coma dressed in Brooks Brothers pajamas with the initials "TJB" monogrammed on the breast pocket. Virginia, Nancy's private assistant, sees that the doctors and nurses are doing their jobs. Most of the time, she sits in a chair positioned in the corner of the room, one leg crossed over the other, with her hands folded on top of a black leather notebook, waiting like the rest of them. Actually, there is nothing to be done for the moment.

"Just wait and see, but it doesn't look promising," states Dr. Houser, with an English accent, a tall wiry haired man in his early fifties.

It appears unlikely Tom will come out of the coma. From frustration and dread, Nancy fusses with the bed sheets, trying to cover up Tom's arms, so the tubes sending intravenous medications into his system are not so noticeable. She wants him to look as normal as possible under the circumstances. Nancy puts on a strong exterior. From what Tom told Trey over the years, she must have learned it from their mother: a true Southern woman, born into a prominent family, raised to marry well. It was doubtful Mrs. Brookston married for love, but rather a merger of two powerful families; not a union true to the heart, but one truer to a love of power and more wealth. With that came a life protected from the rest of the common world, providing an invisible barrier, where nothing bad or unpleasant could touch her. Money and power surrounded her, keeping her safe from the unpleasantness of the outside world. Now, Nancy was just like her — protected by wealth and power. But even that was not enough to guard her from what Tom had done.

"How could anything like this happen?" Nancy asks Trey, over and over again. Adding, "How could Tom do such a thing? He has everything. Tom has wealth. What else could he want?" But she knows more than anyone that it did not always bring happiness.

Prominent southern women, like Nancy, have a way of turning a blind eye to anything distasteful going on under their eighteen karat gold-lined roofs. Such things are swept under expensive rugs. They go about their lives, overlooking the sins of their husbands, and even those of their sons and brothers. It is the women who hold up appearances for the outside, and go about their lives as if the world is truly a beautiful place.

As children, Nancy and Tom had been very close. They were inseparable, an uncommon relationship for most brothers and sisters. Normally, daughters stay close to their mother's side, while sons are glued to their father's hip. In some cases, it is the other way around, but very few opposite sex siblings experience the unyielding bond which they shared. In the beginning, there seemed to be a close attachment between both parents and children. But as they grew out of infancy, the great divide began. Soon, all Tom and Nancy had were each other; their childhood voices and scampering feet at play echoed in the vast stone rooms in an enormous estate in Birmingham built for a king and filled with servants.

Their older brother, Nathan, by eight years — the mirror image of their father in so many ways — was off in boarding school much of the time, and had become mostly a stranger to the younger children. Although, to a degree, Mrs. Brookston was a dutiful mother, she was obligated with garden socials, the country club and charity events. It was her place to be involved in the community, keeping the family name in good standing. These activities also served, for a greater part, as a distraction from the harsh truths about her life: mainly, the lack of intimacy with her husband, which resulted in an emptiness in her heart. Apparently, while Mr. Brookston was busy building up a construction empire, he was also juggling many indiscretions with long legs and big blonde hair on the side.

Reasonably, the emotional absence of their parents is why Nancy and Tom grew close. That lack of intimacy sent both children on a lifelong search to replace it. As an effect, Nancy and Tom were left to a world about which most children could only fantasize. They were attended to and pampered by nannies and servants. Every morning the young Brookstons were awakened, bathed and dressed in the finest of attire. They were given the best of everything, except the attention of their parents. Six years older, Nancy had always taken a parental interest in Tom. When he was born, she put her favorite dolls from around the world back on the shelves with the countless others, and made Tom her baby. Nancy projected the love she never felt from her parents onto Tom, a real doll who could return it.

No, this was not happening to her big and strong baby boy. He would never be unhappy enough to try to end his own life. Now, she grieves from his actions, as if Tom is her child and she is his loving mother.

Nancy never married. Instead, she traveled the world with her mother until Mrs. Brookston died at a ripe old age. Their father had been years gone from a massive stoke. Nancy took over running the family estate, while Nathan successfully oversaw the family businesses at a cordial distance. He married right out of college. To the delight of his father, Colleen was from a huge banking family, the epitome of the social elite. It was another union of power and wealth, but one that seemed, at least appearance-wise, to work better than the generation before. They had two young girls and a son on the way at the time of Tom's attempted suicide. As expected, Nancy became a second mother to Nathan and Colleen's children. Not a surprise to Tom. He often expressed his belief that she was trying to correct the emptiness, which was so apparent in their mother's heart, by taking on the role of motherhood without ever having a child of her own pass from her womb.

There may not have been a cornucopia of love between or from their parents, but there certainly was more than enough money for everyone, more than sufficient for the generations to follow. This over abundance of wealth did pose a problem for Nancy. By modern standards, she was a less than attractive woman. As did the Brookston boys, she inherited the masculine looks of their father: thick coarse hair, bushy misdirected eyebrows — which Nancy and Tom managed to groom very well — and a stocky build. Nancy did the best she could appearance-wise, with what she had to work with. In later years, she went under the knife: a new nose, liposuction to thin out her waist and heavy ankles, all to tame the likes of her father's genetics resulting in a much improved outer shell.

There had been men in her life, even before the cosmetic surgery, but her family money was, and remained, the most attractive thing about Nancy to her suitors. On the inside, Nancy had complete and true beauty which was sadly obscured by her earlier outward appearance. She was well aware of the burden she carried coming from a prosperous family. It was a hard lesson learned at nineteen, from a man who swept her off her feet, only to leave her standing in the parlor of a Justice of the Peace late one night. Derrick was a twenty-one-year-old, storybook-tall, dark, young and handsome. He was a laborer in the distribution center of one of the Brookston's companies. They had been secretly dating for several months before Nancy told her father about their great love. He was not happy to hear the news.

"But, I love him, Daddy," Nancy exclaimed.

"You're too young to get married, and besides, this boy comes from nothing," Mr. Brookston told her.

"We're going to get married whether we have your blessing or not."

"We'll see about that!"

"You can't stop us, Father."

"Are you so sure he loves you, or the Brookston's money, child? I forbid you to see him again."

A month after the confrontation, just enough time for her father to find out who his daughter's suitor was, Nancy and Derrick planned to meet at the Justice of the Peace in the next county of Walker. On the scheduled night, he went AWOL, and she never heard from him again. Instead, one of Mr. Brookston's lawyers was waiting for her. He had paid Derrick ten thousand dollars to leave town, which was a spit in the ocean compared to the family wealth. Nancy was crushed. Her only comfort came from Tom.

After that, she questioned the intentions of the men who came around offering affection. Just how much was her love worth? It took a while, but Nancy came to understand that Derrick was just like her father. It was all about money and what it could buy. He realized ten thousand dollars was all he was going to get out of the Brookston family. From then on, she looked for signs of her father in the men who pursued her. There was no hiding their underlying intentions — money and power. Also, her father's womanizing and treatment toward Mrs. Brookston turned Nancy away from repeating her mother's history — rich, but lacking in love. Instead, she gave that love to her younger brother and nieces. Although Nancy loved Nathan as well, she held some resentment toward him because of his cold-shoulder position toward Tom's sexuality.

She became a woman of the world, savvy in many ways, and innocent in others. Do not be misled, as Nancy became older there were quiet and discreet affairs. Of her choosing, she lined the pockets of many men with her family's money. Some were struggling poets, others artists and musicians. This way there were no false hopes of true love and romance. In return, she bought love for short periods of time. She shared stories of her affairs with Tom during late-night phone conversations from different venues around the world. Little did she know of the emptiness he was experiencing, despite the string of his young lovers. Something Tom managed to keep well hidden from his older sister.

Nancy accepted Tom's homosexuality. It was apparent to her early on in their youth. She was the only one in the family who did not pass judgment on him. Mrs. Brookston did the southern thing, pretending he was otherwise. His father washed his hands of Tom due to an incident that occurred the night before Nathan's wedding. Tom was in his first year of college, and home for the marriage festivities. After a late night of drinking, Mr. Brookston was making his way across the grounds of the estate to a string of small cottages that housed some of the servants, one being his favorite maid. While passing by the pool house, he caught Tom naked with two men and a woman: one a distant cousin and his wife, and some hot number — as Tom described him over the years in his endless retelling of the story — from the gay bar in town. After which, anything but a gentlemen's agreement was made with his father, that he would try to live a respectable life outside of the state upon finishing school, at the family's expense of course. There was a list of stipulations, the main one being not to shame the family name. In other words, keep his perverted sexual lifestyle – as his father stated — hidden. The family was enormously well-connected, both in the political and financial worlds. The Brookston family had more money than any other in the state of Alabama, or the south for that matter. Mr. Brookston did not want the family name tarnished; certainly not by the escapades of a gay son. Apparently however it was acceptable, in his circles, to cheat on his wife, but to have a gay son was not.

As the years passed, his father and brother turned a cold shoulder. The distance between father and son, and brother and brother, grew wider and wider. Tom was not blatant in his mannerisms. From his teenage years into that first year of college before being caught by his father, Tom wanted to be like everyone else, at least by all appearances. He tried to make an effort to date girls, bringing them to the estate for swimming or tennis engagements. Delighted, Mrs. Brookston stepped in to offer suggestions of proper girls he should invite to the country club's winter balls, family summer picnics at the lake home and other events. It was an uncomfortable time for him. Many a gala was spent dancing with the best of debutantes, all the while cruising the handsome men over their shoulders. Tom played along at the frustration of many an unsuspecting girl's desire — and her parents' — to date a fine young boy from the most prominent of southern families.

Years earlier, prep school opened up the world a little wider for Tom. He was away from home for long stretches. It was there his interest in other boys really began to peak. Tom found himself in late-night meetings with a few boys like him, who stole secret moments in dormitory bathroom stalls, while most of the other boys were well asleep in their beds. Many a night, after the headmaster made his last check, Tom quietly slipped out from the covers, while trying not to disturb the sleep of his roommate.

The door to the communal bathroom nauseatingly squeaked, as it always did. His eyes squinted from the introduction of bright fluorescent lights, having to adjust from the dim night light of the hallway. On his first encounter, Tom found himself standing in front of the stalls, the clean white tile cool under his bare feet. With an echo, a low, phony cough breaks the silence of the room. The door to a stall guardedly opens to welcome him in. Tom walks toward it; a hand reaches out to pull his arm in, the rest of his body follows. He eagerly touches the other boy's exposed penis. Tom was fifteen, the same age Trey would be, and like him, the other older, almost seventeen. The stall door shuts, sealing its two occupants from the rest of the world. Innocence was exposed, and eventually, left behind inside those stall doors.

◊

Early into the third week, it begins to seem apparent. Tom's prolonged attempt at ending his life of sixty years will be successful, but now, not necessarily solely by his own hands. The combination of Dalmane and Valium, combined with alcohol, depressed his central nervous system to such a degree that his breathing greatly decreased, sending him into a coma from which he would possibly never awaken. The extreme lack of oxygen has caused brain damage. He has no spontaneous respirations, and is dependent on a ventilator. He exhibits no unprompted movements, or withdrawal from noxious stimuli. Tom does not have pupillary reflexes; his pupils are fixed and dilated. He is being fed through a feeding tube. His heart still is beating, but there is clearly no evidence of higher brain function.

Tom never liked to drag things out, especially if there was a decision to be made, or a situation to be acted on. How ironic that he is lying in a hospital room in a vegetative state. Tom thought pills and booze would be a quick and painless exit. He believed taking them was the best way out, much neater than shooting himself, or jumping off the penthouse balcony onto Park Avenue below. If Tom was anything, he was immaculate about everything he did. There was no way he was going to put a hole in his body, or risk his million-dollar face hitting the sidewalk. After all, why destroy all the great work of one of New York's most famous plastic surgeons. It would be a waste of good money. But his plans had gone haywire. Now the two people he cared about the most, Nancy and Trey, had to make the finial decision, whether to let him go, or continue to hold on to less than a grain of hope. It is not up to Tom anymore.

"But Dr. Houser, there must be something else that can be done!" Nancy cries out, as her eyes began to swell.

She quickly gets ahold of her emotions, the accumulation of tears in her eyes stops. Nancy then takes a deep breath while holding her head back to keep them from running down her cheeks.

"I'm sorry. It's extremely improbable that your brother will ever come out of the coma. And even if he does, he won't be the Tom you remember. He'll be less than a vegetable."

From the hallway, Nancy turns to look at Tom with the tubes connected to his body, like he is some science project in a bad sci-fi late-night movie. Her eyes follow the breathing apparatus running from his mouth to a machine on wheels by the bed. Trey is standing next to it, with his back to the room. He is looking out the window. Unlike Nancy, Trey has been crying all morning. She looks back at Dr. Houser, who is slowly but continually shaking his head.

"It's just his body lying there now," he says. Then adding, "I'm so very sorry Miss Brookston. I really am."

Old Flames Burn Bright

Who really understands the relationship between the human heart and mind? One day someone tells you they love you, life is nothing without you, and then somehow those words slip away into some obscure place never to be offered again by the one whom you so cherish. Suddenly you see a different person standing in front of you — a stranger — but one you have kissed a thousand times. Someone you have opened up your heart and soul to, a person with whom you have stood naked before, offering your body to be his. Your bodies have been locked in passion, mouths opened wide to taste and feast upon one another. You have literally allowed him inside you on so many different levels. Now, you find yourself standing alone. Empty. Your heart feels it will explode with fear and indescribable pain, while your mind is fogged with memories, and you wonder if you will ever hold that person in your arms again.

The subsequent nights can be so quiet when you are alone and desire his intimate touch to take the stillness from the darkness of the room. Moonlight piercing through the crack of the window draperies stirs you in bed. Oh how you do not want to be alone. The realization is that through those draperies, under the same moon, somewhere out there, lovers are making the world turn as yours stands still. You are wondering when you will love again, and if it will feel as intense and be as meaningful as before. You look at the phone hoping it will ring, and when it does, it is not who you want it to be. The desires in you continue to grow as sadness takes hold of your gut.

While pulling a pillow close, you turn on the television to ease the silence. Resting your hand on the nakedness of your body, you wrestle with a flood of emotions, as the clock on the bedside table endlessly ticks into the early morning hours. With eyes closed, you tell yourself to dream of your lost love with all the intimacies once experienced, only to know that after this night has passed, you will wake up alone.

◊

Trey was a fresh face in town. His newness stood out like a zit on a beauty queen's forehead. Even though Atlanta was much bigger than Birmingham, in many ways it was a small town. Anytime someone from out of town stepped in the bars, the locals knew; especially if he looked like Trey. Everything was new and exciting to him. It showed on his face like the involuntary expressions of a child at the circus for the first time.

Although Tom was twenty years his senior, Trey did not see

the span of years between them. Oddly enough, and a surprise to Trey, it was perhaps the strongest draw. Instantly he saw maturity and strength and an extremely handsome, confident, and sexy man with a pair of eyes that looked right through your clothes to the flesh. The smoked-filled air of the bar visibly circles Tom as he leans against the vacant pool table. At three a. m., The Cove, now long since torn down and replaced by a sewage treatment plant, is filled with men who do not want to go home alone after the other bars in the city have flooded their dark interiors with eye-blinding light, sending their occupants out into the dark night. Besides Backstreet, it is the only other private club where members pay fees, which allows it to stay open past the regulated closing time of the numerous gay haunts in the city.

It is a world so far from the one Tom came from. That is why he likes it. The Cove is seedy, nasty and dark, the adjectives his father would use to describe his gay son's lifestyle. It is the last stop and last chance of the night, or rather, early morning, to find someone to take home or to just get off with somewhere on the premises. You can smell the sex in the air, and possibly step in it, as you circle the bar looking.

Tom stands there like a Greek god among his subjects; as with all the rest, he is looking, too. He could be arrogant at times and often perceived as cocky. So much so, one might think Tom is packing a thick twelve-incher in those expensive jeans. Later, closer investigation would rebut that assumption, but a nice package all the same. His facade is mostly an act. Somewhere underneath there is a temperate man trying to climb his way up to the surface.

Even then, at thirty-nine, Tom is a man to be noticed. Still a looker with his muscular stocky build and thick slightly-salted dark hair that falls over his forehead like that of a twenty-year-old every time he turns to the right with a quick gesture of his head. He has eyes that seem to have the ability to look right into your deepest thoughts; they are the bluest this side of the Mississippi. The second Tom spots the newcomer, he knows he is going to have him for the night.

Trey heard about The Cove from some guys he had been hanging out with earlier in the evening. He followed them over in his car, but soon lost the clique in the crowd. The dim light and thick cigarette smoke make everyone look fuzzy to Trey. Tom watches him as he makes his way at a snail's pace to the bar. Trey feels a hand brush across his ass, but it is hard to tell who it belongs to. It really does not faze him as much anymore. Trey is getting used to being grabbed and fondled. He sees it as an initiation into a fraternity.

"What will you have?" asks a sweaty and shirtless bartender, over the noise.

"A Bud, please," Trey strains to be heard.

"That'll be three-fifty," says the bartender, as he sets the beer down.

Trey senses the presence of a large man standing behind him. He can feel him slightly pressing his upper leg against Trey's butt. Before he can pull out the money from his pocket, a hand reaches around him slapping a ten on the counter.

"Make it two and keep the change," Tom says.

Trey grabs the beer and turns around. Tom is a good two to three inches taller, and at least seventy pounds heavier.

"You didn't have to do that."

"It's my pleasure," Tom says, with a grin.

"Well, thanks."

"So you from around here?" Tom asks.

"No, from the Birmingham area."

"Really?" Tom answers in surprise.

"Yeah, Birmingham," Trey repeats.

"Man, you're kidding me. I'm from Mountain Brook."

Trey knows with that information Tom has, or is from, money. It is one of the richest areas in Birmingham, a far cry from Brighton with its trailer communities.

"So you live here now?" Tom asks.

"No, just in for the weekend. Had to take a break from school."

Trey is totally mesmerized. He feels flustered. An odd exhilaration scampers through his body. Suddenly he feels a deluge of emotions: sex, lust and comfort. They repeatedly bang into one another like a school of hungry piranha voraciously ingesting a stunned fish. Tom makes him nervous, but in a good way. The bar is hot, which adds to the delusional effects he is rapidly experiencing. Sweat collects on his forehead. Trey repetitively wipes it off with the palm of his hand. His shirt is sticking to his back as he feels the sweat rolling down from his armpits.

Tom can see he is getting to the newcomer, finding pleasure in it. He is amused and excited. His thoughts are racing too, already having the boy in his bed with his mouth on his dick.

"Let me get you another beer," Tom offers, as he turns to the bar, ordering himself a dry martini and another Bud for Trey.

Less than an hour of trivial conversation passes, along with the consumption of several more beers by Trey and a second martini by Tom. He is moving in for the kill, as he rubs Treys shoulders and back. Just the feel of Tom's strong hands on Trey's body is enough to make him surrender. Tom knows when to make his move. He is a pro. Tom leans in to kiss Trey. It is enough to suck the breath right out of the boy's lungs, while leaving a lingering taste of vodka on his lips.

"Want to get out of here?" Tom asks.

◊

The next morning light floods the room sending Trey's arms in a blind search for the covers to pull them over his face. In a semiconscious state, he tries to continue the dream that earlier put a smile on his face.

"So you decided to stay for breakfast after all," Tom states.

Trey thinks he is still dreaming, until he feels the sheet hurriedly being pulled from his grasp, leaving his nude body exposed. Within seconds a realization flickers in his head like an unstable fluorescent light blinking on and off. Trey is not in his own bed. Still disorientated, he cautiously opens one eye, then the other, to the sight of a devilishly handsome man, freshly showered smelling of lavender soap, wrapped in a thick white cotton robe standing beside the bed.

"Fuck, man," Trey responds in a startle.

He peers over the edge of the bed looking for his clothes.

"We did that already," Tom jokes.

"We did? You seen my clothes, man?"

Trey slides off the bed holding the sheet of which he had regained possession.

"They're already in the dryer. I couldn't let them smell up the house with all that bar smoke residue," Tom informs his bemused guest.

"But, but I'm naked. What do you want me to do, stand around with nothing on?" Trey rebuts.

"Well, you're a pretty sight like that, but I've got you covered."

Tom pulls a pair of blue pin-striped Brooks Bothers boxers and a white T-shirt from a highly-polished highboy chest, and tosses them at Trey's crotch; Trey would have never stayed the night in the first place, if he had not fallen asleep in Tom's comfortable sleigh bed. The late hour, combined with too much drink at Tom's encouragement, and the lushness of a feather down comforter with Tom's big strong arms around him was too inviting. He never spent the night with a trick before, much less had sex with anyone much older. Although still awkward with sex, what Trey remembered was enjoyable; it seemed Tom had been really into him, more sensual and caring than what he had experienced up to now with men closer to his own age. Waking up in someone else's bed is a whole new experience for him. Trey is not sure what the proper protocol is, and has no idea how to act.

"How long before my clothes are dry?" he asks.

"Are you in a rush?"

"Have a history exam to prepare for, so I should be heading back to Birmingham soon."

"Perhaps I can help you study. I was pretty good with history in school back in the stone age."

"Ah, I don't know," Trey says.

"Well the offer stands. Your clothes should be done in another fifteen minutes," Tom responds.

Trey takes another look at Tom. He smells so good. Tom's beautifully chiseled chest covered in dark hair bulging out of his robe is distracting. The hell with studying for a history exam, he thinks to himself. Trey picks up the loaned boxers and T-shirt and throws them back at Tom.

"On second thought, I'm not ready to get up," Trey says.

"Oh, yeah," Tom remarks.

"Yeah."

With that said Tom undoes his robe and eagerly climbs back in bed.

That morning was the beginning of many more weekends of Trey driving his Mustang to Atlanta to be with Tom. It was a passionate relationship while it lasted. Tom was as experienced as Trey was innocent to this new world of men. Before Tom, he had only had oral sex with other men. Tom was the first guy with whom he had anal intercourse. Excitement filled Trey every time they spoke on the phone. His heart ached on the Sunday nights he had to make the two-and-a-half-hour drive back to Birmingham. Trey felt he was keeping a big secret from his parents and friends back in Alabama. But it was a secret he was willing to keep.

Theirs was a timely meeting. In the dawning days of the 1980's, AIDS was just a paragraph in the papers and a blurb on the news. It was the gay cancer that no one really knew much about. Reported
60

cases were in the New York City and San Francisco areas, and had not quite reached the South. A panic swept across the country as more and more information filtered out to the public.

As a young man, having come out before the eruption of AIDS, Tom, like most gay men his age, had experienced the pure raw pleasures of unprotected sex. His sexual experiences for the first years were free and uninhibited. Tom saw the condom as a nuisance. Sure, it was a barrier to keep him from contracting a disease; there was always the fear of syphilis or gonorrhea, but those usually could be taken care of with antibiotics. He viewed condoms as a barrier from freedom; another obstacle to overcome his life in a straight world. He had been screwing guys since prep school without protection.

Before AIDS, Tom would not have thought twice about hooking up with someone and fucking them raw. Men were actually dying from this new disease. Now there was a new fear in the back of his head and those of his contemporaries, waiting to see who would die next, while watching friends and acquaintances getting sick, deteriorating to skin and bone, and then passing. It was a constant fear hovering overhead for many. They waited and looked for signs of the disease on their own bodies. Tom discounted it by telling himself he never had sex with anyone from New York City or San Francisco.

Despite his awareness of testing, it would take him some time after the world knew what AIDS was to get a blood test to check for the virus. Up until then, he would not go to his doctor or a clinic. The very thought of finding out he might have been exposed sent an ice-cold chill through his body. He had seen the mark of AIDS. More and more were sick and dying, and soon almost a whole generation of men would be lost. Tom continued to wonder when he would be next. When was it his turn? What would happen to his beautiful, strong body if he had it? How could he watch it waste away to nothing? He would rather not know. Tom told himself whatever was, was. A test would not change anything.

Before meeting Trey, in an effort to stay negative, he did struggle with using condoms, but it never felt as good as raw sex; he found them too restricting and sex was not as pleasurable. In years to follow, it would become more and more of a problem.

He knew Trey was new to gay sex and continued to fuck him raw. At that point, Trey was so in love, he would do anything Tom wanted, even if that meant having unprotected sex with the daunting gray cloud of AIDS hovering over the gay community. Little did both of them know how dark, ugly and massive that cloud would grow. The fear of AIDS did curtail Tom's interest in other young guys for a time. Trey had everything he wanted: youth, beauty and a sense of unwavering loyalty. But even the lurking fear of AIDS could not keep Tom satisfied by just one guy, no matter how beautiful he was. He finally got tested for the first time, more out of guilt than fear; guilt that he might be putting Trey in danger if he was unaware of his true HIV status.

Three months into their love affair, Trey transferred to Georgia State University and moved in with Tom. He now was a kept boy. His surroundings were very different from the single-wide trailer he grew up in. Trey had crossed over to the other side of the tracks. For the next three years things seemed, for the most part, fine. Trey majored in art, eventually graduating with a bachelor's degree.

In celebration they took a trip, at Tom's insistence, to Miami for the White Party, which would become the future granddaddy of circuit parties. It was Trey's first time in Florida, and other than a brief appearance at a tea dance fundraiser in Atlanta, he had never seen so many gay men in one place. It was at the fundraiser, a few months before the Miami trip, where he saw Tom's appetite for young boys blatantly surface for the first time since they had been together. They were dancing with a group of Tom's acquaintances high on coke. Tom took a snort offered by one of them. Trey passed on it. They were all rubbing up against one another; the two buffer guys focused their attention on Trey, while Tom zeroed in on the youngest one of the group. Trey felt out of place and uncomfortable as they locked him in a sandwich. Tom was dancing close to the young boy, letting him grope his crotch. The tryst was soon cut short when one of Tom's buddies fell out on the floor and began to have a seizure. They spent the rest of the night in the hospital emergency room.

Although Trey was well aware of Tom's roaming eye, as time passed he foolishly hoped that he was giving him all he needed. Things seemed to be going well between them and Tom knew what a looker Trey was. He even seemed to get off on the attention other guys bestowed on his boy. But the resurrection of Tom's appetite for other young men was not much of a surprise to some of Tom's friends. Several were astonished when Trey moved in, regardless of his good looks. They, on the other hand, knew Tom's history and his insatiable hunger for boys.

There were a few times after their second anniversary that Trey suspected Tom might be messing around on the side. Without concrete proof, there was nothing he could say or do about it. He just shrugged it off as having a boyfriend who was a big flirt. He figured, with Tom's age, that he would want to settle down once and for all. Regardless of any suspicions Trey had, Tom continued to be loving and supportive. Little did Trey know there were suppressed desires building up inside of Tom, like a volcano getting ready to explode. When it did, it would be hard to run from the all-consuming heat. Tom brought Trey to the very core of the volcano when they entered the White Party.

Running From the Flames

Trey finds the party to be tiring as it goes late into the night, but admittedly the men are beautiful. He loves the attention they are giving him and hopes that Tom is noticing. Trey wants him to realize what a catch he is and that there is nothing more desirable than a beautiful boy who is totally and unquestionably devoted. Despite all the men and choices, Trey wants to continue to belong to Tom and no one else. But Tom's eyes never stay still at the party, always scanning the crowd like a hawk looking for prey. Trey just pretends there is nothing to it until Tom disappears on the dance floor, later showing up with Mitch, a hot twenty-year-old French boy with his jeans half way down an exposed bubble butt, no underwear of course. Soon, they are back at the Fontainebleau Hotel with Mitch and one of his friends. Everyone is high on coke, except Trey, who is close to drunk, as he finishes off a bottle of vodka in the hotel suite.

The next morning Trey awakens among nude bodies entangled on white sheets, twisted and pulled out from the corners of the bed. The perfume of a long night of sex still hangs strong with a pungent arousing odor trapped in the dim room. Bed pillows thrown on the floor make a temporary obstacle course. Cautiously, Trey makes his way to the bathroom, stepping over the scattered assortment of clothing discarded hours ago in the feeding frenzy. He accidentally kicks a well-used bottle of Motion Lotion. He stops in his tracks to watch it roll over the carpet until it rests against a chair leg. His head hurts; mostly from the alcohol, but partly from the realization of what he has been a part of.

Still passed out, Tom's face is buried in one of the guys' crotch; whose, Trey cannot distinguish. The room is strangely quiet except for an occasional snore and an exaggerated exhale of breath. There is an open condom box on the bedside table. Most of its used contents are scattered on the floor among wrappers, although Trey really thinks none of them were used properly, or stayed on any one dick long enough as might have been advisable by the manufacturer. He cringes at the thought. An ill attempt at least, to be cautious in the age of AIDS.

Trey grabs a bottle of aspirin from the counter, and pops three on his way into the shower. Impatiently he waits for the water to turn warm, still holding the chalky white dissolving pills in his mouth. Finally the warmth comes and he opens his mouth to wash down the aspirin. Now the water is turning hot as steam engulfs the clear glass enclosure, before hastily overtaking the rest of the room. He sits on the shower floor allowing the pulsating water to wash off patches of semi-hardened cum that has taken ahold of the fine body hair of his arms and around his belly button. His head hangs low to keep it from pounding, as Trey waits for the aspirin to do its job.

God, what have I become? Trey thinks, as his hands cradle his head. He wants things to work with Tom, but Trey had not imaged an open relationship of sharing his man with anyone else. He wonders is this what the future holds for them.

It all happened so fast. He wants to please Tom, but the price of doing so seems to be too high. What Trey can recollect from the night before has frightened him. His mood is of loss. It seems he was caught up in a tornado where all the men, drugs, alcohol, music and sex tore through his very soul, and in the process, ripped a hole in his heart. Sure he was drunk, but not enough to have liked the orgy in which he participated hours ago. Why did he go along with it? Trey keeps asking himself, like he is expecting an answer to appear out of the steamy air.

Hours ago he fucked a stranger as his lover cheered him on. At first, it may have been arousing, but the morning has cast a different light on it. Tom is a master of persuasion. The two young circuit boys were easy work for him. They took one look at his strong muscular six-foot-two frame and "Daddy" went off in their heads, like the ring out after hitting the jackpot on a slot machine in Vegas. Trey had the same reaction on his first encounter with him. Standing there talking to Tom, he kept imaging how comforting those well-developed arms would feel wrapped around him, and of course those eyes, which are worth mentioning again; those blue, blue eyes that just stole his heart. They had completely stolen Trey's, and brought him to this point.

The rest is history, as they say.

Tom was all Trey could think about from the beginning. He was his world. Perhaps Trey should have seen the subtle signs as they popped up, but he did not want to see them or the underlying truth. Some people have this magnetic quality that just pulls you in, sometimes against one's own will. That was Tom. Even when something in the back of your brain tells you — in a soft scream — to turn around and go in the opposite direction, you find yourself frozen. Before you know, it's too late to run away.

So Trey ended up in a lavish hotel suite, butt naked with three strangers, one of whom he had known for three years, or had he? But Trey was not totally innocent. After all, even reluctantly, he was there partaking in the feast of flesh: hands grabbing body parts, tongues lapping up sweat, and wet mouths eating lust like it had been laid out on a buffet table.

What the hell was he thinking? Trey asks himself again, with the faint taste of lube on his tongue and the feeling like he needs to vomit. Slowly the night is being rewound in his aching head. Trey is hoping he had used a condom. He remembers Tom fucking him without one, but that was common practice for them, while one of the other guys was sucking him off. For the love of God, he cannot remember, and at this point he does not want to.

The hot shower helps him collect some of his thoughts, although they are still sluggish due to the excess of vodka still in his system. All Trey can think about now is getting out of the hotel room, away from the smell of sex and the morning-after fear.

It is time to make a decision. He knows he was trying to be someone he is not; trying to be the person Tom wants him to be, and do whatever it would take to hold on to the man he adores. He was acting the night before. But all the best acting in the world cannot change him into someone else. Tom is the one who has to change. Maybe it was a test he was putting him through to see if Trey could perform. But that was all Trey was doing: theater. Even in that Oscar award-winning performance, there had been no heart behind the character Trey was playing. They say an actor needs to find some truth in his character. The only truth Trey found was that it was the wrong part for him to be starring in. Viscerally, he knows this is not who he is, or ever will become.

Once out of the shower, he quietly moves past the bed, searching out his discarded clothes. Tom and the others have hardly moved from their positions, but now Trey can tell whose crotch Tom's face is buried in. The loud blond boy Tom had taken so much pleasure in fucking: Chad, or was it Chase? Whichever, it is not important now.

Without concern, Trey mixes dirty wrinkled clothes among clean ones in his bag. Once successfully dressed and packed without disturbing the sleeping trio, he wonders if he will be missed subsequent to their awakening. Or will his absence go unnoticed and the feast pick up where they left off, once the night has worn off their bodies?

Trey thinks about leaving a note for Tom, as he eyes the cream note pad with the hotel logo in burnt sienna centered on the top. He leans over the desk and picks up the pen. It shakes in his hand, as his stomach is feeling sick again. He sits down in the chair and scribbles out Dear Tom in blue ink. Blue like his eyes, Trey thinks.

A cough from someone in the bed breaks the silence of the

room, and then everything goes quiet again.

On second thought, no. He will know why I've left, Trey thinks, and then looks back at the bed.

He scratches through Tom's name and lays the pen on the pad.

A part of him wants to remove his clothes and return to bed before they know he is gone. He can lie down and perhaps that will make his head stop hurting and settle his stomach. If he can just get close to Tom, Trey thinks, he will feel better; especially if he can lie in Tom's arms and they can cuddle like they did back home in Atlanta, where he felt Tom's breath on the back of his neck night after night. But there are others in the bed now, he reasons in his head, others who have come into their relationship, and now it is tainted. Somehow he knows it will never be the same again. He will never feel the comfort and safety he had experienced with Tom before this trip. His heart is pounding; his head continues to feel it is seconds away from cracking open, exposing his brain.

Shit, it is not the same anymore, he thinks. It is an unwelcome realization. Call me old-fashioned, he reasons, but if I wanted to fuck around I would have stayed single. I would have never moved in with him in the first place.

Tom had asked Trey to move in a dozen times before he finally said yes. Now it seems like such a contradiction in his character. From day one, Trey knew the man he loved was a chicken hawk, and he had a slight fear he would be of little use to him after his boyish looks took on some years, but Trey put his faith in hope that Tom would settle down.

After their first year together, he felt cautiously optimistic Tom had changed, and gotten the boy craze out of his system. But now Trey realizes that is not the case. The truth about Tom is lying in the hotel bed. He was just getting warmed up. Last night Trey shockingly saw a different side of him, which made it clear that Tom will never get his fill. He will be running on empty from now on. He will never be happy with just one guy, Trey thinks, his mind trying to reason with his heart. His heart does not want to walk out that door, although all of the fiber in his brain is telling him to.

Perhaps last night had changed nothing for Tom, only rekindling his deepest desires, but for Trey, it changed everything. He is a different person now, and Trey is seeing Tom differently as well. His time is up. Tom has had his fill of him and is moving on. In a way, Trey understood Tom's need to be revived by those eager to let him drink their sweet juice of youthfulness. Things were adding up now, especially considering the last year. Tom had been talking more about becoming an old man, making self-degrading remarks. At first, Trey just made light of them.

"Well, you're my old man, and no one else's, baby," Trey would say.

But that would not pacify the smoldering desires in Tom. The only thing that could would be some new fresh young meat. As long as they were around, Tom felt eccentrically young and alive. Trey witnessed the transformation last night in the hotel room.

The door makes a slight creaking noise as Trey vigilantly opens it. He is tightly wrapped in panic like a belated birthday present. This is it, he thinks, I am leaving now, as if Tom asleep in the bed can read his thoughts and will wake up and tell him not to go. Trey wants to turn his head around to see him one more time, but he knows seeing Tom with the others will make his heart hurt more, if hurting more is possible. He keeps his eyes forward waiting for his legs to move, but they do not. They just stand there, rigid and heavy like he is wearing cement shoes. He holds on tight to his bag, so tightly that his knuckles are turning white. Trey looks at his feet. Move, his mind tells them, but still they do nothing.

He feels something trying to climb up his throat. Trey swallows hard, but the sensation comes again, this time, even stronger. He drops the bag. It thumps to the floor. Trey makes his way back to the bathroom. He feels he is moving in slow motion, dragging his legs behind him. They are weighted down with anxiety, loss and uncertainty.

Finally, Trey makes it and drops in front of the toilet. He does not feel the impact on his knees. Trey feels nothing except angst and the sickness barreling up from his gut. He dry heaves several times before the vomit sensation subsides. Trey wipes a long string of spit from his mouth and chin before coming to his feet again.

He walks over to the vanity and turns on the water, watching it as it fills the sink before splashing some on his face. It is cool on his skin. Trey does not bother to wipe his face and hands dry; instead he makes his way back to the front door, water dripping on his shirt as he passes Tom and the others once again. He wants to cry. They are still asleep.

He tightly takes hold of his bag again and exits the hotel room. The air in the hall is distinctly different, fresher, and he is able to breathe. For a moment, Trey stands on the other side, waiting for the door to shut behind him. He waits until he hears the click of the lock before beginning his walk down the hallway.

The ride to the airport was close to unbearable, seeming to take forever. Then, another two hour wait to get on a flight to Atlanta.

When Tom woke up to find Trey missing, he sensed something was wrong, but told himself that perhaps he had gone for a swim or to the restaurant to eat. It was an excuse to allow himself to revisit the scene from the night before with his guests. After the two guys left, Tom noticed the hotel stationery where Trey started to leave him a note. Seeing his name scratched out told him what was going on in Trey's head. When he saw Trey's things were gone, Tom left a message on the phone machine in Atlanta. It was flashing for Trey when he arrived. Tom called several more times that evening, but Trey was not ready to talk. He stood by the phone listening to Tom leaving message after message.

By the time Tom returned home on Monday evening, Trey had already vacated their house and moved temporarily in with a friend. He had made it easier for Tom, giving him all the freedom he wanted, and there were plenty of young men to fill his time. It was not easy for Trey, but he did not want to compete with every twenty-year-old that might be around the corner. From guilt and confusion, Tom asked Trey to come back. The answer was no. Trey wanted to, but hoped if he stayed away long enough Tom might finally change.

After a few months they started dating again. But that still left too much autonomy for Tom. He had it all now, Trey and the freedom to see other boys. He so loved Trey, but it was too hard to resist a sweet young ass willing to spread his legs for some daddy meat. There was plenty of that to be found — Atlanta was the bottom capital of the South. Even though Tom did not tell him about any of the romps with other boys, he did not have to. Trey could smell them on him, and he could see them in the reflection of his eyes.

The uncertainty became too much for Trey, so much that, on many occasions, he shamefully drove by the house late on the nights they were not together, either to see someone else's car parked in front, or Tom's car gone from the garage.

Eventually, Trey called it off for the second and then a third time. The breakup was harder for Trey, who thought about Tom night and day, wondering who was with him; who was sharing the bed they once christened.

It took a while, but they became friends, good friends. There was no extinguishing the love they had. But Trey could not share Tom in the hotel room back in Miami, and he could not share him back in Atlanta. As they say, time can be a healer, or at best, buffer the pain of lost love. But there are just some things time cannot expunge from the heart's mind.

Following their final split, Trey plunged headfirst into the gay lifestyle after having experienced a small taste of it before their meeting. He soon found that there were too many games to be played, and Trey did not know the rules. It took a long time to get over Tom, so in the interim, Trey was sleeping around trying to fill the void Tom had left. Every new encounter was a risk of the heart, mind and body.

Tom too went wild, sleeping with every beautiful, barely-legal guy that crossed his path, partly to ease the loss of Trey, but mostly to feed his obsession. He went through them like a large economy-size bag of Almond M&M's; the colors may have varied, but the flavors were all the same — crunchy and tasty in the center — feeding his own fading youth.

So far, nature had been good to Tom. For the most part he had good genes. His father had remained handsome well into his sixties. The fact that Tom was a big kid at heart only added to his irresistible charm. But Trey knew it was a matter of time before it all caught up with him. He would wait to see if Tom might slow down as the years grew in number.

Dishearteningly for Trey, a few years after their break-up, he could see Tom's obsession for young men was increasing. It was becoming clearer that for Tom, being with someone around his age, or even Trey's, would have been too much of a reflection of himself, and a reminder that time never stops moving forward without taking with it one's own youth. Trey knew Tom loved him, but he was coming around to the understanding that if he had stayed in the relationship, Tom would be unable to stomach watching the years eat at the layers of Trey's youth. In doing so, Tom would be witness to his own aging. With that new knowledge, Trey tried not to take it so personally. It was a numbers game with Tom. He required the injection of youth like a drug addict needed dope.

Three years after Miami, Tom had his first face-lift to tighten things up a bit, as he jokingly put it. Trey knew there was no joking associated with it. Tom was doing all he could to put a roadblock in nature's way. Trey even helped Peggy look after him during his recuperation until he was ready to go back out into the world again. Although they were still seemingly in the future, Trey started thinking about his own maturing years. Even though he was still beautiful, Trey knew he was not young enough for Tom anymore.

Peggy fought Tom as much as she could about getting the face-lift.

"Now God has a plan for you (her well-used line). No need in you having some witch doctor cut on your face and all," she would say.

Even after the procedure, she still did not let up.

"See, look at you all black-and-blued up. You're going to just mess up that nice face of yours. God gave you that face, I don't know why you want to go and spend all that good money on a face-lift, Mr. Tom. God has a plan for all of us. You shouldn't be messing with his work. Now there is no telling what you will look like when those bandages come off. It's the devil's work, I'm telling you."

Perhaps it is some kind of cruel joke nature and God are playing on the vain, who are not at ease with growing old, Trey thinks, as he watches Tom sleep. His face is puffy, there is bruising around the eyes peeking through the bandages. Trey is reminded of the better days as he sits in a comfortable occasional chair covered in a Fortuny fabric.

He picks up a men's fitness magazine from the side table, looks closer at the cover model, and then tosses it down in abhorrence. It reminds him he needs to do a few hundred more crunches at the gym later that afternoon. Now he is feeling guilty that he cut his workout short the day before to rush over and sit with Tom while Peggy ran errands. He wonders, staring at the discarded magazine — the buff gym stud seems to be mocking him from its cover — is it better to be average and go through life unnoticed, or rather to have the God-given gift of beauty and face the cruel reality of watching it being taken away as the advancing years cover it layer by layer, cutting in lines and wrinkles?

Growing older in the gay community is a big concern for many homosexual men. Tom was a prime example, even Trey was finding he was facing that concern. The culture is drowning itself in beauty and youth. If one is fortunate enough to be born with good looks, it is only a matter of time before it is taken away. For those blessed, as time passes and their looks wilt, they, as with other older gay men, fade into the background only to be soon forgotten by the very culture they once played a vital role in nurturing. Tom was going to do everything in his power to give Mother Nature a run for her money, even making a pact with the devil, if need be, to keep him from growing a day older.

As far as Peggy and Trey were concerned, they hardly noticed much difference in Tom's appearance after the first surgery, but he, on the other hand, had a new lease on life. At least for a while.

Two years later, Tom and Peggy moved to New York City. Tom bought a penthouse on Park Avenue. It was hard for Peggy to say no after Tom showed her the palace in the sky. It had a great separate apartment at the west end all for her, with a private entrance, a bedroom, living area, small kitchen and bath. Despite their differences, he had been good to her in Atlanta, always making her feel like family, and she felt the same about him. Growing up, Peggy, never in a million years could imagine living like this in New York City: a poor close-to-middle-aged woman with a seventh-grade education living up in the sky. Every night before going to bed, Peggy looked out her bedroom windows in awe.

Over the years that followed, Tom became more dissatisfied with his fading looks, which sent him back for repeated trips to the surgeon to make some nips and tucks here and there. The young boys kept coming in and out of his bed. The money helped to continue reeling them in. The fancy address, expensive foreign cars, designer clothes, and free vacations to exotic places became a strong magnet. But they only held them for a short period of time. A few moved on of their own accord, while others, like Trey, did not want to share him, or Tom simply tired of them; usually the latter. He had to have more and more youth to see as his reflection.

A Different Kind of Music

It took Nancy and Trey another day to make the gut-wrenching decision. It was a long and arduous twenty-four hours of regret, hesitation and questioning. She leaned heavily on Trey for strength and assurance that there were no other options but to let Tom go, like he had tried to do several weeks ago. After consulting with other doctors, and her minister back in Birmingham, with Trey at her side, she watched Dr. Houser flip the switch that would stop the machines that were keeping oxygen moving in and out of Tom's lungs and blood pumping through his heart. Peggy, Kyle and Virginia stood in the hallway to witness the sorrow.

Now, the day after, with few words spoken, Nancy, Trey and Kyle ride behind the black shiny hearse carrying the coffin with Tom's body to LaGuardia Airport. Peggy is left with the unpleasant task of closing up the penthouse. Virginia has already gone ahead to insure that everything for the transport of Tom's body has been cleared. It is all Trey can do to hold himself together. Having Kyle with him helps. He is grateful he decided to fly up a week ago, and is there now, for whatever Kyle's reasons may be. The simple thought of being back home in Atlanta with him is all that is holding Trey together until this is over. A hopeful thought it is, but hope will do for the present. He tries to think of more pleasant thoughts as he looks into Kyle's eyes and is reminded of the first time he gazed into them.

◊

Trey met Kyle at a country bar in Atlanta, another Saturday night, in another bar and pushing forty. It was the last place Trey wanted to be, but he promised his buddy, Steve, he would join him out for a night of bar hopping. Hoedowns was the first stop. The bar was at its peak, with a wide assortment of men and women stirring up the mix dressed in everything from western wear to leather to preppy, crisscrossing the bar. The dance floor is full of two-steppers kicking up their heels under a large video screen with a fine-looking Tim McGraw performing. The song being played by the DJ, on the other hand, is by Lee Ann Rimes, not Tim, singing down on everyone, making it appear Tim is doing a bad lip-synching job.

Trey follows Steve through the corral of people. A group of guys race past them. A short muscle boy in a red plaid shirt holds onto his cowboy hat, as if he is running from a wild bull on the loose. Instead, as the DJ is making his announcement, the muscle boy and the others are rushing to get into position for a popular line dance. Steve and Trey step aside to let them pass. Within seconds, the beat of the music changes and, like a well-rehearsed chorus, fifty-plus weekend dancers kick up their heels, while proceeding to twirl and spin their bodies to the music. Hee-haw!

"Hey, that's him," Steve says, as he motions to Trey.

"Where?"

"Over to your right," Steve directs, with a thrust of his head.

"Yeah, he's cute," Trey answers, not really telling the truth.

Trey is referring to a rather average, big-built guy standing in arm's reach to their right. For the past week, Steve had been chatting with him online. After exchanging pictures, they decided to meet at the bar that night. With some encouragement from Trey, Steve approaches him. After a few awkward moments, it appears the preliminary conversation is picking up some steam.

"This is Allen," Steve introduces, as he pulls his new friend over to where Trey is standing bored out of his mind.

"Hey, man. So you're the guy Steve dragged me out on a cold night for," Trey says, with forced enthusiasm.

Allen's response is swallowed up by the music.

Steve and Allen continue to get acquainted. Trey stands next to them, looking around the crowd, thinking how he wishes he were home in bed. His eyes are irritated by the smoke trapped in the bar, as a result of the poor ventilation; another good reason to be home, or almost anywhere else. Steve excuses himself to relieve his beer filled bladder. Trey is left to make idle conversation with Allen.

"So, what do you think about this place?" Trey asks.

"I come here since it's the only country bar in town."

"People seem nice," Trey responds.

It is too hard to talk over the music and loud voices. Besides, Trey has steadily lost interest in the bars over the past years. There was still an occasional night out, here and there, spent dancing at another bar called the Heretic with his shirt off — jeans unbuttoned at the waist and underwear left on the bathroom floor at home — dancing with a variety of men, all showing off their bodies. It was the same scene in every big town across the country on a Saturday night. The Heretic was an easy pick-up place if in the mood. But one did not have to leave the bar to get off. By two a. m., the back poolroom and hallway were filled with men making body contact, the dim lights weakly reflecting off the sweat rolling down their shirtless backs. On almost any weekend night, a group huddled around a man being fucked by another. The two strangers' moans were muffled by the bodies encircling them. A constant flow of men made the rounds, many, like animals stalking prey, getting groped or groping, while others were there just to watch. Public sex was never Trey's scene, but there was undoubtedly a level of arousal from being in its presence.

There had been the passing of many seasons since Trey first drove that Mustang through the late afternoon countryside, watching the day turn into night, wind rushing in and out of the open car windows as he faced an uncertain future with only childhood dreams to guide him. He pursued those early dreams of becoming an artist. After Tom and Trey busted up, he threw himself into his passion. Gradually his art began to do well. Trey found much of his time consumed in the studio, surrounded by the smell of oil paint and varnish. If he was not painting, he was attending art openings and keeping up the illusion of a successful artist. He kidded about his accomplishments saying, when asked what he did, "He just spent his time watching paint drying."

Now, he is looking for something more but does not think he will find it in a bar. Unlike Tom, Trey likes the idea of settling down with one guy. Early on, Trey knew he would be content to be with one man. He wanted the routine day-to-day structure of coming home in the evening to the same person, going to bed and waking up with that person. There was something special about belonging to someone. Trey wanted ownership in a relationship like he thought he had for a time with Tom.

Trey wonders if he can leave soon now that his friend has met Allen in person. He decides to wait until Steve returns from the bathroom to make his egress.

"Hey, doesn't that guy look like Justin from *Queer as Folk?*" Allen says as he points to a young, good-looking fair-haired guy wearing a brown leather shirt and jeans.

Trey noticed the guy a few minutes prior to Allen's acknowledgement. There is no question about it, he is a looker, but Trey is ready to go home. Like Tom, he had his share of short relationships with men. Plus, just like Tom, the older Trey got, the younger the men became. It is interesting how he was attached to older men in his twenties. Now, older himself, the tables were slowly turning in the other direction, where Trey is finding himself waking up with men whose mothers are his age. He refuses to believe he is following in Tom's footsteps.

"The world is full of beautiful men, and I'm going to fuck as many as I can before I die," Tom often said.

Unlike his dear friend, Trey is not intentionally looking for younger guys; it seems they are searching him out. For whatever reason, there was a segment of young men who preferred older ones. Some were looking for money and security, but Trey was not a wealthy man.

By forty, a large number of men on average had let themselves go, pulled down and out of shape by gravity. On the other hand, although both were given a head start at birth, Trey, as Tom had done, kept his body in excellent shape through the years. He was a hot man at thirty-nine. Now, the same age Tom was when they first met, Trey was slowly maturing into a future "daddy" type, but without leather chaps or a harness in his wardrobe. Like Tom and many other gay men, Trey spent six to seven hours a week in the gym to feed the growing obsession, putting more value on his physical beauty than his inner peace. Over the years, his body filled out into a beautiful sculpture of a man. It seemed the older Trey got, the looks matured as well.

Everything in the gay world revolved around the male body. It was all about beauty. Many of those not born with it had gone to great lengths to acquire it. The covers of most gay magazines were adorned by young, buff delicious men from eighteen to twenty-four, staring out from the newsstand shelves. Where were the rest of the men — the average, the plain, and the overweight and older men? Did they not matter? To a large degree, because of AIDS, there was a big part of a whole generation of men — Trey's generation — gone. On any given weekend night, the bars were full of young men in their twenties and thirties. Where were the older ones? Were they at home with their partners and two dogs? Or were they dead?

Trey cannot help but wonder about the really cute guy Allen

pointed out, even though he has decided it is better to take a hiatus from men all together, especially younger ones. Even still, he finds himself looking around the bar to see where this stranger has gone. It will not hurt to have one last look at him from a distance, an image he can keep in his head for later that night when he is in bed beating off before going to sleep. That way, he can relieve himself, wipe off and be done with it. How harmless can that be, Trey wonders? He is ready to leave Steve with his new friend anyway and head home to a comfortable but empty bed. Perhaps this Justin look-alike left as well, and that will end the interest altogether. Why get all worked up over a stranger, even if he is so his type.

As Trey is getting impatient to say his good-byes, he sees "Justin" staring in his direction from the entrance of the dance floor. At first he is not sure he is really looking at him, but possibly someone nearby. Trey looks around, and then looks back at the blonde who is now pointing at him and mouthing, "Yes you. You want to dance?"

Trey shakes his head no and mouths back, "Don't know how to two-step."

The guy smiles as he heads for the floor, just as a new line dance begins to form. At that moment, Trey wishes he knew how to dance to this country music. He regrets not taking the classes the bar offers on Monday and Tuesday afternoons which he entertained doing with a friend several months back. He cannot help but think if indeed he had, he would be out there now with the cute blonde. Trey is not bold enough to try to fake it; these weekend dancers are too good. He watches the boy kick around to the music with the others. For a moment, he feels like he is back in junior high school watching Michelle Douglas dance with some popular guy. The regressive thought leaves his brain as quickly as it entered.

A big muscle guy, standing a few feet away in a black tank, has been staring at him since Trey arrived, but he is not interested in large guys. He is almost annoyed by the guy's persistence in trying to catch his eye. This guy has passed behind Trey three times now; on two of those passes, he took the liberty of grabbing his ass. Trey wants to deck the guy if he does it again.

Steve is saying something to him, but Trey has his mind on the blonde. He is thinking about sticking around for a few minutes to see if he can muster up the nerve to speak to the boy. He is wondering if he should even make an attempt. Trey laughs to himself thinking what would Tom do if he were in town and out with him. He laughs again. This time an ample smile comes to his face. He knows exactly what Tom would do: make a bee-line to the boy; fill him with drinks and invite him to fly up to New York. Tom has no loyalty to friends when it comes to very cute young boys. The only thing that would protect one's boyfriend from Tom would be a chastity belt — one with a very strong lock.

Trey loses sight of the blonde on the floor; too many dancers to see over and around. The boy is short Trey thinks. Hard to tell at a distance, but he looks under six feet. A plus. Trey likes shorter guys. He feels they fit better under him. He does not like long-legged ones; too much leg flying around in the air when he is bedding them. He is amused by his indecision. Less than an hour ago he was over men, and now he is all about this one.

Trey feels someone brush against him from behind again. He thinks it is the muscled guy, and turns around ready to give him a piece of his mind. Surprisingly, it is the blonde. Trey is drawn in instantaneously by the boy's eyes.

"Hey, man. I'm Kyle."

"How are you, bud?"

"I'm great now."

"Why's that?" Trey asks raising his voice above the noise.

"Because you're here. I was getting bored."

"Looks like you were having a hell of a time out there."

"Yeah. How come you don't dance?"

"Never learned."

"Well, I can teach you."

"Looks like you know what you're doing out there. That's for sure."

"And I bet you could teach me a thing or two, as well," Kyle says, giving Trey a coy look.

Trey cannot help but smile.

"I have a feeling you're something else," Trey says.

"I'll be anything you want."

"Now that's a thought."

"So, you want to kick up your heels?" Kyle asks.

"Well, I kind of had that in mind for you, but it's late and I should be heading home. How about giving me your number?"

"Sure, but I don't live here."

"Oh. Where're you from?"

"Boston."

"When you leaving?"

"Tomorrow night," Kyle says with a frown.

The last thing Trey wants is to get involved with someone from out of town. What is the point? Even though Kyle is hot, it would end up being just another mindless fuck. Besides, he can tell he is young. How much so, he is afraid to ask.

"You sure you want to go home without me?" Kyle asks.

"Well, I'm sure I want to go home. With or without you is another thing."

Trey decides to think with his head and not his penis. He wants to fuck Kyle. Oh man does he want to, but it is not going to be tonight. They exchange phone numbers at the bar.

"Okay, bud. Nice meeting you," Trey says.

Can I call you tomorrow?" Kyle asks.

"Sure. That'll be great."

Trey reluctantly turns for the door.

"Hey, wait," Kyle calls out.

Trey turns around.

"Yes, bud."

"Let me give you something to think about."

Kyle reaches up gently grabbing Trey behind the neck to tilt his head downward. Their lips meet. The kiss is long and wet. Trey tastes a delicate fruity flavor rousing in their mouths. He puts his arms around the blonde pulling him in close. Kyle can feel Trey has gotten excited; his penis erects against his leg.

"Damn," Kyle says, as he comes up for air, and he is not referring to the kiss, although it was amazing.

"Okay. Tomorrow then," Trey says, as he turns and heads for the door. He looks back over his shoulder at Kyle, who is watching his departure. They both smile and wave good-bye.

Kyle is disappointed. He wants to have sex tonight. He shakes his head. The night is still young, he thinks to himself, but he doubts there is anyone in the bar that can measure up to Trey. He heads back to the dance floor.

Facing Monsters

Subsequent to their meeting at the bar that January night, Kyle called Trey bright and early for a Sunday morning to meet at the Starbucks in Ansley Mall. Trey was nervous as he walked in wearing a black cable wool crew neck sweater and Levis. Kyle was already there, wearing jeans and a tight long-sleeved T-shirt with Abercrombie across the chest. He was sipping a fat-free decaf latté. Trey planned to show Kyle around Atlanta, but they soon ended up at his house. The next six hours were spent getting acquainted physically, until Trey took Kyle to the airport to catch his plane back to Boston. Less than a year later, Trey drove up to the Ivy League town to bring Kyle and his belongings to Atlanta — all in a Land Rover, pulling a U-haul trailer packed to the gills, boxes of Kyle's clothes strapped in the safari basket on the roof.

They lost the right rear bumper guard and a few pairs of 2(x)ist underwear somewhere in North Carolina on Interstate 75 South in the middle of the night.

Trey was concerned about the age difference. He dated younger guys after his relationship with Tom, but never thought about playing house with any of them. He is surprised it has lasted this long, but things may change once Tom is laid to rest and they are back in Atlanta, and are faced with addressing unfinished business. But for now, Trey just wants to think that everything will be okay. First things first.

◊

Trey and Kyle are flying out of New York with Nancy and Virginia in the Brookston Industries' private jet. Tom's body lies in a mahogany casket lined in cream silk secured in the cargo compartment of the plane. Understandably, the trip is solemn. Nancy carries a look of loss on her colorless face. She is wearing a black Chanel suit magnifying her paleness. Her large diamond stud earrings and the tennis bracelet on her right wrist are blinding even in the daylight. A small gold cross hangs around her neck. Her hair is pulled up in a tasteful twist. Nancy's grooming is flawless except for the few strands that have fallen to either side of her face.

For most of the trip, she sits in her seat looking out the window. Nancy sporadically moves the bracelet up and down her arm. Her assistant sits in a seat toward the back, checking off a list while making final arrangements on the phone. Occasionally, she walks over to Nancy and whispers words in her ear pertaining to Tom's upcoming service. Nancy shakes her head yes or no, and Virginia returns to her seat to continue with the preparations.

Trey feels helpless. His dearest friend is lying in a casket and his sister seems to be in a state of shock. Trey knows there is nothing he can do for Tom at this point, so he tries to focus on what Nancy needs, to help her not feel so alone, now that Tom is gone.

"Can I get you something?" Trey asks Nancy.

"No, dear," she answers, before looking back out the window.

"Well, will you let me know if I can?"

"Yes, but nothing now. Nothing. Unless you can bring Tom back," she answers.

Trey wishes he could. Oh how he wishes he had been a better friend and seen the warning signs. It is apparent to him that her eyes are red from crying. Not that Nancy would have let anyone see the first tear fall. She waited until she was alone locked in Tom's bedroom, so no one could hear the pain of her loss. Even Peggy tried to console her, also seeing the red eyes every morning before Nancy left for the hospital.

"God will see you through this," Peggy told her.

"Thank you for your concern, but I don't know what to think about all this. Tom's my brother. Why didn't he come to me? I would have helped him," Nancy confided in Peggy.

"I know sweetie, I know. But let God take care of things. He has the power to take care of everything. I have been praying for our boy. Now let me make you something to eat. You need to eat to keep up your strength for Tom."

"How could God let him do this?" Nancy asked.

"I don't have an answer, dear. There is so much we can't understand," Peggy said, continuing to be consoling.

Peggy did have a way about her; even with a linebacker's build, her soft soothing voice eased from her lips like warm caramelized sugar. Like aroma therapy, she always had a clean washed smell that lingered after she left the room. Everything about her was comforting. But Peggy's prayers did not bring Tom out of the coma.

Trey respects Nancy's wishes to be left alone and returns to his seat next to Kyle, who is sleeping. The morning flight is smooth. It appears to be a clear day in the making, with a few white bulbous clouds, as the jet cuts its way like a rocket through the sky. A light pink haze envelops the sun rising in the east. Trey cannot help but remember the trips he made with Tom over the years in the same jet. Not too long ago, they flew to Paris together, and a year earlier to the Cayman Islands. Three years prior, they went to London on a shopping spree for Tom's penthouse. On several occasions, Tom sent the jet to fly Trey up to New York. Now, it is carrying Tom home one last time. In a million years, Trey would have never dreamed he would be making this flight under these circumstances.

After dropping Trey and Kyle off in Atlanta, Nancy and Virginia will take Tom on to Birmingham. A service is scheduled in two days. Nancy gives a lingering hug to Trey, as Virginia and Kyle look on. There are no words to describe the heavy hearts that are finding courage to beat in saddened chests. Nancy can no longer restrain the dam of tears, as she holds on to Trey. They both begin to cry, their tears mixing together on their cheeks.

"You were the best thing that ever happened to Tom. I know

he loved you dearly," Nancy whispers in Trey's ear.

"And I loved him."

"I know sweetie, I know," Nancy acknowledges.

They stand locked in the embrace a few minutes longer, before Nancy weakly pulls away. Almost immediately, she wipes the escaped tears with her hand.

"I'll see you in a few days," Trey says as he offers his hand to her.

Nancy reaches out for it, squeezing it as tightly as she can muster.

"Call me if you need anything, Nancy."

"I will, and you do the same."

The taxi drops Trey and Kyle at their home at eleven-forty-five a. m. It is a sleek contemporarily-renovated 1940's split ranch, with a mix of neoclassic elements and fine antique furniture. Certainly nothing on the scale of Tom's penthouse, but a very respectable residence in Peachtree Hills, just north of Midtown, and a long way from the single wide trailer in which Trey grew up. Tom bought it for him after they split up. The house is stuffy from being closed up while they were away. Kyle proceeds to take their bags upstairs to the bedroom; Trey opens up the French doors off the living room to allow in some welcomed fresh air.

Upon his return, Kyle finds Trey standing in front of the large kitchen window looking out on the square pool centered in a well-groomed backyard. The undisturbed water resembles glass, as it reflects the sky and surrounding shrubs and flower beds welcoming the late morning sunlight. The emotional strain is evident on Trey's face. His hands rest on each side of the sink, showing his wide latisimus doris muscles under his shirt, and large triceps as they flex out of the short sleeves.

"Do you want to talk?" Kyle asks Trey.

For a moment, there is no response. Kyle makes a big swallow in his throat. He really does not want to talk about their problem, but feels he needs to give Trey the option to do so if he wishes.

"Do you want me to pick up Buffy and Sam?" Kyle asks, trying to quickly change the topic of discussion.

Their two golden retrievers, Buffy, now four years old, and Sam, two, would usually be waiting for them at the front door. Kyle kenneled them before he flew up to New York the week after Trey.

"Let's get them later. What if we take a nap first," Trey finally speaks.

Kyle is relieved with that response, and walks over to where Trey is standing; he has not moved from his stance at the sink. The mood is tense. Without another word spoken, Kyle stands close behind Trey, slowly sliding his arms around his thirty-two inch waist. He can feel Trey's defined abdominal muscles. Kyle takes a deep breath, as he cautiously rests his head on Trey's broad shoulders.

"This feels good," Kyle says.

"Yes, it does," Trey answers.

With that spoken, Trey turns around with Kyle's arms still around him. He kisses him on the forehead. Both their eyes close for a moment. Kyle feels safe for the duration of the kiss, and the continued embrace. Trey then takes Kyle's hand and leads him to the bedroom. They have not had sex for almost a month. Even the week Kyle was in New York, Trey could not bring himself to. They had been staying with Nancy at the penthouse while Tom was in the hospital. Kyle had been understanding, even though he was unsure if Trey wanted him anymore. Regardless, Kyle wanted to be there for Trey and hoped their problems would be swallowed up by the current events.

During that week, although they did share the same bed, all Trey wanted to do was cuddle, but not throughout the whole night, like they had before. In the past, if Kyle woke up without Trey's arms around him, he would make a whimpering sound like a lost puppy.

"Hold me," he would call out, as he made the sounds.

"Okay, baby," Trey would say, before pulling him back into his arms.

Kyle would whimper again, but in contentment and fall asleep.

Kyle now stands by the bed, beginning to remove his shirt.

"Let me do that for you," Trey offers.

With that said, Kyle stops at the second button. Trey pulls off his black polo shirt, revealing his large muscular frame which still looks close to perfect even after a two week forced break from the gym. His middle to lower chest is covered in light short soft brown hair, which started growing in his mid twenties. It meets at the sternum bone. He stopped shaving his chest several years ago. From there, it travels down between a six pack, enough to bring almost any man to his knees. Kyle knows Trey is the perfect man, or very, very close. He had been such a fool to risk losing him. Maybe it is too late, but they are together now in their own home. Kyle is going to do everything he can to help Trey forget about Tom's death, and his own foolishness, even if only for a few hours. Sex is always the answer to Kyle. He wants to feel Trey inside of him. While in New York, he laid beside him every night craving his touch, hungering for Trey to enter him. At the time, that was the last thing on Trey's mind.

Trey walks over to where Kyle is standing; his boyish blond hair touches his long eyelashes framing deep blue eyes. Slowly, Trey reaches for the third button, and begins to undo his shirt, until it lies open showing a hairless chest and stomach. Kyle's body is natural, never having set foot in a weight room in his twenty-four years. Youth is still on his side. Barefooted he stands five feet, ten inches, a few inches shorter than Trey. He has a swimmer's build. Kyle is a member of the Atlanta Gay Men's Water Polo team. Almost every member – at least the tops, not to mention the spectators — have fantasized one time or another about getting ahold of his round plump bubble butt, accentuated by his Speedos.

Trey slips his hands into the open shirt, feeling soft smooth skin on his fingertips. This instantly gives Kyle an erection. Trey pulls him closer until their bellies touch. Kyle licks his full red lips, as Trey leans in. His body is shaking slightly. He is scared, wondering if Trey still loves him, or if he is just playing with his emotions? Whatever the case, Kyle wants Trey at that very moment and does not wish to wait another second.

"Baby," Kyle whispers.

"What?"

"I'm so sorry."

"Hush," Trey whispers back, before confining Kyle's words by surrounding his lips with his.

The kiss is soft and tender at first, almost hesitant. Trey's lips brush over Kyle's in a lingering tease. Their noses touch, as they exchange the same air. Trey eases his wet tongue into Kyle's mouth, as his hands slowly slide into his pants, moving down until they grab hold of his ass. Kyle releases Trey's belt buckle. He pushes the boxers, along with the jeans, down his legs until they reach the floor. Now Trey is naked. Kyle can feel his heart beating faster. His breathing becomes heavier. The weeks without sex seemed like forever for Kyle. Now it is like the first time they were together. Then, everything was new and exciting. At that time, there were no secrets or lies yet between them. Neither one of them owed the other anything. They were just two strangers caught in a moment of passion and lust. Whereas now, there is more than just sex lying between the sheets.

Trey lifts Kyle up to the edge of the bed and pushes him down on his back. His body makes an indentation in the cream down comforter, as he freely allows his khaki pants and white low cut Calvin Klein briefs to be pulled off his lower body. Trey tosses them aside. Now they are both naked: Kyle on his back, his legs spread wide; Trey standing over him, looking like an Adonis. Both their cocks are hard, Kyle's pre-cum dripping onto his stomach.

"Now, baby, now. It's been too long," Kyle says, his words broken by gasps of short breaths.

His heart continues to race, as Trey makes a step closer, spreading Kyle's legs even wider with his hands, until he can clearly see the pink of his hole. His first instinct is to put his mouth on it. Kyle reaches out to grab Trey's dick. Just the touch of it, much less the sight, makes him want it inside him.

"Please, baby, please," Kyle cries.

Trey effortlessly slides Kyle back further on the bed to make room for him to get in between his legs. He lowers himself, until his lips reach the inside of Kyle's thighs. Trey begins repeatedly kissing his way inward toward his ass. Kyle's eyes are half open, his head back, his face showing the excitement he is experiencing. Trey's strong hands continue to spread his legs, as his tongue makes contact with Kyle's ass. At first, the licks are slow and light, like he is licking ice cream from a cone. His rhythm steadily increases, and the licks feverishly become faster and faster and heavier and heavier. Kyle can feel Trey's saliva making him wet. All he can think about is feeling Trey inside him. His excitement is climbing so much that he is ready to crawl out of his skin. Kyle reaches out to touch the back of Trey's head, forcibly pushing it between his legs.

The licks begin to slow down until they stop. Trey's hands loosen their grip, and begin sliding down Kyle's legs, until they reach his ankles. Everything goes still. They both hold their positions: Kyle waiting to feel Trey's tongue lick him again; Trey resting his head on the bed between Kyle's open legs. A few moments pass.

"Are you teasing me?" Kyle asks.

"No. I just can't right now."

"But, baby."

"I just can't. Let's get the dogs," Trey says, as he comes to his feet.

Making a Good Appearance

Before the guests begin to arrive, Trey stands alone by the coffin looking at Tom's face. He cannot help but think how rested he looks, much more so than the last time he saw Tom. A sad smile expands his lips as he takes note of the dimple in the center of Tom's chin. What a handsome dimple it is, so perfectly centered, and of a good size, he thinks. Trey is taken back to the time they were together, when they both seemed so happily in love. He is reminded of how he used to put his finger in that dimple. They would be lying side by side on the sofa in the den of the house on Penn Street watching a rental movie. Trey would glance at Tom from time to time, just to look at his handsome face. Sometimes, he would put his finger in the dimple and twist it. After doing it repeatedly during the movie, the practice would annoy Tom, but only slightly.

"What are you doing, silly?" he would say, as he swatted Trey's finger away.

"Just seeing if it has gotten any bigger," Trey would answer.

They would both laugh and go back to watching the movie.

Or, on a whim, Trey would do it while Tom was driving the car, or even when they were bathing together in the tub, usually catching him off guard. It was just one of Trey's little ways of letting Tom know how much he loved him. In more intimate moments, he would kiss it. How he loved kissing Tom's strong chin with the dimple. Trey looks around the church to see if anyone has arrived, and is relieved to see they are still alone. He has the urge to kiss it again. Trey leans over to press his lips onto Tom's dimple one last time. He is overcome with grief. His eyes tear up, the droplets fall onto Tom's sleeping face.

He straightens his body. Yet again, Trey looks around the church. They are still alone. He cherishes this private moment with Tom, as he lightly runs his hand over the top of Tom's hair examining how neatly groomed it is. Nancy had Phillip, Tom's personal hairdresser from the ritzy Manhattan salon of Talbert's, flown in to assure every hair was in place. Patterson Funeral Home did a good job making him look like his old self. The two weeks in the hospital drained the color from Tom's face. Now, he has color again, artificial, but all the same, an even tan covers his face and neck.

In his present state, Tom appears every bit a handsome older man in the fall of his life. He now will remain this way in appearance for eternity in the eyes of the living. Tom will not grow a day older.

The years of their friendship softened Trey's feeling of love for Tom, at least on the surface. All the same, those feelings lived quietly under his skin.

"What a waste," Trey says softly, as if talking to Tom, first looking at his body, and then up at the ceiling of the church. Eyes back on Tom, he continues his conversation, "If you're up there, I hope you know just how angry I am at you." He could not help but be mad at Tom for killing himself. But he was more than mad. Trey was beside himself with rage, that Tom would do this to him and Nancy. It left so many unanswered questions and so many regrets. Tom's family and friends aside, there were so many others who wanted to live, but they had no choice but to die. In Trey's eyes, Tom had a choice to live, if nothing else, live for all those who had no say in their lives being cut short. After all, he thought, the end for all would come sooner or later.

Trey tries to pull himself together. He knows Kyle, Nancy and the rest will be arriving soon. Trey purposely came to the church early to have some time alone with Tom. Once all the pomp and circumstance begins, Trey will have to share him again. All this is for Nancy's sake; the open casket, the service in the church, and the crowd of mourners that will soon arrive. It is the way Nancy thinks Tom should have wanted it, but it is more like the way she wants to say good-bye. Although he is dead, she is still fussing over Tom as she did when he was alive. Trey is concerned she will totally fall apart when all the events are over. Understandably, she is having a hard time letting go, even of Tom's physical body. Because of that, there is one final funeral arrangement Nancy is having a huge dilemma over — Tom's cremation. After the service, Nancy has no choice but to let go of his physical body. She knows Tom left emphatic instructions to be cremated, and Trey is there to see that his wishes are honored. Trey knows Tom would never agree to being locked in eternity in the cold, mossy family vault, no matter how morbidly beautiful it is. In life, he watched time eat away at him. Cremation is the only way to end the decay once and for all.

Gradually, the church begins filling up with old friends and business acquaintances of the Brookston family. It hums at a low rumble, orchestrated by the people moving about finding a place to sit. Rising collective voices fade in the grand sanctuary as they are lost in the open rafters. The strong but yielding voice of a young boy dressed in a pure white choir robe sings, *Abide With Me* from the balcony. His voice hovers in midair over the crowd as if he were truly an angel singing from high in the heavens.

The people keep coming; only a few of their faces are familiar to Trey. The majority have no idea of his relationship to Tom, or their personal history, as he stands at the entrance hall handing memorials printed on fine linen paper to each one as they enter. In life, Tom would have never cared to spend any amount of time with most of these people; they were there for their own benefit. These are country club types, big time contractors, developers and sales people, wanting to stay in the good graces of Tom's brother and sister. It is an investment in their futures, both socially and for all-around good business practice.

They know nothing other than rumors. The grand imposing doors of the Crestwood Methodist Church cannot keep the rumors out, nor will being under its holy roof keep them from spreading. Trey is among strangers here. The attendees may not know the whole story of the other life he lived with the son of the richest family in the South back in Atlanta, or even the latter years Tom spent in New York, but they are hungrily fishing to find out. Servants talk to other servants, and some of them talk to their employers. Now the employers are talking to each other, as they subtly point fingers spreading the rumors while Tom's body lies in front of them. They were kept in the dark about how Tom really died. All they knew was what had been fed to them in the Birmingham News. His obituary read he died of a stroke. Nancy felt it better that way, for the family's sake.

Nancy sits in the front pew with Nathan, Colleen and their children. A few cousins and an uncle and aunt, one from each side of the family, sit behind them. Nancy insisted that Trey and Kyle sit with her, but Trey thought it best they take a place in the third row. It makes things more comfortable for him in light of Nathan's strong views against homosexuality, and because of Tom's will, giving so much control of the final arrangements to Trey and most of the assets and money, too. Nathan wanted it all back to the family, which was exactly what Tom had done; Trey was family, as were several other close friends. These friends became family over a span of many years. Even Peggy was more family to Tom than Nathan ever was. Like his older brother, she may have never agreed with his lifestyle; and although Tom may have never followed some of her beliefs, they had been there for each other. She sits quietly next to Kyle at the end of the pew, wearing a distinctively large lacy white hat and matching gloves, holding her prayer book with both hands.

A rumble moves through the church pews as a stunning woman makes her way down the aisle. In this community, even with the many well-dressed attendees, she puts them all to shame without even trying. It is obvious she is from out of town. Two mature ladies sitting in the back of the church notice her first.

"Look, Louise. Who's that woman?"

"Never seen her before, Gertrude."

"Is that one of the Henderson girls?"

"No, no. She's too tall. They're all short you know."

"Hum. She must be a Hollywood actress. Oh my. I think she was in that movie we saw last month."

"No, no. I think she's one of those New Yorkers. Must be a friend of Tom's, God rest his soul," Louise corrects.

She is neither a Hollywood actress, nor a New Yorker. Lee Ann tenderly pulls along a shy eight-year-old red-headed boy as her husband, George, and an older son follow closely behind. Because everyone in this upscale community knows one another, it is easy to pick out a stranger in the crowd. She is dressed in a finely tailored black suit, with a long sheer maroon scarf fashioned around her neck. It floats several feet behind her as she walks with an air of reserved confidence in four-inch black Manolo's that show off her long, well-toned legs. Trey has been anxiously watching for her. They had been great friends back in the Atlanta days. Their lives since had taken them in different directions, but their bond kept them in contact over the years, occasionally getting together for a holiday or birthday. She owed Tom a lot, as he did her.

Trey talked with Lee Ann many times on the phone after Tom took the overdose, but had not seen her since his third successful art showing in New York at the High Gallery, about a year ago.

Tom flew her up along with some other friends for the opening, and for an elaborate pre-party at the penthouse where they mingled with a select group of New York's "A" list.

A warm smile comes to Trey's lips upon seeing her. The slight commotion caused by her entrance continues, as more admiring eyes follow Lee Ann's gracious walk down the aisle. Trey observes Nathan also taking note of her and the fuss her entrance has caused as she finds open seating on the other side of the church several rows back from the front. She has indeed become a beautiful woman, with an unmistakable air of elegance. There is something special about her, a goodness shining out from every clean pore of her body. Lee Ann is understated, as if she is holding an endless amount of beauty inside. Each time you look at her, you see something more and are amazed.

Her long, just below shoulder-length brown polished hair follows the movement of her head as she turns around scanning the unfamiliar crowd for a friendly face. Her look is passionate but serious; Lee Ann's skin wrinkles between her eyes as she searches. Suddenly after spotting Trey, the concerned wrinkles disappear, and her skin is once again smooth. After a second of relief passes, Lee Ann's face comes alive. A radiant smile explodes on her. It is warm and inviting. The occasion is a sad one indeed, but she is happy to see him.

Her smiles come freely now. There is an obvious easiness to them, where in years before, they had been almost nonexistent. Trey returns a smile of equal measure. He mouths, "I love you. You look wonderful," to her over the heads of the guests. She softly blows him a kiss, pushing it along with a hand gesture. At that, Trey's smile grows even larger as his eyes begin to tear.

Lee Ann's two bright-eyed children sit between her and her husband. George is handsomely tall and stocky, with a slightly receding hairline. The younger of the two boys kicks his legs, as if he is sitting on the edge of a dock splashing up the water. She gently places her hand on his knee and leans over to whisper something in his ear. With that, the little boy stops his imaginary splashing. Lee Ann turns back around to offer Trey another smile. He has never seen her happier. For a moment, it helps lessen his loss.

Following the service, Nancy puts on a big to-do at the family estate.

"Just as Tom would have liked it," she said.

The sky is as blue as Tom's eyes. Almost everyone who attended the church service has come. Few would miss an afternoon at the lush gardens of the Brookston estate, eating and drinking fine food and wine.

Nancy is still having trouble with Tom's decision to be cremated.

"Are you sure?" Nancy asks Trey.

They stand on the edge of a stone pond; a large single bolder jets up from its center, with water cascading over it. Trey reaches out to hold her hand.

"It's what he wanted, Nancy. You must respect that," Trey answers.

"But, Trey."

"Nancy, it's almost done. You must honor his request. Tom wanted to be totally free. To keep his body in the grave would be an insult. Let him be free in death, as he tried to be in life. He ended his life to stop the decay of his body. We can't fail him now."

Her eyes look at the ground.

"Yes, you're right, you're right. He would hate that. Why should he be any less vain in death than he was in life," Nancy smiles.

It is the first smile Trey has seen on her face in many, many weeks.

"I'll go personally to get his remains, that is, when it's done," Nancy says.

"Why don't you let me take care of that? You've gone through so much," Trey insists.

"Whatever you think," Nancy concedes.

Tom told Trey years ago about his wishes to be cremated. He made him promise to see that it was done when that day arrived. It was one of the reasons Tom made Trey executor of his estate. He knew if left up to his sister, she would go against his wishes. Tom's body was already on its way to the crematorium. In a few days, another but smaller ceremony would take place at the Brookston family's mausoleum, where his ashes would be placed, or at least that is what Nancy was led to believe.

Two of Nancy's socialite friends unknowingly interrupt the in-depth conversation. Trey excuses himself to allow them to give her their condolences.

He walks over to Lee Ann, where she is sitting on an ornate cement bench, watching her two boys playing with some of the other children. She has kicked off her shoes, wiggling her toes in the dense green grass. Ten feet away, Nathan looks on. He is standing by a tall row of manicured hedges that dwarf him. He has been watching her for some time, since seeing Lee Ann at the service, wondering who this beauty is and what her relationship was to his departed brother.

"Trey, it's hard to believe so much time has passed," Lee Ann says as she starts to stand.

"Please, don't get up."

He motions with his hand for her to remain seated.

"Of course," Lee Ann responds, offering him a seat next to her, as she makes a quick turn of her head in the direction of the children.

"They are such good boys, Lee Ann," Trey comments.

"Thanks, I'm so fortunate to have them and George of course. Would you ever believe this was possible? It's truly a miracle I have a new life."

"I can see that you're happy."

"Yes, very."

"Good. You deserve it. All of it."

Lee Ann leans over to hug Trey.

"I have something for you," he says.

She looks at him puzzled, as Trey pulls an envelope from the inside pocket of his suit jacket.

In the distance, a child's voice calls out, "Look at me, Mommy."

Lee Ann turns her head again, while tucking a section of hair back behind her ear. She acknowledges her older son as he performs cartwheels on the smooth green manicured lawn.

"Be careful, darling," she says.

Lee Ann bites her lower lip in a manner that a concerned mother would do. Proudly, she lightly claps her hands together before turning her head back to Trey.

"You make a great mother," he says.

Trey can see the beaming pride in her eyes.

"I hope so. Thanks for saying that. I feel like a mother, even if I never carried them in my body."

"That's beside the point. You're their mother. The best mother they could ever hope to have."

It was a childhood she never had. Now, Lee Ann is giving it to these two boys. She will go to any lengths to give them a safe and secure life. Trey can see that. He and Tom were at the boys' baptisms. Tom joyously took the honor of becoming their godfather. It had been a happy event, one much different from Tom's and Lee Ann's first meeting. She had come a long way since that unforgettable night, running for her life through a frozen black winter's night. She will forever be grateful to Tom for saving her in more ways than one. In some ways, she was the one who saved him, at least for a while. Because of Lee Ann, Tom found a missing part of his heart, and learned how to give it to a stranger. With that, he discovered he was not better or worse than anyone else, and not so different either.

Trey hands her the white envelope. Still puzzled, Lee Ann looks at him, and then at it, before taking possession.

"What is this all about, Trey?"

"Something Tom wanted me to make sure you got. You were very special to him. He wanted you to know that."

"Trey, I know. I know he loved me, and I owe so much to him."

Lee Ann holds the envelope for a moment before cautiously pulling at the seal. Inside, she finds a bank book in hers and the boys' names. Lee Ann's mouth opens, as she reads the balance, but the words are inaudible. She is speechless.

"But, Trey?" she utters, as she stumbles for words.

"He wanted to make sure that you and the boys are well taken care of. Tom wanted them to get a good education, and have a good start in life. A better one than you had."

Lee Ann rests the papers on her lap, and looks back at the boys. Her eyes water until they cannot hold anymore. The tears generously pour out and down her cheeks.

"Hey, no need for those," Trey says.

"I know, Tom never liked me to be sappy."

Trey removes the white handkerchief peeking out of his jacket pocket and hands it to her.

"Is my mascara running?"

"No. No streaks yet."

"Well, at least I'm using better make-up these days."

"Speaking of sappy, have you noticed Nathan checking you out?" Trey asks.

They both giggle.

"If only he knew," Lee Ann comments.

"God, wouldn't Tom get a kick out of that," Trey states.

"I think he is," she responds.

They both look up to the sky and laugh before looking over at Nathan again.

Making Amends

Tom's heart had not always been open to others whose struggles he never experienced, perhaps a result of the privileged and sheltered life he was given at birth. He saw himself on a higher level than most, something he surely inherited from his father. His attitude was totally unconscious; it was second nature, and partly the reason he acquired few close friends. Sadly, people were drawn to Tom because of his wealth and good looks, but not his personality. Like his father, Tom would walk into an establishment, whether it be a restaurant, a department store, or the like, expecting to be waited on hand and foot, as if he were the king of the land.

Several years before Tom met Trey, he purchased an old southern home in the heart of Midtown Atlanta. After he spent over a hundred thousand dollars and diligently supervised a crew of skilled workmen, it stood proudly once again on the oak-lined street. Tom had brought it back to life, regaining its original beauty with many added upgrades. Almost as a hobby, and partly out of boredom, he began buying up other houses to renovate and resell. Midtown Atlanta, as other in-town communities of large cities across the country, was left to deteriorate during the great migration to the suburbs in the 1950's. Once that happened, these beautiful homes were chopped up into apartments, boarded up, or left to weather the years without much love and care. As a result, they became overrun with crime, prostitution and drugs. Tom led the way, as many gay men did in the late 1970's and 1980's, to revitalize these communities. His plan was to single-handedly regenerate Midtown by pushing out the riffraff and cleaning up the area. In his eyes, there were a few obstacles, but nothing money and hounding City Hall and the police department could not accomplish.

One of those obstacles was prostitution. It ran rampant in the bordering areas, as well as in his new Midtown. Tom hated prostitutes. He went as far as chasing them down the street if need be, waving his hands like he was swatting flies away, every time they encroached on, or near, one of his properties.

"I'm calling the cops if you don't leave," he would yell.

Tom hounded the Atlanta City police and city council members. Because he was a man of influence, they tried to accommodate him as much as possible. But despite the patrols, and even with Tom standing sentry in front of his well-manicured house, the flesh peddlers continued to return at dusk to sell their souls to anyone who would buy. The johns came slowly at first, driving their cars looking for sex throughout the maze of Midtown streets. By the early morning hours, their numbers increased, as did those of the prostitutes.

On his second-story porch, camouflaged by the tall developed oaks, Tom guards his domain. At the first sign of a prostitute, he steps out into the dim light thrown from the street lights.

"Find another street, you WHORE. You're not going to bring this one down," Tom yells.

Over time, he came to know many by name. First, Tom tried to reason with each one to take their business elsewhere. There were all kinds of hookers on his street: male, female and some like Lee, a seventeen-year-old transsexual. He had been on the streets for several months after being kicked out of his parents' house due to their inability to accept that their son believes he is emotionally a girl. He has felt this way as long as he can remember. By all appearances, he is. Lee looks, walks and talks like a girl. In the fifth grade, he unflinchingly told his parents he wanted to be called Lee Ann. Being uneducated in such matters, and not willing to be, they saw him as a freak of nature, as did his classmates and those of the poor south Atlanta community in which he lived.

As an effeminate child, Lee was called a sissy, a fag, and every other name in the book; even some by his parents. There was some irony here; his parents are a mixed racial couple — African-American father and Caucasian mother, dealing with their own internal prejudices, as well as those from the outside. His mother struggled with being the wife of a black man in the south, where there was a history of zero tolerance for mixed marriages. There were the long stares and crude remarks like, "you nigger-loving cunt," "skank whore," and "coon-loving bitch." In their community, many of the white men hated the thought of one of their women being with a man of color. There were death threats, broken house windows, car vandalisms, racial words of hate painted on the front of their house in the middle of the night, and even a cross burning. His parents saw Lee as another problem they did not need.

He had been abused by some of the older boys in his neighborhood. On several occasions, forced to perform oral sex, and another time, just shortly before being kicked out by his parents, Lee had been gang raped by three boys. The streets became his home, sleeping in abandoned houses or in dark alleys. Sometimes he would stay with gay men for short periods of time, trading favors for a warm place to sleep. He hung out in the local gay bars to keep from feeling so alone and discarded. Lee knew he had to find a way to survive, leaving him little choice but to sell his body in order to get food to live. He found himself alone with no one to turn to for help. The only hope Lee had was hope itself, but that seemed to be running out fast.

His natural skin tone is a golden honey color. Lee's abundant long brown wavy hair is wild, growing from his scalp like the branches of a willow tree. His five-foot, eight-inch frame is lean, and appears tall and lanky in the shabby scratched-up high heel shoes he found in a dumpster. Lee's beauty is untamed with emotions running wild and scared, trying to find out who and what he is in this world; trying to find out how to endure. He walked the streets of Midtown, picking up unsuspecting men fooled by his looks, offering blow jobs for ten dollars a pop. Under the disguise of dark, Lee made a beautiful Lee Ann.

Tom yelled and chased Lee away like he did all the rest. In his eyes they where all trash. A few nights would pass until Lee and the others came back, moving in and out of the weak, yellow glow cast by the street lamps. Despite the "no-cruising" signs posted throughout the neighborhood, the johns still came. They drove their cars, circling the streets, looking in anticipation and desperation with their eyes wide open.

One December Sunday, just hours before the sun begins to chisel its way through a frigid morning sky, Tom is awakened by what sounds like a woman running in narrow heels. Their vibration hitting the pavement quick and hard echoes through the night, bouncing from house to house in rhythmic pounds down the street. Of course in this neighborhood, it could just be a drunken drag queen leaving one of the bars in close proximity, but it is not.

In desperation, a voice calls out gasping for oxygen from the icy air. Lee's breath lingers, almost frozen, as he races past it. A car slows for its occupants to view the lack of clothing covering his body, but they do not stop to answer the calls for help. The car's red taillights flash bright for a second, then dim as it speeds off. The commonplace sedan moves forward until it disappears down the street. Lee's dress has been ripped at the waist, exposing his panties. His face is red, as blood runs from a split lip. His heels hurriedly skip over the road, making the scuffling noise. Lee is running from an abandoned lot a few blocks from Tom's.

"Someone help me," he calls out, in the lifeless night.

Two men chase behind, one carrying a knife, its silver blade wheeling above his head.

"I'm going to cut you, bitch," one of the pursuers yells.

119

"Oh God, help. Please, someone help me," Lee calls out.

"We'll get you, bitch, and cut you a vagina," the other screams.

Lee's heart races, his sweat soaks what little clothing clings to his body. As he turns his head around, he can see the silver blade of the knife, the sight amplifying his terror.

The two men relentlessly continue their pursuit. They are furious they had been fooled. The transvestites walk the streets with the real female prostitutes; most were obvious, with their large frames and masculine features covered in heavy make-up and unrealistic wigs. On the other hand, Lee's small frame, his own long hair, and feminine face are very convincing. His attackers had more than a blow job on their minds. When one of the men reached to rip off Lee's panties, he got an unexpected surprise. Now, the two men are almost on his heels.

The commotion grows louder as Lee approaches Tom's house hoping to find a hiding place in the well-shrubbed yard. Tom walks out on the second-floor porch of his bedroom, wrapping his robe tighter to his body, double-knotting its sash, to help keep out the cold.

He is stunned. Even in the dim light, he recognizes Lee being chased by the two men. Tom sees the hard polished edge of the knife, and hears the screams. They are just a few feet from his front yard. Tom yells out, as the man with the knife catches up with Lee, pulling him to the ground.

"The police are on their way," Tom forcibly informs, although he has yet to call anyone, but hopes they will believe he has.

But, it is too late.

Lee screams again.

"My God. STOP. STOP," Tom yells, as he witnesses the knife cut Lee's wet flesh.

Faint police sirens introduce the morning. A neighbor had been disturbed earlier by the screams and yelling, and had alerted the authorities. The two men scamper out of the light provided by the street lamp, disappearing in the still dark air. Lee lies on his back looking up at the stars in the crisp chilly sky. His clothes are now bloody. Lee's body is numb all over. He cannot feel the blood making its escape and pooling around him.

Tom runs down to the yard.

"My God, what have they done?" Can you hear me?" Tom asks.

Lee's eyes remain wide open, but unresponsive to his voice. They continue to stare up toward the sky. Tom unsashes and removes his robe and lays it over Lee.

"Can you hear me?" Tom asks again, as he leans over him.

Tom gently shakes Lee's arm.

"Don't hurt me," Lee suddenly speaks.

Intense fear washes over his face. Lee tries to look down at his stomach where the knife cut, but finds it hard to move his head.

"I'm not going to hurt you," Tom answers.

"You hate me, don't you." Lee states.

Tom can see black tears streaking down Lee's face, as he tries to talk. His make-up is messy, mascara crisscrossing down his cheeks.

"I think you shouldn't try to speak. Help's on its way."

"Why do you hate me?" Lee asks.

Tom has never witnessed anything so horrible in his life. Suddenly he is afraid for Lee, whereas before he could have cared less about him. On one of the winter's coldest nights, two very dissimilar people have come face to face, in a life and death situation. Tom's expensive silk pajamas intensify the cold. He continues to lean over Lee watching his robe turn redder and redder with blood. Nothing can protect them from what is happening in the night. He feels alone even though the sirens grow closer, yet still seem to be days and nights away from arriving. Tom knows he must do something more. He tucks the robe tighter around Lee's body, and puts pressure on the cut with his hand. The blood is surprisingly warm on his skin. Lee's life begins to run between Tom's fingers. He finds himself praying to God to help him. It is the first time in his life he has ever said anything that resembles a prayer. Tom desperately wants to change what is happening, to keep the life inside of Lee. He places his other hand on Lee's cold forehead, whose eyes are still wide open, as if frozen by the concentrated cold.

Tom feels panic overtaking his body. He wants to run back in the house and close the door leaving all this ugliness out in the cold night. He feels he needs a drink at that very moment, and the warmth of a roaring fire to sit in front of. He wishes Peggy were home, but she is in Birmingham, at a bible retreat, and will not return until sometime tomorrow. Why is this happening to him, he wonders? He is above all this. Things like this do not happen to people like him. He told Lee to stay away, and now look what has happened. His mind races with thoughts. Lee could have run in any number of different directions, but no, he had run to him. Now Tom has to deal with it. Somehow he knows he has to make things all right. He tries to think what Peggy would do. He begins to pray to himself again, while putting more pressure on the cut. He knows he has to fight the desire to flee and leave Lee lying alone. Tom knows he has to either help, or take his hand from Lee's stomach. Suddenly the panic leaves him. His thoughts are bringing him to the understanding that this is not happening to him, but to Lee.

The first light of morning begins to push a golden glow up from the dark horizon. It is a welcomed sight, perhaps a sign. For the first time, his rich, spoiled life has meaning. Tom has a chance to be unselfish, and do something to help another human being. Before, he saw Lee as a whore, as trash, but now he is forced to look into the eyes of a stranger he previously detested, and see something totally different, and at the same time, look at himself as well. He sees his reflection in Lee's glassy eyes. Tom now sees him in a different light.

"You're going to be okay. I don't hate you," Tom says, trying to comfort Lee, as he continues to look into his eyes.

At that moment, Tom realizes he never really looked at Lee in times past. He saw what he wanted to see, and nothing else, never bothering to look any deeper than the facade of make-up with which Lee covered himself. He never saw Lee as a person made of flesh and bone with blood running through his veins. His eyes carry a sadness, one Tom can relate to. A sorrow that being different brings, and with it, the longing of wanting something that seems so out of one's reach. It is a sadness staring back at him in the mirror of Lee's eyes. Tom knows he can do something to change Lee's fate, and possibly his own.

The ambulance takes Lee to Grady Memorial Hospital. Tom follows in his car. They are oddly connected now. Lee has a deep stab wound, which cut his large intestine. After a week in the hospital, Tom brought Lee to his home. There, a friendship grew, that was born out of a cold winter's night. A year later, Tom paid for Lee's sex change operation, and a new life began for Lee Ann. The police never caught the two men who attacked Lee. It was in the past now: a horrible act of hate that changed two lives forever, and gave birth to a new beginning, for Tom and Lee Ann.

After the sex change, Lee Ann took steps to leave her painful past behind and find a quiet place in the world. In doing so, she also abandoned the gay nightlife that once gave her shelter. Tom and Trey were the only gay friends with whom she kept in contact. After all, she was never gay. She always liked men, and she always felt female. She was "miss-assigned" at birth. Now, she is a success story. Her outside appearance fits the inside.

Lee Ann got a job in Rich's couture department at Lenox Mall. It was a good fit at the time. She was surrounded by girly things. Her beauty was admired by both employees and customers alike. Ironically, two Decembers later, she met George, an accountant from Chattanooga, Tennessee. He was Christmas shopping for his mother and sister. Lee Ann helped him with his selections. George was instantly attracted to her, and after she rung up his purchases, he asked her out.

Lee Ann told him on their third date about her past while they were finishing their main course at The Pleasant Peasant on Peachtree Street. There were only a few couples left in the quaint Midtown restaurant. George sat next to her with his eyes wide and his mouth slightly open. He was astounded, and at first thought she was making a joke. She pulled out a photo of Lee from her purse and handed it to him.

"This is your brother?" he asked.

"No. It was me, but only of my outer self. The inside has always been the same. I don't know why I keep the picture. Maybe I feel like I owe him (referring to the picture of Lee) something, and I don't want to throw him away like my parents did me. After all, he is the one that had to endure all the pain, misery and loneliness.

With that explanation, George knew she was not joking. The color of his face went pale. Lee Ann was fearful of his response. He was the first man she had been out with since her operation. She prepared herself for rejection while they both sat at the table covered with white linen. Lee Ann waited for George to say something or just get up from his seat and walk away. The waiter approached to remove their dinner plates, while another scraped the table with a silver crumber.

"Can I interest you in a tasty dessert? Perhaps our Chocolate Intemperance or some southern apple pie topped with cinnamon ice cream?" the waiter asks.

"Give us a few moments," George speaks up.

"Certainly sir," the waiter responds, and walks over to another table.

George is stunned like a deer caught off guard by the headlights of a car squeaking to a halt on a dark zigzagging mountain road. He shakes his head as he fumbles for words. In lightning speed deliberation he goes over what Lee Ann has just told him but none of it makes sense. He slept with her after their second date; she is all woman, every inch of her, from what he could tell, and he would know. George is no virgin.

Lee Ann had not planned on having sex with George right off the bat. She was afraid of how her new parts would work. They looked and felt real, but she had never tried them out except for practicing on herself in the shower and in bed. But sooner then she had planned, it did happen. After their first date they talked for a week on the phone every evening until well past one a. m. The following weekend George came to see her again. They spent every minute together like they had known one another for years. It was love at first sight. After a full Saturday they ended up at George's hotel room getting ready to go out for dinner. Needless to say, they had to order room service.

To Lee Ann, George was everything she could hope for in a man: physically strong, handsome, good-natured and tender. The moment he entered her was bittersweet. It was her happiest by far, but at the same time she knew she had a secret, one that could shatter the fairy tale she was just beginning to live. To George, Lee Ann was the sweetest, most beautiful woman he had been with. Never in a million years would he have thought of her otherwise.

George looks at her across the table, the picture still tightly gripped in his hand; all he can see is a woman he is quickly falling in love with. He is touched by her tales of past hardships. An overwhelming desire to keep her safe swells inside of him. Others might have been disgusted, felt ticked or come after her like the two men had on that dark winter night; the memories still haunts her at times in her sleep. But George was different.

"You know we can never tell my parents," George says.

A smile comes to Lee Ann's face.

"Does this mean you want to see me again?" she asks.

"Yes. Nothing can keep me away," he answers.

Lee Ann is totally surprised by his reaction. She could have been successful at keeping the past secret, but she felt he had a right to know. George reached over to take her hand before gently kissing her on the lips.

A year later they married and settled into a life in the conservative town of Chattanooga, George's hometown. His parents welcomed Lee Ann with open arms, and to this day do not know the full story of the boy in the picture. George bought a silver frame and put the picture of Lee in it. It sets on the dresser in their bedroom. On the night George proposed, he handed her two gifts. One was a beautiful emerald-cut diamond ring; the other was the picture frame.

"I want you to give Lee a resting place in this frame. Because he is a part of you, he is a part of me now. I accept him as I accept you. I want you to be my wife. Will you marry me?" George asked, while down on one knee.

Lee Ann burst into tears of joy before answering, "Of course I will. Yes, yes and yes."

Most might see her life as boring, but it was all Lee ever wanted from the time he was a little girl in a boy's body: to be a girl, get married and have children. The adoption of the boys, two brothers, came soon after the marriage. Lee Ann now had the perfect American family.

Putting Things to Rest

A string of expensive cars and limousines tag silently behind the white Rolls Royce carrying Nancy, Peggy, Trey, and Kyle. Nathan and Colleen follow behind in a black Lincoln stretch with the Brookston Industries' logo on the front doors. Lee Ann and George are in the third car back, while their boys are at the estate being watched with the two girls by the Brookston's nanny.

They follow the black hearse carrying a Biedermeier-like, six-inch by eight-inch box, all making their way over the cracked cement road that had been laid well before any of them were born. The cracks in the road remind Trey of the wrinkles of an aged man showing the years of his existence. Like a road map, the cracks run the course of his journey, crossing many times as the years advance. Some of the lines are delicate, and others more pronounced. Some slightly crease the surface of his skin, while others are deep and hard like they have been cut with a trawl. There are some smooth areas on the road like those between the lined horizontal wrinkles of the aged man's forehead, but those are few and far between.

Cautiously, the cars progress over the cracks of the winding road, as so many had over the years. They move ever so slowly over them, followed by another and then another. The only sounds made by the fall day are those manufactured by the faint whistle of moving tires, and the crushing of leaves, as the wheels flatten them. Every few feet, the cars roll over the expansion joints in the road making a double thumping noise, as the front tires and then the rear ones pass over them. There is an orchestration to the combination of sounds: leaves crackling, a thump, a slight detectable pause, more leaves crackling, and then another thump. The next car in line repeats the rhythm, as the caravan of headlights, faded by the bright noon sun, makes its way along the narrow aged road; the lights are noticeable only under the shade of prime thick willow trees, in the beginning stages of shedding their leaves. They stand like mourners — the willow trees — lining both sides of a stretch of road. The cars continue, soon crossing over a wooden bridge. Below, the life of stirring water gently making its way on a different journey adds to the composition of sounds. The cars pause, approaching a turn in the road, where two massive oaks flank either side; like guards, they reside strong, almost insuring the visitors do not awaken the dead.

A homeless man has made camp in one of the old abandoned mausoleums. Conceivably, the family line died out, and there are no relatives living to be concerned with its unkempt condition, or that someone living has made it his home. Its marble walls, aged as the road, still hold elegance. Three-quarters of the mausoleum is covered in thick angry vines embracing the architecture of the structure, leaving most of the family name, "Francisco," exposed over the pediment.

Two nude figures stand outside the mausoleum's entrance, one a woman and the other a man. Their bodies are slightly twisted reaching for one another, as if in grief, their marble flesh sexual and alluring, their reach frozen in time. The twisting of their bodies appears strained, as if the very marble itself is being extracted by two souls locked in rock refusing to be separated by death. The expressions on their faces are that of loss and confusion. Almost childlike and innocent, they seemingly stand full of desire to touch each other, but yet not quite able to reach out far enough, locked in a spell of lust and craving for one another. As the years turned into decades, they have slowly reached out inch by inch getting ever so closer and closer. Once chiseled and polished by the hand of an artist, time gradually was turning stone into flesh and blood.

Trey can see the bearded man, holding his ground in his unwashed gray tattered clothing, through the tinted glass of the car window. He is well camouflaged in his surroundings. As the motorcade slows, Trey engages the electric window to get a clearer look. It opens halfway before he takes his finger off the button. Even then, he feels he is invading the man's privacy. Trey looks into the stranger's eyes and sees nothing, as a gush of cool air enters the car. It soon dissipates, after he hits the button to close the window. The vagrant peers through a rusty black iron gate, past the frozen lovers and out to the road. His grimy hands, black with dirt, grip the gate tightly, pulling it shut to keep a safe distance from what he perceives to be intruders. Unnoticed by the caravan (except for Trey), he stands there silently in his home among the dead.

"How dare they come," Trey believes the man must be thinking, as the forgotten soul retreats back into the shadows. In doing so, he stumbles over a raised square section of the cement slab floor, its levelness disrupted over the many passing years. Roots of the mighty oaks have torpidly forced their way through the ground of the cemetery, giving life and movement to this dead place, while making their way in hundreds of directions, sprouting into the graves, and slowly surrounding the coffins. In a caress, the roots hold the dead, cradling them in the arms of mother earth.

Unfortunately, Trey had made this journey too many times; more than he cared to remember for friends and good acquaintances that passed, many before their time. This one is harder to the point of unbearable. The senses of anguish and grief are raw and unforgiving, growing in him like a malignant tumor. Trey looks over at Kyle, as he feels the gentle touch of his hand collecting his. It still manages to incite a tingle in Trey's chest, in spite of his uncertainty about the future of their relationship.

"How're you holding up?" he asks in a sweet whisper, his blue eyes clear and alert as they pass over Trey's face.

"I'll be fine once we put him to rest."

"Maybe we should head back to Atlanta tonight. Nancy will understand," Kyle suggests, his voice taking on a concerned manner.

"Yeah, perhaps that's a good idea, babe. We need to get home. We've been gone too long," Trey answers.

The Brookston mausoleum is large compared to the others in the memorial park, looking more like a small aged Roman temple. A row of low manicured shrubs line the stone walk leading to its entrance. An ornate bird bath, centered in equal distance between the road and the gates, stands in a circular section of the walk, welcoming thirsty birds now disturbed by the visitors. Like the walk, it is covered in moss, its water green and murky. Overgrown rose bushes cover the façade, surrounding the tall heavy double iron gates with the family crest. They cry open as the minister separates them.

Nancy, carrying the box, follows him with Trey, then Kyle behind her. Nathan, Colleen and the rest lag behind. The gates lead into a marble entry with a twenty-foot arched ceiling depicting cherubs, in faded paint, hovering in the clouds. Two thick dark smoked-glass doors, mimicking the shape of the iron gates, lead the mourners into the burial chamber. Trey looks up in amazement at the gold dome ceiling overhead. A small concave skylight in its center allows a beam of light to illuminate another family crest inlaid in the floor. Many generations of Brookstons are laid to rest inside these stone walls. Now, there will be another, almost, that is.

Because of Tom's dislike for his father, he made other arrangements. Several years back, at Mr. Brookston's own service, Tom made a decision that he would not allow any part of his physical body — fully knowing he would be cremated when the time came — in this place. In a secret addendum to his will, Tom instructed his attorneys to have the majority of his ashes switched with those of a beloved dog, Nipper, a Rhodesian Ridgeback, which died before he moved to New York. For ten years, Tom kept the dog's ashes in a marble urn on the mantel in his library, with a picture of him and Nipper beside it. The bulk of his ashes were willed to Trey to disperse as he saw fit. It was also a way to get back at his father, who never allowed him to have a dog as a child, no matter how much he pleaded for one. Mr. Brookston hated animals.

The burial chamber is cool and damp as the minister stands in front of the vault where the Biedermeier box and its contents will soon be laid to rest. George puts his arm around Lee Ann to comfort and warm her.

"Please, everyone come closer," instructs the minister.

The small congregation rallies around Nancy. Nathan and Colleen prefer to stay in the back as the minister begins a prayer. Peggy gives a reassuring rub on Nancy's arm.

With a nod from the minister, Nancy carries the box over to the open vault. She looks at Trey, and then back at the opening. He wants to tell her about the switch, feeling he is deceiving her; but through Tom's attorneys, Trey was told not to tell anyone in his family, not even Nancy. Tom made it clearly understood that only a teaspoon of his ashes were to be mixed in to keep Nipper company, and he knew Nancy would, in the future, especially on holidays and birthdays visit his remains. He knew an empty vault would not console her, and she would not understand his need to be totally free, even in death, so that is why he instructed only the teaspoon. At least, he believed, that was something, an essence of what was left of him. He could not allow his remains to be restricted, confined inside these dark, damp walls locked up from the rest of the world behind heavy iron gates. It was a final act of freedom, from his obsession, the wealth that fed it and his father's distaste for him.

It would be too much like returning home for the last time. Tom never spent more than a few days at a time visiting the estate when he was alive, and it was not going to be any different now.

"God bless the soul of Thomas James Brookston," speaks the minister.

Nancy hesitantly places the box in the open vault and steps aside. The minister makes a sign of the cross in the cool air with his hand in front of it.

As instructed earlier, Trey and George pick up the cement block covered with a marble plaque with the engraving:

Thomas James Brookston

Our beloved

1945 — 2004

"We entrust his soul to you, God," finishes the minister's prayer.

"Amen," speaks everyone.

The block of stone is heavy as Trey and George slide it into place, sealing the box in the vault.

Peggy's soft voice fills the burial chamber as she begins to sing *Amazing Grace*.

Spoiled Milk

Trey is in a state of disbelief as he sorts through a shoebox of cards collected over the years from Tom. There are birthday cards, I miss you cards, I love you cards and even a get well card from when Trey had a bad cold. Mixed in are some red and silver foil wrapped Kisses Tom had once covered their bed with one Valentine's Day. There had been hundreds on the bed; Tom and Trey made love and ate chocolate Kisses throughout that night. Only the few that survived made it to the box of memories. They have long since gone stale, but Trey's love is still semi-fresh even after all these years.

There are loose photographs as well waiting to be put in picture frames. The odds that they will make it out of the box except on rainy days reserved for reminiscing are slim. More likely, the box will be the only home they will ever know. Still there is hope for a few photographs to make their escape to carefully selected sleek frames, but Trey wonders if he will have any hope of understanding why Tom, a man who owned a large part of his heart is no longer alive.

Trey gently holds a card Tom sent to him in Birmingham shortly after their first meeting. It is one of those funny juvenile ones, where when you open it a cartoon figure jumps out at you. The print below reads: I REALLY LIKE YOU! CAN YOU COME OUT AND PLAY WITH ME?

He struggles to understand everything that had happen from the time they met up to their many past phone conversations. Looking for answers that will give him some resolution.

◊

A herd of leaves skips across the grass as if by their own force. Without hesitation, they migrate over the blunt dull green blades for some undisclosed destination as the October sun strains to warm the cool morning fall air. Trey watches, fully knowing it is the unseen wind that pushes them along. Regardless, he prefers to believe the leaves are self-propelled, as if each one has a heart and a soul of its own, and invisible legs, or some ability to fly just above the ground in order to move along wherever they wish and for whatever reason. In the crisp air, with just the slightest hint that winter will be moving into the landscape, the leaves continue to move. Some are whisking along, while a few seem to be agitated, darting back and forth over the same ground, making little progress on their journey to somewhere or nowhere. Others appear more determined to arrive at their objective; steadfast, they glide out of sight.

Encroaching clouds move overhead altering the intensity of the sun's light on the ground. Trey continues to watch from the window in a daze, his ear becoming numb from the long conversation, as he listens to Tom. He watches the digital clock on the stove, which tells him that Tom has been talking for almost an hour. He cannot help but think while listening, with as much understanding as possible, that he is glad it is Tom's "dime." The conversation is not unlike the many they have had over the span of years since Tom moved to New York City. They were all usually about men. Very young men.

"I got a permit for a gun," Tom blurts out.

"You what?" Trey questions.

"Yeah, a GUN," he clarifies, with more amplification in his voice.

"What, you feel unsafe? Tom, your penthouse is like a fortress."

"I'm, I'm tired of trying anymore," he cries out, and then quietly sobs into the phone.

"Stop this kind of talk, man. We've gone through this before. So many times," Trey reminds him.

"I know, but what's the use? You would be better off without a friend like me. One less crazy in your life," he says.

"Tom, you're being dramatic. You and I both know you're not going to shoot yourself. It's the alcohol talking."

Trey knew Tom hated guns. His father was a hunter. The first time Mr. Brookston took his young son on a hunting trip, Tom threw up all over himself when he shot his first and last deer.

By now the years were racing by. Trey and Tom had been close for seventeen of them. Trey knows this time Tom is not necessarily joking, because unlike before, there is an underlying tone in his voice that is direct and to the point; a direction that had been absent in the previous talks. This threat is enough to make Trey start worrying more. He had been around long enough and talked with Tom enough to know something was about to happen. He had seen the subtle changes in his attitude toward life; they seemed to be mounting and consuming his friend. Trey had gotten a small taste of Tom's self-degrading remarks on growing older when they were lovers; now as friends, and as the years collected under their belts, it was getting worse.

"Maybe you should talk to someone," Trey suggests as he takes a seat near the window.

"You mean a shrink?" Tom laughs.

"Might not be a bad idea."

"I'm not crazy. Just old."

"Come on Tom, it might help."

"I'll think about it," Tom patronizes.

Trey lost count years ago of Tom's lovers. As their own relationship settled into a friendship, he felt jealousy from listening to Tom's stories of his young conquests. But he loved Tom, and if he could not be his lover, then he would have to settle for being his friend. Eventually, Trey got to a point where he had to surrender that kind of love for a friendship. He knew Tom had an obsession to the point of being an illness; and what kind of friend would Trey be if he turned his back on an ailing friend? Over the years, he gradually came to see Tom in his true pathos.

A realization which caused Trey to have pity on him.

But Trey did not totally blame Tom for this sickness that ate at him. Trey, too, was growing older, but the changes in his body were insignificant compared to the ones Tom was experiencing. Trey directed some responsibility for the ills of growing old to the community in which they lived, not only the gay community, but straight society as well. It really was not just Tom's appetite alone; it was being fed by the magazine covers, gay and straight alike; it was the so-called mainstream television commercials using innuendos of sex to sell the likes of anything from cars to toilet paper. Sex sells, and it was being advertised like Futures on Wall Street.

Advertisers pushed the miracles and dreams of their products with the half nude iconic perfection of sexual desire that belonged only to youth and beauty. These leaders of the pop culture continued to make conscious decisions to ignore a majority of the population by surrounding it with a non-stop barrage of youth. Be it advertisers, bars, or sex clubs, they all played a hand in putting suffocating sex in the face of every man, woman and child. Putting a half-nude person holding a product in their hands on a billboard, now that's some innovative good advertising, Trey sarcastically thought.

Still, it was Tom's money. All that money. The boys could smell it like sweat from a lumberjack's armpits. They threw themselves at him for a chance to get something of value in return: a car, a new wardrobe, their rent, or just some cold hard cash.

"I hope you will, Tom."

"Yeah, or maybe I will get lucky and a New York City bus will run me over."

"That's nonsense! NOW STOP THIS!" Trey insists, getting up from his chair to pace the floor.

He hears Tom begin to sob again.

"Trey. I just can't," he begins to say, and then there is silence on the other end of the phone.

"Tom. Tom are you still there?" Trey asks in a panic.

Again more silence until Trey can hear a series of muffled sniffles.

"He left. Alif left last night. He took some clothes and that stupid stuffed animal and left."

Trey can hear the ice cubes clank in Tom's drink over the phone. Most likely a vodka martini on the rocks.

"'He'll be back, Tom. What happened? What did you two have a fight about this time? Was it over money again?"

"No, not money. Although he spends it like it grows on trees."

"Well, in your case it does, Tom."

"He said he wouldn't stop dancing at the club. So I told him to go."

Trey wants to scream out, "Let him go! Good riddance!" But he does not.

"God, Tom. How many does he make?" he asks instead.

"I don't know," Tom answers. "But he is a looker."

"Tom, they're all lookers. And there are plenty more where he came from."

◊

He met Alif in Provincetown. Tom had gotten a real beauty this time: an olive-skinned, black-eyed boy of Indian descent, living in Hamilton Heights. Alif was a student and a dancer at Rhino's in the meat-packing district. It was a quick engagement. Within a few months, Alif moved into the lush penthouse with just a backpack, a toy stuffed green cat and a world of worry for Tom. Alif was raised in the Muslim faith. His father owned a chain of small neighborhood grocery stores in the city and New Jersey. Mr. Ahmed immigrated to the United States with Alif's mother, shortly after their marriage.

Alif tried to keep his sexuality from his parents. But after moving in with Tom, it was hard to explain relocating from a dingy two bedroom, one-bath seven-story walk-up with three roommates and rats, to a Park Avenue address with a much older man. Alif tells them he is house-sitting for an extended period of time. He is careful to cover his tracks, but not careful enough. His father has been suspicious for some time about his son's sexuality and hires a private detective. Shortly after, the shit hits the fan when Mr. Ahmed is supplied with photos that leave no room for dispute. His only son has been caught kissing an older man in front of the Roxy, a gay club. He confronts Alif in the back office of the main grocery store.

"They kill homosexuals back in our country," his father screams with a red face.

An average-looking man in his mid fifties, it is hard to imagine he has produced such a gorgeous child. Although very well dressed in black wool slacks, a light gray shirt and a black and gray patterned jacket, Mr. Ahmed has an unevenly round face and a bit of a belly overly stressing the buttons of his shirt. His eyes are larger than normal, perhaps as a result of the increase in his blood pressure concerning the intensity of the moment. At first, Alif feels like a mouse caught in a trap, but instead of a steel rod, he feels the weight of his father's anger on his tail, leaving him squirming in the chair.

Mr. Ahmed forcibly pushes the few long strands of hair back over his bald spot. Alif focuses on his father's large forehead reflecting a low sheen of light. His mind wanders as his father continues to badger him, occasionally flailing his arms — in fast motion — into the air like he might be directing traffic on a busy street. Minutes later, after Mr. Ahmed has started talking, Alif fades him out. He stares at the floor, his eyes tracing the wood grain of the wide planks under his feet. Now he finds it almost funny that his father is on the verge of a heart attack, and all Alif can think about is how grateful he is that male pattern baldness generally is carried down on the mother's side of the family. Mrs. Ahmed's father and grandfather both sported full heads of hair. A slight internal smile comes across his lips as he runs his hands through his thick hair, like a headband in a subtle act of reprisal.

"Son, are you hearing a word I'm saying?" Mr. Ahmed demands.

Alif looks up as he removes his hands from the top of his head and rests them on the table. His hair falls forward covering most of his forehead.

"I don't know what to tell you, Father. Nothing I say is going to make you happy. You're overreacting," he scoffs, sliding back in his chair.

"You are a disgrace to your mother and me," Mr. Ahmed says, while slamming his fist on the table, hitting it hard enough that two of its legs jump up a few inches off the floor.

It startles Alif, but he is not frightened by his father's anger anymore; instead, he's rather amused. He sits back up, quietly hoping he can leave soon.

"And who is this older man?"

"No one, Father."

"Don't expect me to fund this sinful lifestyle you're living. You'll need to get a job if you want to continue your education and eat!" he yells, unaware his son is a stripper in a gay bar. A detail the detective had yet to discover.

"But Father," Alif pleads. He is acting.

"No, this is final until you turn your life around."

"May I go now, Father?"

"Remember what I've said, Son. There are consequences to your actions."

It is easy to be drawn in by the exotic beauty that God so generously bestowed on Alif upon his birth into the world. Even his father realizes this truth sitting across the table, being amazed and bewildered by how it radiates from every part of him. Only a few humans are truly given such magnificence. At one time Mr. Ahmed was proud of having a son who possessed such human beauty. Now, he sees it as something else. It is possibly a curse, of sorts, to be so stunning and wanted by so many.

Any curse associated with Alif's physical beauty would fall on those taken in by it. He was one of those young things with a hunger for attention. Always in need of being reminded he was the best-looking one in the room, much like a younger version of

Tom, Alif refused to stop dancing at the club for the sole reason that he needed the attention. Tom continually fed him compliments, like sweet chocolates, filling his gut, but that was not enough. Like Tom, he had to get it from more than one source. They fed on one another; Tom wanted to own him and his beauty, and Alif wanted the attention and money. There was nothing lasting about their relationship. It would soon spoil like milk left out of the refrigerator on a hot August day in the deep South. There were plenty of penthouses and flashy cars in New York to go around. It would take more to keep Alif in his bed. Tom had met his match. They were a lot alike, wanting to be noticed and desired twenty-four-seven.

More so than before, Trey's phone rang in the lean hours with a drunken distressed man on the other end. Now that Alif was not around, most of Tom's nights were spent drinking expensive liquors while watching porn. Other nights he would venture out to Strips, a bar frequented by older, wealthy men. There was no lack of younger guys looking for a sugar daddy. They numbered a hundred to one. Soon Alif would be a memory. There were plenty of nice round butts in New York City waiting to be filled, and dicks to be sucked by Tom, and others like him. If it were a taxable commodity, New York City would have been out of the red years ago. Most were legitimate pretty gay boys looking for a life of leisure, while others were gay-for-pay. Tom was guaranteed a date for the night, only to find an empty wallet the next morning. But there was enough of that too for every sweet ass he could find. Even if Alif had stayed, it would only be a matter of time before Tom grew bored and found another boy. There was always another boy to be bought.

Keeping Good Measure

It is hard to keep an erection without the blue pill. Frustration races across Tom's face as he strokes his flaccid cock, while watching a Fuck Fest Video. Two hot buff guys are taking turns screwing a smooth thin Latin eighteen-year-old boy with full lips and big brown eyes. Pure pleasure washes over his face as the tag team enters him again and again. It is one of Tom's favorites, released before the onset of AIDS. There is a worn spot on the video in one of the scenes where Tom has repeatedly rewound and played it countless times. Pure raw sex, no condom covering blood-engorged dicks moving in and out of a sweet juicy ass. No added lubricant needed, just sweat, spit and pre-cum. Skin on skin. Tom's eyes remain glued on a close up of the Latin boy's ass being fed. Lately, even the intensity of barebacking on the television screen cannot bring a rise to his dick. Nothing.

He rubs his muscular chest with his left hand, feeling the hairs running between his fingers, while continuing to coax blood into his penis with the other. Tom adjusts the black leather cock strap wrapped around his ox balls and dick. Again, NOTHING.

He fast forwards the video. The remote is slippery from lube. The brown-eyed boy is now on his stomach with his big wet lips around the taller man's cock; the other's face is buried in the Latin's sweet round ass. The audio is on loud. Peggy has retired for the night to her apartment and will not venture back into Tom's domain until morning unless otherwise called. The moans of the boy fill the bedroom, as the cheesy background music builds.

Tom imagines his mouth on the boy's ass, licking up the pink, pushing his tongue into it like a penis. Tasty, Tom thinks. A loud moan escapes the speakers of the audio system, as cum ejaculates over the face of the Latin boy. He is covered in dripping white. His tongue slips out of his mouth to taste the frosting. Tom's eyes are big. His penis is half erect now. He concentrates harder on the boy licking up the cum from around his lips. He can almost smell it permeating the air and taste the boy on the television screen. He has had many like him — smooth, brown skin, with fresh tight bodies and round asses like ripe tasty cantaloupes.

The Latin boy then wipes his face with his hand where his tongue cannot reach and precedes to lick the cum finger by finger. The frame of the video moves to focus on the movement at the other end of the boy. A tight, mature large well-developed ass is moving up and down on the screen. Up and down on the eighteen-year-old boy. A respectable dick moves in and out of him, as the moans continue to spill from the boy's wet cum-soaked mouth.

It is now the man who is moaning, being encouraged on by the other.

"Give it to him," he orders.

The boy continues to moan.

"Plow his ass, man. Feed that hole."

The frame is now on the man's masculine face. His eyes are closed, mouth opened to release the pleasure he is experiencing as a result of the warm hole his penis is invading. Tom watches as if this is the first time he has seen the video. More blood moves into his dick. His strokes become longer and harder. He blindly reaches on the bed for the bottle of lube, his eyes still watching the cock entering the boy's ass. His excitement mounts. Tom wants the boy. He wants his dick in the Latin's ass. He wants to be the one pounding deep inside of him. Tom has been there hundreds of times and it is still never enough.

Mesmerized, he manages to squirt more lube on his own dick before discarding the container somewhere on the bed. Moments later the container annoyingly rolls back to his side, but Tom swiftly pushes it away. The cock strap feels tight now, as it holds in the blood, trapping it in the shaft. Now he is at full erection and proud of every inch. He slaps his erection repeatedly against his stomach. The bedroom fills with the sound of him beating his cock, the moans of the Latin, and the pounding of his ass.

The boy screams out, "Give it to me harder. Fill me up big daddy."

The frame moves from his face to the penis pulling out of his ass. A close-up of a hand stroking a wet penis fills the screen as cum explodes, shooting all over a well-fucked Latin ass.

Tom's frustration rises. The video is not enough. He wants the real thing as the credits roll on the television. Tom feels a sense of urgency as he sits up on the edge of the bed. He has not ejaculated yet. He strokes his cock a few more times before stopping. He lies back on the bed while reaching for the remote. Tom rewinds to the last scene with the close up of the Latin's ass being fucked. He freezes the frame and then sets the remote aside. Tom spits in his palm and begins beating his meat, as he thinks about the boy and what it would feel like to be raw inside his ass until a gush of white cum spills out of the head of his dick.

Moments later he unsnaps the strap, discarding it on the bedside table as he stands up. He catches the cum dripping from the head of his penis in his hand, carelessly wiping it and his crotch area with a towel he had gotten earlier from the bathroom. Tom is still not satisfied and now he regrets ejaculating, just in case he decides to go out, or the possibility of an online hook-up arises. It will be hard to cum again, at least for several hours. Tom walks from one end of the bedroom to the other, pacing like a caged animal. There seems to be no rhyme or reason to his movement. He puts on a robe and continues his walking. There is still lube and cum on his penis, it sticks to the silky material. He makes an adjustment, but it only last a few seconds until the robe sticks to him again.

Tom pushes the door wide open as he exits the bedroom. He heads down the hall and suddenly stops in his tracks. He turns and walks in another direction, into another room, walking then stopping again, looking at everything he has acquired over his lifetime. Tom came from a long lineage, traceable to the fine old plantations of the South, where his ancestors first made their money on the backs of slaves. There was so much wealth, so many things carried down from generation to generation — so much stuff, beautiful stuff. More stuff than any one family would or should need. Like his ancestors before him, who enslaved to build such wealth and beauty, Tom was enslaved to it. He was enslaved in a cocoon of wealth and privilege, decades of it — at the expense of others' pain, keeping him at a distance for anything real or true, and at that moment, he would freely trade it all for the boy in the video.

Tom eventually makes his way to the library. He tries to rub the late hour irritation from his eyes as he sits down at his desk. He can smell the cum on his hand and wipes it on his robe. The sleek flat computer screen beams its light into an otherwise darkened room, stylishly decorated by some well-known designer, whose talents frequently covered the pages of Architectural Digest and various other high-end interior design magazines. Pricey artworks, well-placed throughout for drama, are dimly lit. The air of the penthouse, well-removed far above the activities of the city below, is remarkably crisp. The hour is now late, well past midnight; his robe falls off his left shoulder. The music of *La stete di vivere* (Thirst For Life) plays from the stereo, filling the penthouse with a surreal mood, as wicks of candles in the living room burn low, their light barely strong enough to reach into Tom's adjacent library. His hands slowly run through his freshly dyed hair, still thick as a teenager's.

He moves the mouse until the arrow locates the AOL icon. Tom double-clicks, and waits for the sign-on screen to appear. He types in Olderatpark4younger and his password. Tom is online now. A whole world waits inside the lighted box in front of him. He activates the chat room list and searches until he finds NYCm4m3 has a vacancy. At the same time, he has entered match.com checking out the profiles like he has done on countless occasions before. Tom clicks from picture to picture while reading their clever profiles of what they are looking for: body type, sexual position, age range, etc. It seems to him no one wants to date anyone over thirty-five, much less someone over fifty. Tom returns his attention to the chat room as he scrolls down the list of screen names in the room, checking out more profiles, making mental notes of the ones he finds of interest. He has not changed his own profile in years. It still states that he is forty-nine (he was lying then about his age), six-two, 240lbs of muscle and hung. He sees no point in changing his age. He thinks a "few" years off is of little concern. After all — it is AOL anyway. It is more likely he does not want to deal with the fact he is years older since he first executed the profile. The rest of the information is correct.

Suddenly, an instant message pops up.

Hotnwet25: What you looking 4?

Tom eagerly checks the profile and is happy to see it also has attached pictures of a cute guy. He quickly responds.

Olderatpark4younger: A nice piece of ass.

Hotnwet25: Are you a top?

Olderatpark4younger: Yes.

Hotnwet25: Where you located?

Olderatpark4younger: On the Park.

Hotnwet25: Nice address.

Olderatpark4younger: It'll do.

Hotnwet25: Can you get to the Village?

Olderatpark4younger: No, not into going out tonight. I'll pay cab fare over and back.

Hotnwet25: Cool. Do you have any pics?

Olderatpark4younger: Yes.

Hotnwet25: Any X pics?

Olderatpark4younger: Yeah.

Hotnwet25: So how hung are you?

Olderatpark4younger: So you're a size queen. LOL. How hung do you need me to be?

Hotnwet25: Nothing queenie about me, bud.

Olderatpark4younger: Just kidding. 8.5 and very thick with a mushroom head.

Hotnwet25: NICE. Okay. Send please.

Olderatpark4younger: Give me a second.

Hotnwet25: K.

Tom hurriedly searches through an array of disks in the bottom right side desk drawer. Retrieving one, he holds it in the light provided by the screen. After taking a closer look, he exchanges it for another with a single X written in the middle of its white label. Tom pops in the disk and selects two cock shots and a body picture.

Olderatpark4younger: Sent.

After a few minutes, which seem longer to Tom, the instant message rings.

Hotnwet25: Nice body and dick man.

Olderatpark4younger: Glad you think so.

Hotnwet25: Cool. Looks hot. Any face pics?

Olderatpark4younger: Sure.

Tom's hand revisits the drawer filled with disks searching for another. His most recent pictures were taken two years ago at a beach in Marbella on Costa Del Sol. He has never been a fan of getting his picture taken, always shying away from the camera, afraid of the truth it will tell. He pushes the disk in the computer and proceeds to open up Photoshop, quickly reviewing the pictures before selecting two that he thinks make him look good and sends them to E-mail.

Hotnwet25: You still there?

OlderatPark4younger: Sent.

Hotnwet25: Just how old are you?

Tom responds without thinking.

OlderatPark4younger: 59

Hotnwet25: That's not what your profile states.

OlderatPark4younger: A slight oversight.

Hotnwet25: You can say that. Man, that's some old dick. How old are your pics?

OlderatPark4younger: My screen name indicates that I'm older. You don't have to be such an asshole. You'll get there one day if you're lucky.

Hotnwet25: Yea, maybe. Later dude.

Tom increasingly spent more and more time online looking.

Hours and hours went by on the internet eating up the night as he cruised in pick-up sites like AOL chat rooms, man4mansexnow. com and gay.com, reading profile after profile. The latter had been one of his favorites until it became overrun with cyber whores with webcams. They popped up on his screen as frequently as insects hitting a bug zapper at a Friday night summer cookout.

"Two hot college guys ready to get in on. We love to fuck and you can cum with us."

"Get a real job you WHORE," was his usual response before hitting ignore.

He finds interesting the choice of words many use to express what they are looking for, a common phrase being, "NO OLDIES!!!" – as if older men are something to be scorned, he thinks to himself. Tom feels they are zeroing in on him personally. "NO OLDIES" rings out in his mind over and over again. After a while, he begins believing that he is useless. At fifty-nine he sees himself as an old used-up piece of shit — and the negative profiles are not helping matters any. For Tom, if he cannot get into the pants of a guy under twenty-five, then what is left in life?

In distress, Tom makes another late-night call to Atlanta. This time Kyle picks up the phone. Without speaking, he nudges the receiver into Trey's side to wake him out of a sound sleep, sure that either someone has died, or, more likely, Tom is on the other end.

"Hello?" Trey answers half asleep.

"They all think I'm an oldie. A FUCKING OLDIE."

"What are you taking about, Tom?" Trey asks, trying to wake up.

"I'm old. Used up. An antiquity."

"Are you drinking again? Where is all this coming from?"

Kyle rolls his eyes and turns back over on his side.

"That's what they're saying in their profiles."

"Whose profiles, Tom?"

"Online. They don't want any oldies."

"Oh, you've been online again. Don't pay them any attention. Some of those young guys are clueless. You're still a hot man, Tom."

"Yeah, but you're biased."

"Well, biased or not, you're still hot. Now turn off that computer and go to bed. It's late."

Trey was biased, but he meant what he said. He had run across the same kind of attitude online, too. He had seen the profiles with "NO OLDIES, FATS, OR FEMS." Trey took it very personally as well, believing this choice of wording sad and disrespectful. He wondered if these guys had any understanding of the cycle of life, a heart, or any respect for older men — men who had built the community in which they lived today.

Trey questioned if they understood that a community is built, supported and nurtured. It was his understanding that the gay community came about in this way. Perhaps more subconsciously than consciously, but before he moved to Atlanta many years ago at nineteen, there existed a diverse group of individuals who had laid the foundation for the city's gay community, as in other cities across America. Trey saw them as "pioneers of sorts," this older generation of men. It is because of their efforts, joys and heartaches, that there exist gay bars, gay bookstores, gay softball teams, and gay support groups today. All he had to do as a young lad with excitement in his eyes was pack up his car and steer it east. With big dreams and a strong desire to find others who were like him, Trey made the pilgrimage to the gay Mecca of the South.

Time moves on, and with it comes new generations of young men, not much different, and in many cases, very much the mirror image of those earlier pioneers, looking to find a home in communities already established. Many of those pioneers have passed, but thankfully, some are still around. Trey is grateful for what they have given to the gay community, which he calls his own, that has grown into a diverse collection of individuals. These earlier men stood strong at Stonewall, held partners and friends dying of AIDS close to their chests, started the ongoing fight for equal rights, and fought wars abroad, all benefiting the freedom that gays enjoy today.

In a world with a history of horrors and an uncertain future, Trey is glad to have a community of experienced friends and mentors to whom he can turn for acceptance, advice and even love. These "OLD MEN" deserve respect because they are still a part of the gay community. Trey feels passionate about his belief, hoping those with "NO OLD MEN" stated in their profiles will become enlightened and realize it is those old men who brought gays to where they are today. It is also his wish that they find a better choice of wording, by stating the age range, body type and mannerism in which they are interested. Trey takes comfort in thinking that, after all, it will not be long before they see an old man looking back at them in the mirror. Then they will know the loneliness men like Tom are feeling. The loneliness, and even fear, he can hear in Tom's voice. One day they will see the face his long-time friend sees in the mirror and know. Trey feels bad for Tom, and even a little for himself. He knows in the back of his head that it will not be too many years down the road that he might have to endure the same heartless rejections.

"Sorry to wake you. Tell Kyle I'm sorry too."

"Just get some sleep, Tom. I'll call you tomorrow."

Trey had run across similar experiences in his online adventures. Before meeting Kyle, he had an AOL account, TOPMuscl4U with a pretty conservative profile:

White male

Single

37

Muscular/225lbs. /6ft../green/brown

Looking for a nice, cute, slim bottom / no games — no drugs — no couples.

He also had three pictures, two taken at the beach and a head shot.

He could have included that he was hot or very good-looking, or that he had a perfect body, but he was too modest. The pictures would tell the story. He did not want to come off as an arrogant asshole. He found many of the screen names humorous, such as Jockstud456, or any profile name with jock or stud or hot attached. He wondered if there was some kind of exam one had to take to be certified as a "Jockstud."

Trey's screen would light up like a Christmas tree with instant messages, especially after guys got a look at his pictures. What are you looking for? How big is your dick? Man you are HOT! Anymore pics? One of those instant messages was from a twenty-five-year old, good-looking personal trainer named Cody. His screen name was Trainme25 and his profile stated:

25/white/smooth gym body/very good-looking

5'8"/170lbs

Looking for a hot top in excellent shape ages 21-30.

PLEASE No fats, fems or oldies.

Trey is in the chat room for less than a minute when Trainme25's instant message pops up.

Trainme25: Stud!

TopMuscul4U: Hey, bud.

Trainme25: Nice pics, man.

TopMuscl4U: Thanks, yours are pretty nice too.

Trainme25: You looking?

TopMuscl4U: Might be. Why?

Trainme25: You're HOT, man. Would like to hook up.

TopMuscl4U: Did you read my profile?

Trainme25: Yeah.

TopMuscl4U: From your profile, looks like I'm a little old for you, bud.

Trainme25: What do you mean?

TopMuscl4U: I'm 37 and your cut off is 30 looks like.

Trainme25: Man, that's just a guideline. I'll make an exception for you dude.

TopMuscl4U: I'm flattered DUDE, but if you set limits you need to live by them.

Trainme25: Dude. Come on man. I'm really hot looking.

TopMuscl4U: And full of yourself, too, I see.

Trainme25: Come on.

TopMuscl4U: Sorry man. Later. Have a good one.

As much as Trey wanted to hook up with that little Trainme25 and fuck the hell out of his tight gym ass body, he was not going to, no matter how horny he was. He did not want anyone to make an exception for him, especially someone who was so insensitive to have something like: no fats, fems or oldies in his profile. He was too big of a man for that.

Trainme25 was persistent over the next few months after their original online chat, having buddy-listed Trey without asking. Every time he signed on, Trainme25 instant messaged him. But Trey did not give in until he adjusted his online attitude. Soon Trainme25 got the message and changed his profile to:

Only interested in guys that are in great shape and masculine.

After that they hooked up a few times, and Trey did indeed fuck the shit out of Trainme25. Cody did have a hot body, but a big coke habit as well. The last thing Trey wanted was a drugged out guy in his bed, no matter how good a fuck he was.

Comfort and Company

Tom returns the receiver to its cradle and takes a deep breath before getting up from his chair. Both elbows creak, sending razor-sharp pain up his arms. He pauses, sternly biting his bottom lip to hold back the grunt climbing up in his throat, not wanting to acknowledge the arthritis is getting the best of him. A few moments later, he continues to push up with his arms despite the disconcerting pain. His hands tightly grip the armrests, as a look of anguish swells on his face. Knees now straight, Tom's hands slowly release their death grip.

His sexuality managed to estrange Tom from his father, but it did not free him of the family ailments. In their later years, both of his parents suffered from an array of health problems. Before his father's death, Mr. Brookston was virtually confined to a wheelchair as a result of severe rheumatoid arthritis. The crippling disease was slowly surfacing in Tom's body, his advancing years gradually eating away at his once-Adonis appearance from the inside out.

Finally on his feet, Tom heads in the direction of the living room and the wet bar that separates it from a formal dining area. He does not want to go to bed as Trey suggested. Tom's hands are shaking as he reaches for a finely cut crystal glass from the bottom shelf of the bar. The full bottle of Sky vodka makes a scuffing sound as he drags it on the counter's granite surface to introduce it to the glass; a loud clang rings out as it meets its rim. Tom brings the full glass to his lips. His mouth opens to welcome the clear liquor until the glass is empty. He makes a bitter face as the vodka burns on the way down. As if getting more courage to go to war on AOL, Tom fills the glass again before heading back to the library to wage another battle.

The faint sounds of sirens racing on the avenue below barely take Tom's attention from the computer screen. The second glass of vodka, now almost empty, waits close to the keyboard as he continues a desperate search well into another night.

Tom clicks on Boy4hire1 and waits for his profile to fill the screen. It reads as follows:

Name: I will let you know that when I want you too.

Age: Young, but legal.

Occupation: Giving pleasure at a price.

Hobbies & interests: HOT all American looks/6ft./170lbs./ blonde/blue/swimmer's build/naturally smooth/ boyish/ 7cut / bubble butt to die for!

Favorite quote: VERY discreet. Serious only. Don't waste my time or yours. If you are lonely and need some comfort and company, you won't be disappointed. Hit link to view body shots.

Tom decides he has nothing to lose, except another lonely night.

Olderatpark4younger: Hey man, what's up tonight?

Bing. After a few moments, the silence in the room is broken by the instant message ring on the computer.

Boy4hire1: Just hanging

Olderatpark4younger: Are you having a good night?

Boy4hire1: No complaints here. What about you man?

Olderatpark4younger: Feeling like I need some of that comfort and company you mentioned in your profile.

Tom's right hand leaves the keyboard and moves to fondle his dick through his boxers, as Boy4hire1's web page begins to open. A series of headless nude pictures fill the screen.

Boy4hire1: Hey man, know the feeling.

Olderatpark4younger: So, you do this for a living?

Boy4hire1: Do what man?

Olderatpark4younger: Prostitute.

Boy4hire1: Escort.

Olderatpark4younger: What's the difference?

Boy4hire1: Well, if you're a cop, a lot.

Olderatpark4younger: Not a cop.

Boy4hire1: Well, in that case, not a whole lot. LOL. So you interested?

Olderatpark4younger: What's it going to cost me?

Boy4hire1: Depends on what you want.

Olderatpark4younger: Sex.

Boy4hire1: Well, that's a given.

Olderatpark4younger: What will it cost to fuck you?

Boy4hire1: $500.00 and if I come to you, cab fare both ways as well.

Olderatpark4younger: What about to stay the night or what is left of it?

Boy4hire1: $1000.00 for the whole night.

Olderatpark4younger: Do you have a face pic?

Boy4hire1: Don't send those out. You understand in this kind of business I have to be careful. No one has turned me away yet.

Olderatpark4younger: Do you want one of me?

Boy4hire1: Not necessary.

Tom directs his eyes to the bottom right-hand corner of the computer screen making note of the hour.

Olderatpark4younger: Well, its 3:20 a. m. When can you get here?

Boy4hire1: What's the address?

Olderatpark4younger: Park and 52nd. The Imperial. You know it?

Boy4hire1: Yeah. Give me 45 minutes.

Olderatpark4younger: What's your name? Need to tell the doorman you're expected.

Boy4hire1: Andrew.

Olderatpark4younger: See you in a bit.

◊

The cool water briefly washes the late hour from Tom's face. He reaches for a plush gray hand towel from a stack of several with his monogram in black. Soothing light, from the overhead recessed cans, hangs in the room of the master bath, flattering Tom's mature face as he looks at its reflection in the wide slick modern gold mirror hanging over the black marble sink. A collection of scented soaps are piled high in an antique rust colored urn next to an onyx picture frame housing a younger version of the man now looking back at him. Reluctantly, Tom picks up the frame to take a closer look at the captured image of a youthful man standing on a nameless beach, tan, muscular and unquestionably handsome. He now stands in a state of disbelief, wondering, how could the years have taken such a toll? How could they have escaped him so quickly?

It only seems like yesterday, perhaps just a few years, since the picture was taken, he thinks.

The reflection in the mirror, although still handsome, does not lie. Tom now looks like he might be this person's father, rather than the person in the picture. In spite of all the expensive elective surgeries, the trips to the doctor every two weeks to get injections of testosterone to keep up his levels so he can maintain his muscle mass, the hours spent in his personal gym, the trainers, and the body and face skin treatments, Tom can still see the lines and wrinkles that had been smoothed out. They are still there under his skin, waiting to come back again like a sleeping enemy, waiting to rise and take over his appearance. Every time he catches a glimpse of himself in the mirror, or his passing refection in a storefront window on a busy New York street, he hears them screaming out at him, "You are old, used up and of no use anymore." No amount of money or doctors can keep them from coming back sooner or later, or keep the voices in his head quiet.

He takes a deep breath; the fragrances from the scented soaps mix in his lungs. He so wishes he could go back in time to that very beach and dig his feet in the sand in the precise place where the picture was taken. Still in disbelief, Tom halfheartedly returns the picture to a spot beside one of him and Trey on a similar beach. He watches the mechanical movement of his hand as he places it back on the counter. Tom picks up the other picture. A slight smile comes to his lips as he remembers the vacation they took together. He can even remember the exact moment the picture was snapped by a stranger they asked to take the shot, and how intense the sun was on their faces, and how invigorating the breeze was coming off a blue ocean they spent hours playing in.

He remembers how good Trey looked in those black Speedos, and what a perfect tan line they left on him by the third day of lounging many hours away on the white sand. Like it was yesterday, Tom sees Trey standing naked in the hotel suite after a sun-soaked day on the beach. A constant gentle breeze flowed into the room from the open balcony doors that looked out onto an incredible pink and orange sunset erupting over a tranquil ocean. Trey had just removed the Speedos before stepping into the shower to wash off the sand and suntan lotion from his body.

Tom watched him from the balcony before joining Trey in the cool refreshing water. He remembers how much Trey was in love with him and what a great feeling that was to have someone so full of life so into him. For a short time, Tom saw a different world through young eyes: a world full of excitement and new adventures. Trey had brought so much pleasure and happiness to Tom, but it all became lost in an obsession. He knows things could have been different. Now he wishes they had been. Tom lets out a sigh of what could be interpreted as regret.

Curiously, he raises both hands in front of his face to eye level. There, they remain frozen for a time, hanging in the air as if detached from the rest of Tom's body. Positioned side by side, he notes that they still appear large and strong despite the recurring age spots that freckle them. His eyes dart from one hand to the other, then back again following the raised veins running under his skin. He makes a mental note to secure another appointment with Dr. Kline, his dermatologist. The coolness of the marble floor under Tom's bare feet becomes apparent to him, distracting him from the examination. He takes another look at his reflection and moves his body, turning it slightly to the left and then to the right repeatedly until he gets what he thinks is a more flattering angle. Suddenly, his regret turns and a sense of excitement runs through his body. Tom remembers Boy4hire1 will be there soon, he must shower and dress.

Now all cleaned up, wearing a tight black Kenneth Cole T-shirt, cream casual slacks and black slides, Tom walks into the bedroom stopping at the bedside table. He opens a highly-polished wooden box containing an assortment of prescription bottles. He rattles through them until he finds the one containing blue pills.

"How are my little friends?" he mumbles, as he coaxes out a Viagra into the palm of his hand. Tom looks at it as if expecting a response before gently clenching it in his fist.

Returning to the library, he takes another swallow of vodka from his glass and lays the pill on the desk. Tom knows he has to time it just right. It will take a good twenty to thirty minutes for it to take full effect. Taking the pill too soon or too late will kill the opportunity to get a nice erection. He looks at the silver Raymond Weils watch on his wrist, a gift from Trey years ago. He decides he will give it another few minutes and then take the pill. Tom sits back down at the computer to look again at the pictures of Boy4hire1 still up on the screen. He takes the last swallow in the glass, ice clanks against his lips. Tom picks up the phone to call the doorman, Anthony, to inform him that he is expecting a late-night guest. He is an elderly man, very prim and proper, who usually works the night shift. Tom has always tipped him well to insure Anthony will keep his late night conferences in the strictest of confidence.

"Good evening, Mr. Brookston."

"Evening, Anthony."

"Yes, it is a fine evening, sir. What may I do for you?"

"I have a young guest arriving shortly. His name is Andrew."

"Very good, sir. I will be sure to show the gentlemen up."

"Thank you, Anthony. Have a good night."

"And you as well, sir. A very good one indeed."

Tom hangs up the phone and walks back to the bar. He fills

the glass again before returning to the desk. He pops the pill into a welcoming mouth, chasing it with a swallow of vodka from the freshly-poured glass, the third one tonight. He opens the top middle drawer of the desk and pulls out a handful of one hundred dollar bills from a bank envelope, folds them in half and slides them into his pocket. His attention returns to the computer screen that had gone black in his absence. With a tap on the sensor, Boy4hire1's pictures come back into view.

Tom spends the next fifteen or so minutes studying them like he is preparing for an exam. He is wondering if this boy is truly as amazing as his pictures depict and if his face is as exquisite. He gently rubs on his penis in anticipation. Soon he feels a tingle, as blood swells his penis. Tom unconsciously wets his lips with his tongue. The Viagra is doing its magic. Tom had become addicted to it, never leaving home without a bottle on his travels. It made it easier to recapture the erections enjoyed in younger days. His drug use, especially sleeping pills, Valium and an occasional party drug took them south. He had been known in his earlier years to do a line of coke here and there, partly to forget he was getting older, but mostly because many of the younger guys liked to "party." Tom has a reliable source to supply an occasional bag — one of his past young lovers.

◊

The doorman rings to announce the visitor. Tom stands in the entry waiting for the elevator doors to open. For a second, it appears to be empty before a shadowed figure steps out from the side into the dim light of the center of the elevator. Tom takes a deep breath. His eyes open wide to bring the youthful figure standing several feet away into focus.

"It's Andrew, right?" Tom asks, already knowing the answer.

"And you must be Tom?"

"Welcome to my humble digs," Tom greets, extending his hand out in hospitality.

"Some digs, man," Andrew speaks in a laugh, as he walks closer to Tom.

"Yeah, I call it home."

Because of the late hour, Andrew thought his worn Levis and white T-shirt with New York Yankees in blue lettering across the chest appropriate. There was no need to try to impress his new client with a selection of choice pieces of designer clothing. This was not a dinner date, rather a sex call, the fewer the clothes to hassle off — and then on, after the encounter — the better. No point in dealing with fancy buttons or lace-up shoes to fumble over when trying to make a quick and easy exit. Although some of Andrew's clients liked to be seen with him, either at a hot new club or one of the many fussy restaurants that Manhattan offered, Tom is not in the mood for dancing or food, at least not the kind to feed the stomach.

Many of those clients were like Tom: older and well-established with the means of dangling the offer of "the sky's the limit" to any exceptionally good-looking young man who would take the bait and dress the part. Andrew's client resume included married men, bankers, lawyers and even presidents and CEO's of Fortune 500 companies. One of his regulars, the head of a major television network, had been happily paying Andrew for about three months. Of course, they never dined out or went to any high-polished clubs. Andrew always met him at a nicely furnished apartment on the Upper East Side, which was acquired to enjoy the pleasures of young men for hire.

Some of these wealthy men offered at one time or another to set Andrew up in his own apartment with a fine monthly allowance, health club membership and various other perks. He tried it once with a New York Stock Exchange banker, only to feel trapped. It was a strict arrangement. No other johns, always at the banker's beck and call day or night, and total secrecy. The arrangement lasted less than two months. Wisely, Andrew kept his old apartment just in case. It was just as well. He never planned to make "call boy" a long time vocation.

There was nothing unique about his story or how he began turning tricks. The only thing special about Andrew was the way he looked. He thought his beauty would be enough to help seal his desire for fame. After moving from Michigan to the Big Apple two years earlier to be an actor, Andrew found the life of sharing a closet-sized apartment with two other struggling performers a near impossible feat. Barely able to meet his share of the rent and have enough money left over to provide basic necessities, he fell into the world of sex for hire almost by mistake.

He had stardom in his eyes, a bright face and a diploma from the University of Michigan in his back pocket; he was a theater major, who usually got the lead in every production since high school. Before puberty, Andrew had been told time and time again that he was good-looking enough to be in the movies. Once he got to New York, it did not take long to find an agent, but the parts were few and far between. New York was full of fresh and bright faces like Andrew's. Sure, it was just a question of being in the right place at the right time, and landing that one role that would skyrocket him into stardom. But the line for such dreams is miles and miles long. The bigger questions: How would he feed, clothe and shelter himself in the meantime?

On one casting call for a commercial, the producer took a liking to this faired-haired, small-town Michigan male starlet. Andrew got the part, got paid and things were looking up for the moment. Three months, and countless casting calls later, there was no work. In the meantime, Andrew was waiting tables at an expensive steak house with fancy chandeliers and overstuffed booths. One evening, the same producer came into the restaurant. A week later, he called to invite Andrew out to dinner to, as the producer put it, discuss a pending project that he thought Andrew would be perfect for. They ended up in a hotel room. The next morning Andrew woke up with five hundred dollars next to him and no producer.

◊

"Can I get you a drink?" Tom offers.

"I never drink on the job," Andrew says, with a chuckle.

"Suit yourself, I think I'll have one," Tom says, as he motions for his guest to follow him into the living room.

Andrew smiles as he nods his head in acknowledgement.

"Have a seat while I get something to take the edge off," Tom says, as he makes his way toward the bar to pour number four.

There is no response from his late-night guest. Instead, Andrew watches Tom walk across the room. He is curious about his new client, wondering what he did to acquire all the wealth that is represented by the surroundings. Is he married or divorced? Does he have a lover asleep in one of the bedrooms of the impeccable penthouse? Or is his wife or lover out of town? Or is Tom just a house guest of a rich friend? Whatever the answer, Andrew has a feeling that Tom is different from the rest of his paying clients. He quickly begins to analyze the many possible scenarios of Tom's identity. Andrew concluded, if Tom was single, he certainly did not seem like the type that needed to pay for sex as some of his more unattractive clients did. He was older yes, but very sexy. Perhaps, his thoughts continue, Tom does not want to deal with the bar scene and finds it more convenient to pay for his sexual pleasures.

"So, do you do this a lot?" Andrew asks.

"Do what?"

"Hire young men to come to your penthouse – that's assuming it's yours – in the middle of the night?'

"Yes, it's mine. And, no, believe it or not, you're my first."

"Well, I can believe it. You're quite handsome."

"Do I have to pay more for compliments?"

"No, they're on the house," Andrew laughs.

Tom smiles as he turns away from the bar and walks toward Andrew.

"I guess I've paid for it one way or the other, or at least it seems that way of late."

"What do you mean?" Andrew asks.

"Well, let me put it this way. It seems like it would be easier to just put everything on the table or the bed rather, so everyone knows what they're getting," Tom explains with a chuckle.

"I see," Andrew says.

"Are you sure I can't get you something to drink?"

"Well, maybe some water."

Tom returns to the bar. Andrew watches him again, examining the broadness of his shoulders and his thick neck. He is very attracted to him, thinking he is the most handsome of all his clients. Andrew is intrigued by how laid back Tom appears; how casual he acts surrounded by all the stifling wealth.

Quietly, Andrew walks over to where Tom is standing; Tom is unaware of his approach, as his back is still to him. Andrew reaches his arms around Tom's waist, pulling his massive back against his chest. He is impressed by his new john's muscle mass. Tom puts the bottle of water back on the counter next to his glass of partly consumed vodka. He feels Andrew's breath on the back of his neck.

"What's this all about?" Tom asks.

"Getting down to business," replies Andrew, as he releases his embrace long enough to remove his T-shirt.

Tom turns around. His eyes focus on the well-defined chest in front of him. A nervous lump begins to accumulate in his throat. Tom swallows hard to send it down into his stomach. But it resists, and he has to swallow again. Tom decides not to speak and instead moves closer to Andrew until his shirt is against bare skin.

"Feels nice," Andrew says, sliding his hands under Tom's shirt, slowly moving them up his stomach toward his chest.

"Yeah, it does," Tom responds.

"You must work out a lot," Andrew says, as he feels the massiveness of Tom's pectoral muscles.

"Yeah, I do. I have my own gym in the west wing."

A slight moan slips past Tom's lips as Andrew proceeds to pull the black designer shirt from his body. Tom consciously tries to control his breathing. The room is feeling hot as the short light hairs on the small of Tom's back collect sweat. They are now standing bare torso to torso. Andrew begins kissing his chest. Tom's arms are around his waist, gravitating toward his butt. Andrew looks up directly into his eyes as he slips his hand into Tom's pants, grabbing his fully-erect penis, wet with pre-cum.

"Nice package, man," Andrew comments. "Perhaps I should be paying you," he adds in jest.

"That would be another first," Tom says.

Tom reaches for the top snap of Andrew's 501 jeans. In one swift jerk, the top three metal buttons pop open. With both hands, one just below either side of Andrew's waist, Tom begins to move them until he feels two nice firm cheeks. Now fully captured in his large hands, all Tom can think about is his tongue deep between them.

"Man, those feel hot, let me take a good look," Tom requests.

Without a response, Andrew turns around and slowly releases the remaining buttons. He pushes down his jeans. Tom's mouth is watering as he gazes upon what he perceives as two ripe melons ready to be eaten. Sliding his hands down Andrew's well-defined legs, lightly sprinkled with hair, he drops to his knees. Perspiration begins to collect on his forehead, as he centers his nose in Andrew's crack. Tom inhales deeply. The smell of freshly washed ass fills his nostrils. He savors the odor while continuing to hold firmly on to his legs. The smell is intoxicating. It is the scent of youth that Tom craves filling every inch of his lungs until he is dizzy with desire.

Tom slowly begins to follow the crack of Andrew's butt with the tip of his tongue. By now the sweat from his forehead is running down his face. Andrew feels it on his skin. It is warm and wet. He reaches back to spread his cheeks wider. Now it is easier for Tom to lick his hole, licking it like he is a thirsty dog lapping at a bowl of water.

"Before we get any further," Andrew interrupts, as he reaches down to pull his jeans back up, "Why don't we get the financials out of the way so we can enjoy the rest of the evening."

Tom begins to feel edgy. He comes back to reality. He has never paid outright for sex before. The thought of exchanging money for what comes so naturally to him has never entered his mind until tonight.

It's only money, Tom thinks. He quickly returns his thoughts to Andrew and the beauty of him. This is worth paying for, Tom reassures himself.

Andrew holds on to the waist of his jeans as he waits for a response.

"This should take care of it," Tom says, as he pulls the bills from his pocket.

Without counting, Andrew quickly slides them into his right back pocket, then lets the jeans fall back to the floor. He steps out of them. He is now totally and beautifully naked. Every inch is pure perfection. The boy is flawless; Tom thinks to himself, maybe he is worth it.

Tom leads Andrew into the bedroom, where he instructs him

to lay stomach down on the bed. He removes his pants. The soft light of the room throws a warm glow on two naked bodies. One: young, firm and the epitome of beauty. The other: one of masculine maturity, confidence and full of lust. Both have two different agendas; one to give pleasure for pay and the other to receive it for a price.

Tom buries his face into Andrew's round, white bubble ass, and continues the licking he started earlier in the living room. He runs his tongue from Andrew's scrotum to the small of his back. The saliva in Tom's mouth flows like water from a raging river. Andrew can feel his five-o-clock shadow beginning to rub his cheeks raw. He does not say a word; his face is turned to one side as his eyes scan the room. Tom says something, but the words are muffled by the boy's cheeks.

Andrew feels weak. His ass had been eaten by many clients, but Tom's technique is by far the best to date. Normally, this is just "another night at the office," but there is so much passion and desire in this john's aggression.

"Roll over, man," Tom instructs.

Andrew obeys.

Tom wipes the spit from his lips and chin before going down on Andrew's dick. He licks its head and then takes it whole into his mouth. By now Tom has forgotten about the money, or that the person in his bed is a prostitute. Andrew looks up at him, then at the ceiling. His body twists in pleasure.

Tom pulls Andrew's legs apart and up into the air before laying his massive body on top of his. In reflex, the boy's legs wrap around his waist. Tom's penis is hard and full of desire to be inside Andrew's warm wet hole. It appears massive compared to Andrew's average one, but it is still beautiful and perfect to Tom. Size is of little importance; Tom is a face and ass man. His body engulfs Andrew. He begins rubbing against Boy4hire1, pretending to fuck him, as his hands firmly hold onto his ass.

"Man, I want to be inside of you," Tom calls out.

"Is that what you want?" Andrew responds.

"You know it boy."

"You have protection?" Andrew asks.

Tom does not answer, but continues his movement on Andrew, their pre-cum making a slippery mix. Olderatpark4younger's attention turns to Andrew's large red nipples and begins to suck on them, alternating from one to the other, like a hungry baby suckling milk from its mother.

He has hit Andrew's weak spot. The harder Tom sucks, the more aroused Andrew becomes. The boy's legs spread even wider as Tom's big hard dick rubs on his stomach and against his penis. For a moment, Andrew forgets this is a job. He has forgotten he is in the sex business where personal involvement is dangerous. Andrew tries to control his emotions, not wanting the situation to get the best of him. At all costs, he has to be in control, regardless of whether it appears like he is or not. The bottom line is that he is in this position to make money, not get emotionally connected with a client. But the more Tom continues, the more Andrew wants him inside of his hole. He wants to feel it thrust into him, giving pleasure and pain.

Tom collects a large amount of spit in his mouth, which he lets run out between his lips onto Andrew's hole as he lifts the boy's legs up over his head. The smell of sweat, spit, and the odor of man saturates the air collecting over the bed and infusing in the sheets. Tom's lungs fill with the intoxicating mix, arousing him more as he begins to rub his cock lower and lower until its head is pushing on Andrew's anus. With increasing force, Tom continues to move his body between Andrew's legs. He is so much stronger than the boy, even at fifty-nine; Tom is still every bit of a man in control as he imposes his strength on Andrew.

Harder and harder Andrew tries to remain in character. Now, the head of Tom's penis slides inside of Andrew. The boy gasps. The force of the surprise penetration causes Andrew an intense, but brief, pain. For a moment they freeze and lay silent, with Tom cradled between Andrew's legs. Fear has caught them for a brief time, both not knowing what to do. Tom is waiting for Andrew to welcome him in, wanting to push all the way inside to feel the full pleasure and warmth that is just inches away.

Tom smothers his lips on Boy4hire1's, pressing hard until his mouth opens and welcomes in his tongue. The collection of sweat on Tom's hairy chest drips down onto Andrew's young smooth skin. The boy makes a meek attempt to push Tom's pelvis away, but wants him to continue to enter him all the same. The deep kiss is making it hard to resist, but Andrew finally manages to take back control of the moment.

"Man, you have to use a condom," Andrew repeats, as he severs free of the kiss and gets the strength to roll out from under his new john.

Old worries come back to haunt Tom. Is it worth the risk of unprotected sex? He now is reminded he is with a prostitute. The lingering thought crowns in Tom's head along with the knowledge that age has hindered his ability to remain hard with latex, but the blue pill helps. The older Tom gets, the more he longs to be free of any restrictions. Andrew is also afraid, but for different reasons; he is in the sex business, safety is a priority. Every time he engages in sex, he is putting his life at risk, even when a condom is being used.

"Sure," Tom answers.

He reaches for the handle to the top drawer of the bedside table.

To Forgive or Forget

Having returned from Birmingham late last evening, Trey is at a junction, more like a crisis. He feels he has been involved in a bad emotional car wreck. The dogs bark playfully in the back yard tugging at a toy that squeaks sporadically, as they romp on the lawn sprinkled with morning dew. The sun is easing its way into the awakening house as Kyle and Trey sit across from each other at the kitchen table, not speaking any words of importance. They spent the night on either side of the bed with a void between them. Several times Kyle moved his foot to appear to accidentally touch Trey's, but his partner just moved his further away.

Kyle overly butters his whole wheat toast, as Trey hides his face in the Atlanta Journal. It seems they both want to avoid any discussion of the unpleasant night of sleeping alone in a bed they shared.

"I need more juice. Can I get you something while I'm up?" Kyle asks as he slides his chair away from the table.

"No thanks." Trey forces an answer.

Kyle walks over to the stainless steel refrigerator, pulling out an almost empty gallon container of Tropicana Select. He pours what is left in his glass before slamming the carton down on the counter.

"So, Trey, how long are you going to give me the silent treatment? It has been weeks now. You have barely touched me."

He looks up from the paper. Trey is not really trying to give any silent treatment to Kyle. He just does not know how he feels about the apology; not sure how sincere it is, or if there is going to be another indiscretion in the future. Everything was put on hold when Tom tried to kill himself. Things were further interrupted with his death and the funeral.

"Just how many guys have you cheated on me with?" Trey asks.

Kyle looks at him while rubbing his forehead as if he has a headache.

"I was drunk, and I'm not sure anything really happened with Eric and Kim."

"So that makes it okay?"

"Trey, you must know how sorry I am. Like I said, I'm not even sure anything happened."

"Well, condoms tell the story."

Trey returned home from a business trip early in the afternoon on Monday the day after Tom took the overdose. He had been away for three days doing a corporate art installation in Dallas. Kyle was at work, at his job as a computer consultant for a large investment company. Trey was greeted by the dogs and found one of them chewing on a condom, and soon after discovered three packaged ones slightly chewed up under the bedside table. He was perplexed and upset due to the fact that Trey and Kyle had not used condoms in two years, and to his knowledge, there were none in the house anymore. After both having a negative result on their HIV tests, it was clearly understood they were in a monogamous relationship. Trey tried to reach Kyle at his office, but was told he would be in a meeting until later in the afternoon. It was just a short time afterward that Trey received the call from Nancy about Tom. He had to focus his attention on getting back to the airport.

Kyle had wanted Trey to bareback him for several months after they started their long-distance dating. Although Trey liked the idea, he felt Kyle was still young and would be too tempted to stray. He wanted to wait until Kyle moved to Atlanta, then reconsider the whole issue about condom use.

Soon into the romance, they had been spending almost every weekend together racking up Delta frequent flyer miles. On one Monday morning, they consummated their relationship in the raw. The alarm went off at six-thirty. Trey hits the fifteen minute snooze button. Kyle is scheduled on the nine-sixteen flight back to Boston, but is not disturbed by the alarm. He is still fast asleep lying on his stomach, his perfectly round ass peeking out of the covers, causing Trey's dick to stand at attention. He sees it as an invitation and begins kissing Kyle's butt, slowly working his lips toward its crack. Soon Kyle wakes finding his boyfriend licking and softly biting him.

"Baby, I love it when you do that," Kyle speaks, in a sleepy tone.

"Did you not hear the alarm go off?"

"Alarm? Who needs an alarm when you're around?"

He continues licking Kyle's hole. Buffy and Sam lay their heads on the edge of the bed, wanting to be fed and let out. Trey kicks at them to go back to their own bed in the corner of the room.

Kyle slowly gets up on his knees, weak from the intense pleasure he is receiving. In an acrobatic move, Trey flips him over on his back while still eating his ass. Now his dick is rubbing against Kyle's lips; within seconds, he takes it in his mouth. Like a pro, Kyle takes all of it.

"Man, I can't get enough of you," Trey speaks, in excitement and goes back to his eating.

Kyle's mouth is full and responds with a moan, as Trey's saliva runs down his crack. The two dogs obediently sit up in their bed watching their master, thinking he is romping with a playmate. Sam lets out a whimper before Buffy gently paws her in the snout. They are soon distracted by their own play, losing interest in what Trey and Kyle are doing.

The alarm goes off again indicating it is six forty-five. Trey reaches over to turn it off while Kyle rolls back over on his stomach.

"We need to get up, or you're going to miss your flight."

"Screw the flight. Better yet, screw me," Kyle says, with a laugh.

"Oh, yeah," Trey says.

"Just a little longer baby. You know you have to fuck me now. There is no way I'm getting on that plane until you fuck me."

"Is that so?"

Trey reaches for the box of condoms still on the bedside table from the night before with his free hand; the other one has a strong hold around Kyle's waist. He shakes the box over the bed.

"Damn. It's empty."

"Ah, baby, tell me you're joking."

"I wouldn't joke about that," Trey answers, as he throws the box across the room. Sam and Buffy scurry to retrieve it like a play toy.

"Just rub on me," Kyle requests.

Trey lowers his body down and begins rubbing his cock over his ass wet with saliva. Trey's dick is oozing pre-cum like a leaking faucet in need of repair. His arms are wrapped around Kyle's body with both hands firmly planted on his chest as he forcefully kisses the back of his neck. The passion is high, the combination of saliva and pre-cum makes for a very slippery and intensely dangerous situation. They are both caught up in the moment, having totally lost concern about running late for the nine-sixteen flight to Boston.

"Oh, baby. I want you in me," Kyle calls out.

Trey rubs faster and faster. The kisses become more aggressive

185

as he bites his back and shoulders. The head of his penis hesitates for a brief second at Kyle's hole, then moves over it again and again.

"Put it in, put it in. You're making me crazy."

"We can't."

"Just for a second. Please, I want you."

The moment is fervent, almost holy. The head of Trey's penis slips into Kyle's hole. Trey freezes for a minute. A feeling of pure raw pleasure races through his body. They are both breathing heavily; sweat from Trey's body is dripping onto Kyle's back.

"All the way in, baby. Please don't stop now," he says, thrusting his butt up, not giving Trey a choice.

His penis slides deep into Kyle, who screams out in pure bliss as it fills him up. Trey freezes again; the raw sensation is rich with the combination of pleasure and guilt. He knows he should pull out, but he cannot. There is an angel and devil fighting in his head. The good telling him to stop, the bad insisting he continue to plunge deeper and deeper to fulfill his desires. Trey feels helpless between the devil and Kyle urging him on, while the angel is losing ground, fading into some coal-black space in his mind. With every inward thrust, Trey becomes more of a prisoner to the movement, while Kyle and the devil in his mind are the wardens.

Now the pleasure has taken over, replacing all responsible behavior. All reason is lost to primitive animalistic desires; Trey's penis has overpowered his mind. His buttocks contracts and expands with every thrust of his pelvis. In a flash, Kyle roles over and wraps his legs tightly around Trey's muscled body as he grabs ahold of his lover's dick to guide it back in. His short manicured nails dig into Trey's back to take hold, as if he is riding the belly of a bull. The bed knocks against the wall with each precise, almost violent plunge. Trey can feel he is about to come; with each thrust he gets closer. He tells himself to pull out, but it feels too good. Trey is overly excited by his partner's verbal expressions of pleasure. Kyle's hands are now holding on to Trey's butt cheeks, pushing him in deeper and deeper. Kyle is in ecstasy as creamy white cum floods his hole. They are both gasping for air. Kyle's legs relax slightly as Trey's movements stop. He is frozen on top, his penis still inside. Kyle makes a combination of sighs, acknowledging his blissful state. Trey begins to pull out, but Kyle's anus tightly holds on as the last of the semen seeps into him. For the first time in their relationship, Trey has come inside of Kyle.

As the pleasure subsides, the angel reappears from the dark place in Trey's mind, and now the devil retreats, laughing as he fades away. With the angel comes the burden of guilt. Trey knows they had crossed the line, but he loves Kyle, and now he has made him his. He has bred him. Unlike his younger lover, who is too lean in years to understand, Trey knows the injustice they have shown to all those who have entered this place before them, becoming lost in the world of AIDS. Kyle has no guilt. His youth foolishly protects him. He has not seen what Trey has seen: friends dying, dreams lost in just moments of uncontrolled passion, and hearts broken. He is just a boy in a world where he sees only what is good and beautiful. He has a man who loves him, who, at all costs, will keep harm from his door. Trey knows now there is no going back. He will have to make this act of injustice right. Although he is aware of their HIV status, Trey feels it would be the dutiful thing for both of them to be tested again. If only for all those who had lost themselves in such moments, and were forever marked and forever changed.

Now the fairy tale had a new twist, other characters had entered never-never land. Trey would have spent the rest of his life faithful to Kyle. Sure, he had been tempted to cheat many times. But at his age, and unlike Tom, he had fucked all the strangers he wanted. Trey had always been a one man's man. He wanted to come home to the same guy night after night. He wanted the familiar and the comfortable. He also wanted to be free of the fear of sexually transmitted diseases. The fact that Kyle was so beautiful made it easier, too. He never loved anyone, other than Tom, as much as he now did Kyle. In fact, he loved them equally in different ways: Tom had been the older lover in his life and Kyle the younger, and he had taken on a different role with each. Tom introduced him to the gay world, and Kyle reminded him of his own youth, somehow forgotten over the years.

At the end of his life, Trey wanted to remember one great love, not a string of sex partners. He wanted to have memories with someone, which would make the journey into the uncertainties of old age easier. Or at least that is what he thought. Now he was uncertain if Kyle would be that person.

◊

"Looks like a fuck fest to me, Kyle. I told you to watch out for those guys. They have hit on us several times, and they are always checking out your ass at parties. Guys like them have no respect; they are detritus on the face of the earth. That ring on your finger doesn't mean shit to them and apparently not to you either."

"Like I said a hundred times, Trey, they gave me a ride home from the charity auction Sunday night after Steve left with some guy. We stopped off at The Red Chair to have a few drinks. I think one of them slipped something in my beer. I don't know, but it got fuzzy after that."

"Yeah, keep going."

"I remember they came in the house with me. I really didn't ask them in. They just followed me. Kim asked for a glass of water. We were hanging out in the kitchen. They started making out next to me, and one of them reached over and started feeling on my chest. You know how hot they are. Eric pulls Kim's tank top off right in front of me. I told them they needed to take themselves home."

"I'm listening," Trey says, as his face gets red.

"Well, then Eric puts his hand up my shirt and starts kissing on me, and before I know it, they are all over me. I kind of forgot myself for a moment. Kim said he wanted to watch Eric fuck me, and pulls out a string of condoms from his pocket and slams them down on the table."

"And then what happened?" Trey asks, looking like his head is going to spin off his shoulders.

"I told them to leave and that you would beat the hell out of them when I told you. So they left. Really."

"And what about the condoms."

"I guess they left them on the table. I went to bed. One of the dogs must have gotten them off the table. I overslept on Monday and was late to work, so I didn't notice them."

"So you made out with them?"

"Just a little bit. Then I came to my senses."

"Yeah, but you still made out with them."

Eric and Kim were notorious for fucking every cute guy they could lure into their web. They had been together for eleven years, both in their forties, nice looking, with your standard issue gay pumped bodies. Now Kyle, willing or not, had managed to be added to their list of possible conquests.

"I just need some time. Tom's death has really affected me. I should have been there for him. It's a waste that he killed himself."

"He was old," Kyle says.

"How can you say that?"

"Well, I just mean he was tired of living, that's all I meant."

"Well, old or not, he was my friend. Our friend. And fifty-nine isn't old."

"Our friend, as you put it, has grabbed my ass a time or two when you weren't looking, Trey."

"I know. Tom was a dirty man. He liked a good-looking boy."

"I'll say he was a dirty old man."

"There, you said it again. Stop referring to him as old, Kyle."

"Sorry, I don't want to make you any more angry than you already are, but he was always chasing guys half his age and younger."

"So, it's okay for a younger guy to chase an older one, but not the other way around? Is that what you are telling me?"

"Well, I guess you have a point," Kyle concedes.

"Tom had a lot of life left in him. A lot of life. And what does that make me? I'm almost eighteen years older than you."

"Yeah, but I chased you," Kyle clarified.

Trey could not help but smile. It was true; Kyle pursued him from the beginning. He even moved across eight states to be with him not long after they started dating; now it has been two years. Trey resisted at first, not really outwardly, but on the inside. His brain told him not to get involved with a younger guy. In all honesty, he knew he was hooked almost from the first time they slept together.

Trey knew in some respects, he was no different than any other gay man when it came right down to sex. He had been tempted time and time again, even since Kyle and he had been together. His striking good looks and exceptional muscular build attracted many a man to test his loyalty. But his conscience would never allow him to cross the line; that is what made Trey different – a gay man with a conscience.

Maybe nothing really happened, except the petting. But that was still cheating to him. They had their mouths and hands all over his boy. He was not going to just let it go at that. His heart tells him there was more to the story than what Kyle was willing to divulge. Trey can see the guilt on his face.

Eric and Kim had not returned any of Trey's phone calls. He was ready to go over to their house and settle the matter once and for all. Trey was ready to beat the living hell out of those overgrown party boys. He would beat them within an inch of their lives. Trey was tough and had a temper. They knew that and were trying to avoid a beating.

Now the feeling of great loss was consuming Trey: the loss of Tom and, as he saw it, the loss of Kyle's faithfulness. He felt deserted and alone. He was grieving two deaths. Trey was left not knowing what to think or feel and perhaps Tom's death was causing him to overreact.

Feeding Monsters

A moderate breeze whistles through the open doors leading out to the posh balcony, giving life to the sheer draperies, the curtain rod unable to restrain their dance into the room. Like overly-large wings of butterflies, they waltz up toward the ceiling, pausing briefly somewhere in the middle to do a ballet. It is a beautiful dance like two lovers engrossed in a ritual of foreplay. They tease one another in lighthearted amusement, touching and twisting together in midair before untangling. Over and over again they twist and untangle in the soft light of the room. The draperies hover effortlessly in the air before making their minuet back down toward the floor. Wide awake, Tom watches until the breeze stills, and the drapes return to their hanging state. They now stand motionless as the breeze's voice hushes. He continues

193

to watch them in their frozen state until the breeze kicks up again, whistling into the room, and the draperies' foreplay continues, puppeted by the wind.

The rest of the room remains quiet and still as two nude bodies find repose in a late afternoon bliss. Soon the night will slowly begin to pass through the same open doors into the room, where Tom is in a state of contentment as Andrew slumbers soundly in his loving arms. It is becoming a familiar state of serenity, where many afternoons pass in much the same manner. Unquestionably, Tom is in love. It is a strange and forbidden affection, this love he feels, where he has lost control of his emotions, and any reality — his existence up until now — may have once bestowed on him. For years Tom has resisted love to the point of running away, but now it has become a master of him. He feels it in the pit of his stomach where it grows out of control. Like a parasite, it has made him weak, forcing him to surrender everything practical or sane. Like the draperies dancing in the air at the mercy of an outside source, Tom is at the mercy of an uncontrollable force: his obsession.

Lying there, he wonders if his skin had ever been as smooth and clear as Andrew's. Tom's large hand completely covers the boy's as it rests on his. He tenderly brushes Andrew's hair away from his sleeping eyes. This is a moment few men will know, Tom thinks to himself. He is grateful to have Andrew in his arms, grateful to be holding such beauty in them. Tom gently presses his lips to the perfectly even skin of Andrew's face. Their bodies reflect a more golden brown hue than usual as a result of the past week they spent on Fire Island. Like a visitor to a museum, Tom's eyes follow the lines of the boy's body, as if he were studying a famous painting by some renowned artist. A work of art, he thinks to himself. Andrew's slumber continues; he is unaware of such admiration being directed toward him.

Time's clock is ticking loudly in Tom's head. Not the clock on the bedside table, but the invisible one that he fears; the one that no man can slow down or stop. Tick, tick, tick it continues, without the aid of batteries or electric current. Tom so wants the night to never come. Because with its arrival, it brings the knowledge that time is moving too fast. If only he can freeze the hands of this invisible clock.

Andrew's body is silk against his as they lay on the twisted sheets, warm and slightly damp with sweat. Tom's stomach presses against Andrew's back. The faint sounds of the boy's breathing hum in the air, as Tom moves his hand to rest it on Andrew's hip. Tom's penis, still partly erect, is wet and sticky from being inside Andrew. It now has found a resting place on the crack of Andrew's round butt.

Tom can see that what is left of the daylight is beginning to wane. He knows the night has started its entry into the room. It eases in so slowly at first, before eventually rushing in, absorbing all the light into its blackness, into a deep endless pit of darkness like a hungry monster that can never be satisfied. This monster eats up the light until there is none left. Even then, it still hungers for more.

Andrew continues to sleep and Tom continues to hold and engulf him with his arms and eyes. This is heaven. That is how Tom sees him. He has just entered heaven, and now he is holding it in his arms.

Soon, the night will completely invade the room. Tom is

helpless but to let it in. Like the invisible clock he so fears, he cannot stop it. He can close the doors to the balcony and lock them shut, but that will not keep out the night. It will make its way through the minutest of cracks. In order to keep out the night, he would have to stop the world from turning. Tom watches the sky making its progression from light to dark to black. Their bodies will not move until the morning forces the hungry monster to open its black mouth and spit out the light into the world again. No matter what happens. No matter if the monster never opens its mouth again, or if the world stops turning, at all cost Tom will hold on tight to keep his heaven close.

◊

As usual, Tom told Trey everything, not holding back any details. At times, during these long deliberations, Trey felt he had been in the room watching, listening and smelling, like a welcomed voyeur, at least welcomed by Tom. Years earlier, he would not have been able to bear knowing of Tom's conquests, then still holding on to so much love in his heart for him. Now, Trey could not help but feel envious and jealous, wanting them both, wanting to be Tom and wanting to take Andrew's place.

"I'm crazy for the boy," Tom tells Trey during one of those late-night phone conversations.

Trey laughs.

"You're crazy for every pretty boy under twenty-five, Tom."

"Yeah, but this one's different," Tom answers.

"How?"

"You really want me to answer that one?"

"Yes, of course I do."

"You might find it strange for me to say this."

"Yeah, I'm listening."

"He reminds me of you, Trey."

"He what?"

"Yes, he reminds me of you. I should have never let you go."

Trey is taken aback. He is almost stunned by Tom's explanation.

"Now you tell me."

"You're happy now with Kyle. I want to be happy again, too. Like I was with you, but too stupid to realize."

"Well, we have our problems just like everyone else."

"What do you mean, Trey?"

"Nothing. Don't worry about it."

"Well, you know I love you."

"Yeah, I do. But about this Andrew guy?"

"Yeah. What about him?"

"He's a prostitute for God's sake, man," Trey rebuts. "Do you really think he feels the same as you?"

"I don't know, Trey. I just have to be with him all the time," Tom confesses.

"Are you still paying him?"

"Yes, yes of course. But I am hoping he will stop seeing the others," Tom says.

"The others?" Trey questions.

"Clients. His other clients," Tom clarifies.

"You mean his other johns," Trey sticks him with a jab.

"Whatever," Tom says.

"Well, Tom, you're a very handsome man and it's crazy you feel you have to pay someone. Maybe he is attracted to you. From what you have told me he seems to have a "daddy complex." But all in all, I'm sure he's more in love with your money."

"I don't care, he's worth every penny," Tom confirms.

Trey begins to laugh again. Tom's comment takes his mind off the earlier confession.

"What's so funny?" Tom asks. "I ignored the first one."

"When is the last time you even had a penny in your pocket? I can remember in the early days, when we were together, you would never take change from a purchase. It was always "keep the change" because you couldn't be bothered with such small things. It would drive me crazy. I can remember seeing you throw pennies away in the trash can. I bet there is not one penny in that whole penthouse of yours."

"Funny, Trey," Tom remarks.

"Man, if I'd only kept that extra change you threw away, I would be a rich man by now," Trey continues.

"You're not doing so badly, Trey."

"No, things are good in the art world. My last show here in Atlanta, which you missed by the way, was a pretty good success."

"Sorry. I wanted to be there, bud. I'll be sure to make the next one."

Trey was doing well. His art had taken off over the years

with work in many major corporate collections, as well as some very highbrow private ones. He did not need to save his pennies either.

◊

Tom had signed on as a regular "client" of Andrew's. It started out as a financial understanding: a thousand dollars if Andrew spent the night, five hundred for an afternoon or evening visit. Trey found it rather interesting how Tom used to complain about Alif's spending, but on the other hand, he never heard a grumble in regard to buying the services of Andrew. Trey began to see the boy as therapy for Tom. After all, he had suggested he see someone about his problem. Although, a shrink would have hopefully helped Tom deal with the real deep-seated issues that needed to be addressed, Trey had not seen Tom happier.

The late-night phone calls were becoming less and less. Perhaps Andrew was not cheaper than a psychiatrist, but Trey was sure he was a hell of a lot more fun. It was obvious there was an air of glee in Tom's voice and their phone conversations were more enjoyable. Trey was able to stop worrying about Tom's state of mind. On the other hand, there were tell-tale signs, slips of the tongue, and lots of "we this" and "we that," which gave Trey concern that Tom might really be falling in love with Andrew. If that was the case, he was just waiting for it to end, or until the money ran out. Luckily for Andrew, the latter was very unlikely to happen. Mr. Brookston, Trey thought, must be rolling over in his grave, knowing that his younger son was spending his money on a male prostitute. Little did anyone realize that Andrew was just compounding Tom's illness to the point of no return.

Waiting and Wanting

Yes, Tom is happier, but not when Andrew is with another john. It has been five days since Tom last saw Andrew. His odor still clings to the bed sheets, which Tom has ordered Peggy not to change. A black T-shirt — left by Andrew — hangs off the arm of a chair in the corner. It has been that many nights Tom has gone without much sleep. He counts the days until Andrew will be coming back; another client has taken him to the Caribbean for an extended weekend. Tom cannot help but feel jealousy. It rages through his veins. He offered to pay double if he would cancel, but Andrew still left him with a soft kiss on the lips, telling Tom, "There's plenty of me to go around."

Tom wants it all. He wants all of Andrew. Paralyzing desperation comes over him, body and soul, when he thinks of his boy with anyone else. Each heartbeat is intensified. He struggles to remain calm, but the blood moves faster and faster through his body, pushing out the walls of his arteries, stressing every vein until his capillaries are ready to explode. He feels like a man in a straightjacket: trapped. He wants to scream out for Andrew like a madman, but knows it is pointless; his screams would only eventually fade into the night that will not allow him sleep. Tom tells himself there are other boys, so he searches online to find a replacement. A new boy comes to the penthouse, takes his money, but Tom is left only wanting more of Andrew. On the fourth night, another one comes, but he, like the other, is nothing compared to Andrew. It becomes pointless as Tom stares at the computer screen. There is only one Andrew, and he is with someone else for the moment. All Tom can do is wait for his return.

His obsession with Andrew is mushrooming, minute by minute, hour by hour, and day by day. More and more, he feels like an old man. Tom fears his days of bedding young men are coming to an end. Every time he looks in the mirror, he sees one looking back. It is not a true reflection. Tom is still strikingly handsome and strong, but his fears will not allow him to see reality. Rather than seeing a man maturing, with the help of modern cosmetic surgery, he sees his fears. Every line and wrinkle is magnified many times over. How Tom hates those two words: "old man." He sees Andrew as his last chance to hold onto youth.

◊

Several months into Tom's arrangement with Andrew, Trey and Kyle made a trip to New York. The 301 Gallery in Soho had taken on Trey's work. Tom had invited the owner to a party at his penthouse, which housed four of Trey's paintings. Over the years, Tom became a big supporter of his art, having been the catalyst for its becoming part of the collections of several prominent people in New York, as well as Los Angeles. For that, Trey was grateful.

It was an unusually searing hot day in New York, the city air not moving between the tall buildings. Despite the heat, Trey was excited he was in the Big Apple and getting ready for his first show to open in four hours. He had barely seen Tom since his arrival, except when he picked him up in the limo at the airport. There was so much work and worry involved in hanging the show. One of the pieces had been slightly damaged in shipment and had to be repaired. Finally, everything appeared to be ready.

By opening night, a western wind had fortunately swept through the city, pushing the hot stagnant air out to the ocean. Trey was preoccupied with concerns about whether anyone would show up. Tom, as well as the gallery owner, assured him the turnout would be great. That night, a steady variety of New Yorkers and others began to fill the gallery as Trey stood off to the side watching the activity. He was relieved to see they had been correct about the turnout.

Later in the evening, Tom approaches Trey from behind, taping his shoulder. Much relieved by the interruption, Trey excuses himself from a conversation with a young admirer who wanted to discuss some new art movement which Trey could care less about, and eagerly embraces Tom.

"Man, you saved me from that one," Trey tells Tom.

"He looks like a cute one," Tom says.

"Funny. You mean that art student?"

"Yeah. Did you see the butt on him?"

"Didn't notice," Trey says, as he rolls his eyes.

"Does he want you to give him some guidance?"

"No. He was talking about this new direction in the art world. But you saved me all the same."

"Saved you from what?" Tom questions.

"From making a fool out of myself, talking about something I know nothing of," Trey responds. "You know how long I've been out of school?"

"Don't remind me, but I'm glad I could be of help."

"You have done more for me than you can imagine," Trey says as he offers Tom another hug.

Trey's stomach is tight with excitement as he watches the gallery owner's assistant place another red dot by a painting.

"Well, how many have they sold?" Tom quizzes.

"I think that makes five," Trey answers with a big smile on his face.

"Great, and the night is still young."

"And again, I owe it all to you, Tom."

"You did the work, and it's wonderful at that," Tom compliments.

"Okay, okay, enough about my wonderful self, so where is this guy?" Trey asks.

"You mean Andrew?"

"Who else would I be referring to?"

"Over there, by the door," Tom directs.

"So tell me Tom, are you going to introduce me to him or am I supposed to just stare at him?"

Andrew is standing near the entrance. In any situation he would be hard to miss, but the red long-sleeved shirt he is wearing really makes him stand out in the crowd of art lovers, who are mostly dressed in combinations of gray, black and white attire. Andrew appears to be waiting for someone, like a late arrival, as he stands stiffly with his hands in the pockets of his gray pants. Trey cannot help but swallow at the sight of him. If there was a physical description for an "All-American Boy," it was standing twenty feet from them.

"He appears to be everything you said he was, Tom."

"Everything and more," Tom corrects.

"No doubt," Trey offers.

"Well, is he going to stand over there all night?" Trey questions.

"He's a little concerned about what I've told you," Tom informs.

"What? You mean his profession?"

"Yeah. He knows about our past and that I tell you everything. He's a little uncomfortable."

"Well, I don't have all night," Trey blurts out, as he observes Andrew watching them talking. He can see the boy is nervous as he rocks back and forth on the heels of his shoes. Trey is nervous, too.

In a surprise gesture, Trey waves his hand for Andrew to join them. At first, the boy looks puzzled, taking his hands out of his pockets and pointing at himself. Trey nods his head in reassurance, waving his hand again before Andrew shyly begins to make his way over while returning his hands to his pockets for comfort.

"This is Trey," Tom introduces.

"It's nice to meet you, Andrew. I've heard lots about you," Trey says, as he offers a handshake.

"And I of you as well."

Before anymore awkward starter conversation can be exchanged, Kyle makes his way back from the bar carrying two glasses of wine.

"This should calm you down," he says, as he hands one to Trey.

"Thanks, baby."

"Hello, I'm Kyle."

"Oh, sorry, this is Andrew," Tom speaks up.

"Nice to meet you. Are you a friend of Tom's?

There is a long pause before Tom speaks up.

"Yes, I've know Andrew for several months now."

So, what do you think about my husband's work," Kyle asks.

"It's spectacular work," Andrew responds.

"Well, you have great taste in art, as I see you do in men," Kyle says, as he makes an exaggerated glance at Tom.

Everyone offers a forced laugh.

Trey finishes off the glass of wine in two swallows. He is edgy on several levels: one, on meeting Andrew for the first time; and two, he left Kyle in the dark about the small detail that Andrew is an escort.

"Baby, would you mind getting me a refill?" he asks Kyle.

"The server will be around in a minute," Kyle insists.

"I know, but I need to talk to Tom about something. Alone."

"Oh. I can take the hint. You don't have to hit me over the head with one of those metal sculptures," Kyle says, referring to some other art in the gallery, as he turns back toward the bar.

"I'll go with you," Andrew offers. "Can I bring you back a drink, Tom?" he adds.

"That'll be great. Thanks," Tom answers.

From the closer observation, Trey could see there was something special about Andrew. Something even surpassing the all-American looks. Maybe it was worth paying for. Whatever it was, it was subtle. Even from a distance, Trey saw an innocence drawing you in, coaxing you to get closer. This "something" about Andrew seemed familiar to Trey, but he could not quite put his finger on what it was. With the exception of different-colored hair and eyes, he could be looking at himself twenty years ago. Then it dawns on him: Tom's confession.

Trey feels his blood pressure rise, making his face red. Out of all the boys that had come and gone in Tom's life since their break-up, Trey suddenly felt the most jealousy toward Andrew — not spurred by this meeting in person at the gallery, but from the many conversations with Tom over the previous months concerning the boy. It had been slowly growing in his core, this jealousy. It was seeded many years ago in that hotel room in

Miami. Now he had come face to face with it. At that moment, Trey knew he had to get a handle on it. He fought to suppress it, to shrink it down to a manageable size. He reminded himself he was not in the hotel suite looking at Tom with the two party boys. That was in the past, but now he realizes he has never let go of that disappointment and loss. For now, Trey fights to come back to the present and not allow the past to spoil his night. He prefers to believe he is lucky. Perhaps, he thinks, both Tom and he are lucky, at least for now.

Something else dawns on him as well, as he watches Kyle and Andrew walk toward the bar. More than anyone, he is well aware of Tom's obsession with holding on to the appearance of youth. Trey knows he is no different. Every time he looks at Kyle, every time he feels his skin, kisses his soft full rose-colored lips, and every time he makes love to him, Trey is reminded of his own youth. Now he sees that just like Tom, his eyes have searched out beauty and youth.

Taking Chances

They say the love of money is the root of all evil. Those who have it hang on to what they have while making more; those who do not, just want some of their own. The have-nots say if they only had money they would have no problems. Tom never worked for a penny of the bulk of what he had. He did make some investments just for the fun of it, and his buying of houses and fixing them up for resale in Atlanta did make a profit, but that amounted to nothing compared to the trust from his family. He was just lucky enough to be born into wealth. Some people have all the luck, or do they? The one sure thing about having an endless supply of money is not worrying when it is going to run out. Money can buy a lot of things. Another old saying — money cannot buy love — may or may not be true. At least for

Tom, it can buy something pretty damn close. That is how he was beginning to see it.

It was a good thing Tom was rich. This relationship with the boy was costing lots and he was hooked. Eight months passed and Andrew was spending at least three nights a week at the penthouse: a three-thousand-dollar-a-week habit, not including trips, dinners and gifts. Although Peggy pretended not to have an opinion, at times she could not help but let something slip, usually quickly dismissed by Tom. Over her long employment with him, she had seen young boys come and go. Countless mornings were spent making them breakfast, finding their underwear under the bed, hearing moans and groans and hoots and hollers at night escaping past his bedroom door if she was up wandering around trying to catch up on the household affairs. She knew what was going on, but all she could do was pray for their souls. Peggy thought Tom was going to hell for his homosexual lifestyle. But like a good God-fearing woman, she would leave the final judgment to her maker.

Peggy and Tom practiced two different types of religion: one dealing with saving the soul, and the other the flesh. Peggy's, like Tom's, roots were in the deep South. She was the great, great, great, granddaughter of slaves, and it was a sure bet that many of her distant relatives broke their backs in the fields of plantations owned by ancestors of the Brookston family. Despite their hardships and her own personal ones, she, like those before her, worshiped an invisible God, putting all her faith in the teachings of the Bible. The harder life got, the more they believed. She had been raised in the church where every Sunday her mother cradled her in God-fearing arms while proudly singing the gospel in a small white wooden church in rural Alabama. Peggy believed, as those before her, that her soul could only be saved by the Almighty. Life on earth was a test, where a passing grade would grant entry into the golden gates of heaven.

Tom never gave formal religion much reflection. He worshiped the god of beauty, where sacraments were performed in the bedroom. His confessions were not heard by the ears of religious fathers, but by the ears of those just on the other side of innocence. Peggy was baptized in a country stream a quarter mile behind the church; Tom's baptism was made in the sea of flesh. As they say, all waters eventually run together.

Besides, her past was not so squeaky clean. Peggy had no room to judge anyone, knowing she was not without sin, but it was still hard to witness what she believed to be a crime against her religion and say nothing. Peggy had been working in the Brookston estate for seven years before Tom went off to college. Shortly after he moved to Atlanta, on one afternoon visit home, Tom caught her going through his mother's purse.

"What are you doing, Peggy? Isn't that mother's purse?"

"Mr. Tom, it's not what you think."

"What I think is you're stealing."

"I know, Mr. Tom. I was just thinking about it. I need some extra. See, there is this pretty dress I saw at the store. I was ashamed to ask Mrs. Brookston again for a loan cause she gave me fifty a while back and told me just to get it out of her purse. I was just thinking about it. Honest."

"How much does my mother pay you?"

"Well, not a lot, but I'm grateful for what I get."

Peggy puts the purse down on the dressing table and takes a step back. She is visibly shaking as her eyes look at the floor. Tom thinks for a moment. He knows Peggy is a good person, and it is hard to work in all the opulence of the family estate and not want more for yourself if you are an outsider. If Peggy were to take money from his mother's purse, Mrs. Brookston would never miss it. Tom knows, more than anyone, his mother is not always that generous to the staff, most likely underpays most of them.

"Tell you what, Peggy. I could use someone in Atlanta. Why don't you come to work for me. I'll be sure to pay you more than mother does," Tom offers, knowing the money comes from the same source.

"Are you serious, Mr. Tom? What will I tell Mrs. Brookston?"

"I'll handle it. So, is that a yes?"

"Well, exactly how much are you talking about?" Peggy asks with her ears perked.

"Let's see. I'm talking live-in help. You cook and clean. Laundry, too. Two hundred and fifty dollars a week and an apartment over the garage. It's a nice apartment, I assure you."

Peggy had heard good things about Atlanta. They had an African-American mayor and that had to be a good thing. It had to be better than living in a shack on the outside of town.

"You have a deal, Mr. Tom. Thank you, thank you, thank you."

Peggy started looking after Tom a week later, in more ways than one. It did not take her long to pick up on Tom's desire for young men. She was well aware of the rumors from the staff back at the Brookston estate about him and how much his father all but disowned Tom because he was a homosexual. Peggy saw it as a sign. God wanted Tom to catch her debating over taking money from Mrs. Brookston's purse. He wanted her to steer him down the holy road. Peggy soon learned it would not be an easy calling. Their two religions clashed.

◊

"Are you sure this one is legal? I know they do things differently here, but you know they can put you away for that back in Alabama," she offers with concern.

"He just looks young. He told me he was eighteen. I believe him."

"Well, he looks mighty lean in years to me, Mr. Tom. I hope you know what you're doing."

"Woman, hush your mouth," Tom says.

"You know what the Good Book says about lying down with a man like a woman," she preaches.

"I must have skipped that part," Tom rebuts.

"I can show you," she says.

Tom usually did not let those types of conversations go much further. It was easier to let her have the last word. Besides, she could cook and clean circles around the best. Despite her religious fanaticism, Peggy grew on him quickly, but he would not let on that was the case. As time went on, they developed an unspoken understanding; she would try to hold her tongue, and Tom would tune her out when she was unable to. With the last word in, Peggy would go about her business singing one of her hymns. They helped calm her; she believed they kept the evil spirits from the house. Like a good servant, she slipped back into the background, singing and praying for Tom. Although he had no concrete belief in her God, Tom figured having someone praying for his soul could not hurt much.

Not being very enlightened in such matters, Peggy thought that perhaps Tom's homosexuality was a curse put on his family generations ago for their sins. She remembered a great aunt who also worked for the Brookston family. Peggy's aunt retold many stories passed down from generations back, by relatives enslaved on the southern plantations. One was about a many-times-over distant grandfather of Tom's, who owned one of the largest plantations in Alabama. This aunt spun one story in particular about a slave boy named Malcolm. As she told it to Peggy, the master bought him from the auction block for little money.

He was a light-skinned boy with a lot of manhood for his fourteen-year-old body. The master brought him back to the plantation and made him his houseboy. The slaves talked about how he was in love with the boy. After the master's second child was born, he stopped sharing a bedroom with his wife. He would lie with the boy like he once did with her, while she slept in her own room at the other end of the great hall. Many times the boy would sleep at the foot of the master's bed when he was finished with him for the night. Several years later, the wife died from a fever. The master never remarried, although there were plenty of fine women available who would have been happy to take his hand in marriage.

After slavery was abolished, many of the freed slaves went north, while others stayed and continued to work for the master.

He gave the ones who stayed on some acreage. As her great aunt told it, Malcolm stayed, too, until the master died ten years later. The master left him a hundred acres with a house, ten horses and some livestock. Malcolm eventually married and had five children.

◊

Although she does not, in any way approve, Peggy is kind of relieved Andrew is coming around a lot. Somehow, it is better to have the same boy in the house rather than a different one from week to week. Andrew is well-mannered, in fact very polite, saying yes ma'am and no ma'am and please and thank you. She knows he has been raised right, so she wonders why he is with Tom, and why they do the things they do together in the bedroom. She can smell the sex left on the sheets as she changes the bed, wearing rubber gloves. Peggy can only imagine what goes on, the things her Baptist upbringing tells her are unholy. But his attitude is very different from some of the others; many have not acknowledged her presence in the house at all. A few of them scared her, and she worried for Tom's and her safety. Because of her concerns, Peggy always locked her suite at night.

She still liked Trey the best of all the boys. Peggy took a liking to him after he moved in with Tom, back in the Atlanta days. She could not help but be saddened when they broke up. If Tom was going to be a homosexual, a part of her wished he had stayed with him. Peggy wondered why Tom would want so many boys around. Trey was a good-looking guy she thought — good-looking enough for Tom or anyone else; she often told him he had the face of an angel. Besides, at least Trey seemed more mature and not of some questionable age to be having sex with such an older man like Tom. But of course he and Trey were much younger back in Atlanta — and the age difference was not as apparent — as it is now with Tom and the newer boys. In her eyes, he was having sex with children; legal or not, they were children. In the back of her mind she hoped Tom and Trey would get back together. Perhaps she was becoming more open to Tom's homosexuality as time went on, as long as he was with someone of whom she approved.

◊

Over and over, Tom kept ingeniously pressuring Andrew to have unprotected sex. Even with a cock ring and a dose of Viagra, he was having trouble keeping it up the second the condom went on. Andrew slipped up a few times letting Tom enter him raw briefly during foreplay, but he always managed to push him out. Tom even offered to pay Andrew more, but he was trying to hold his ground, even though he was finding it harder to say no when caught up in the moment, sometimes even forgetting Tom was one of his johns. The call-boy life was beginning to wear on Andrew. More and more he began to hate himself. He was continuing to lie to his parents about work. They had been repeatedly asking Andrew when they could come to see him in the play he was supposedly performing in Off-Off-Broadway. Sooner or later he would have to tell them another lie: the show closed early.

To escape from the realities of prostitution, Andrew was spending most of his time with Tom, putting off some of his regulars. At least with Tom, he did not feel so much like a whore. If Tom had his way, Andrew would soon belong only to him.

In the meantime, Andrew saved up a lot of money, mostly thanks to Tom. For some time now, he had been seriously thinking about packing up and going to grad school. He could take his "day job" anywhere, so why not take it west? A few weeks earlier, Andrew received an acceptance letter from the University of California for the spring of 2005, and had just taken his physical exam. He was considering getting a masters degree in theater and possibly teaching after, getting out of the sex business once and for all. Andrew knew he might have to turn a few paying tricks in Los Angeles if funds got low, or maybe he would do better out there with his acting, but he would somehow make it work. He was going to wait until the time was right to tell Tom. Until then, he would remain in New York through the winter. Then the unexpected happened.

◊

Tom has been waiting all day to see Andrew. The last few weeks he has been walking around with a spring in his step. He has gotten the boy to agree to go away to Paris next month for a week. It looks like things are going Tom's way. He calls Andrew to see when he is coming over so they can go to dinner. He picks up on the third ring. Andrew seems distant to Tom.

"Is everything okay bud?" Tom asks.

"Sure."

"You sound kind of out of it."

"No, I'm fine. Maybe a little tired. That's all."

"You still coming early for dinner?"

"Sure."

"Good. We can walk somewhere. I feel like walking in the city. Okay."

"Whatever you want, Tom, is fine. See you in a bit."

Tom hangs up the phone still concerned about the tone, or lack of it, in Andrew's voice. He gives it another thought, then shrugs it off.

Andrew shows up a few hours later. Tom has already worked out and showered. They walk to a little Italian place about fifteen blocks from the penthouse. Taxis race up and down Park Avenue alongside long black limos carrying occupants to one place or another.

They walk unhurriedly side by side with little conversation, as other New Yorkers rush to nowhere and everywhere. As earlier on the phone, Tom notices Andrew is not as garrulous as he usually is, but he is happy just to be with the boy. Occasionally glancing over to look at Andrew, he is still as awestruck as he was on their first meeting.

The evening air is cool giving the false impression of a soon-to-be approaching fall, but it is only a freaky cold front passing through. The dangling bell hanging above the red and white café curtains announces their entry into the old-fashioned restaurant. An overwhelming aroma of fresh-baked bread floods the night and their nostrils the second the door opens. The host, a short bald man with a rosy chuckle and marinara sauce on his white shirt, gives a big welcome and seats them at Tom's favorite table by the bay window looking out onto the street.

Tom fills the dinner conversation — while eating a hefty portion of chicken fricassee with porcini mushrooms, sautéed in white wine and tomatoes — with places to see during their up-coming trip to Paris. He, of course, has been there several times, and is excited about showing it to Andrew, who has never been.

218

The boy sits quietly picking at the plate of ossobuco nin bianco in front of him.

"Babe. Are you sure everything is okay?" Tom asks.

"Yeah, really. Now tell me more about Paris."

Tom goes on for the duration of dinner like he is a seasoned travel guide describing in detail all the places they will go. His excitement is palpable in his voice as he looks forward to walking down the Jardin des Tuileries to the Louvre, and later along the Seine with the boy who has captured his heart, soul and mind.

The stroll back to the penthouse is as non conversational as the one going to dinner. But the night air is almost magical to Tom. The premature fall-like weather still excites him. Fall in New York is his favorite time of year and for him a welcome relief from the hot New York sticky summer days which will more than likely show up again. With the abrupt change in temperature, the city seems to be taking on a whole different attitude, and Tom is as well. He looks forward once again to long blustery walks in Central Park, especially now that Andrew is around. The night air is even crisper than earlier, and the city has quieted down a bit. There is less hustle and bustle on the wide sidewalk and less traffic up and down the avenue. An Asian boy on a delivery bike passes them. For the next few minutes, the smell of sweet and sour pork hangs back in the air.

Peggy is in the kitchen when they return to the penthouse. She has just finished baking an apple pie.

"That smells so good," Tom says.

Peggy is happy to see him in such an agreeable frame of mind.

"Well, just wait 'til you taste it, Mr. Tom. But none 'til tomorrow. It has to set. Okay. Now hands off the both of you."

"Yes, ma'am," Tom acknowledges.

"I'm off to bed. You both have a good night," Peggy says, as she covers the pie with a clean cloth towel.

She gives a hand wave over her shoulder as she heads in the direction of her suite. Peggy drags her feet, in big fluffy light blue slippers, on the floor. It is a sign her legs are hurting from standing too long.

"I'm ready for bed. How about you, Andrew?"

"Me, too. I just want to take a shower first."

"Sure, but you just had one before you got here, didn't you?"

"Yeah, I know. Just want to rinse off first."

"Okay."

Tom brushes his teeth as he watches Andrew get into the shower. Every time he sees him naked, a tingle of excitement shoots through his body. Tom continues his gazing for a few moments and then heads towards the bedroom.

Twenty minutes later, Andrew stands over the bed, beads of water on his chest glistening in the soft light of the room.

"That was a lot of rinsing," Tom says.

"The water felt so good, I guess I didn't realize I took so long."

"You're amazing," Tom speaks.

"Glad you think so."

"Oh, I more than think so. Get in bed."

Tom props up on his elbow. Andrew lies down on his back and looks up at the ceiling.

"I need to tell you something, Tom."

"What is it?"

Andrew hesitates for a moment.

"I."

That is all that comes out of his mouth. Just the word "I" and nothing following it.

"What?" Tom asks.

Andrew opens his mouth again.

"I," he pauses yet again, swallows and says, "I had a nice time tonight. That's all. Thank you."

"I had fun, too. And we'll have a hell of a good time in Paris."

Tom leans over and begins licking off the beads of water still clinging to his chest. Within minutes he is on top of the boy. Andrew is still looking at the ceiling, his arms spread out above his head. Tom's penis is hard as he rubs it against the boy's. He had taken a blue pill while Andrew was in the shower. The night air and walk with Andrew to and from the restaurant invigorated him. Tom feels like a young man again.

He reaches for the handle of the drawer to the bedside table. Tom pulls out a bottle of lube and does not waste any time squirting some on his penis. He takes the residue and rubs in on Andrew's hole, working in his finger. Tom then leans back over on the boy and begins rubbing on him again, still fingering his hole.

"Man, that feels good," Tom says. "All nice and warm."

"It does." Andrew responds with little emotion, but Tom is too engrossed to notice.

Tom moves his dick over Andrew's hole until it begins to slide inside. Andrew reaches down to stop him.

"Aren't you going to use a condom?"

"Oh, baby. Come on. It feels too good."

"We go through this every time! I want you to use protection!" Andrew demands, looking just past his face, unwilling to make eye contact with Tom.

"I want you, baby. I want you free without a condom. Trust me, I'm negative. I had my doctor do a test and I can show you the results."

"I don't want to take any chances, Tom."

"There are none to take. We have gotten so close before. Let me go all the way."

"Tom. No."

Andrew lets out a deep breath he has been holding inside his lungs. He knows the time has come to tell Tom something he has been keeping inside all day. He wanted to tell him at dinner, then when they first got into bed, but he could not formulate the words in his head.

"I guess I should have told you already, Tom," Andrew begins.

"Told me what?" He asks.

"I'm not sure how to tell you."

"Just speak what's on your mind," Tom says, as he raises himself up off the boy.

Andrew looks further away. Tom can see the concern fill his face. He gently turns Andrew's face back toward him with his hand.

"I tested positive."

"Come again," Tom asks.

"I tested positive. I was going to tell you, really I was."

Andrew covers his eyes with his hands, as Tom lies down on his back. They are both facing the ceiling now.

"How? When did this happen?"

"I don't know. I thought I had been safe. I've had a few past rough experiences with some of my johns. Maybe the condom broke and I didn't notice it."

"I was getting my physical to start grad school, no more trying to be an actor. I was going to tell you that as well, but they called me to come back to the doctor's office yesterday."

They both go silent. Tom sits up and pulls Andrew into his arms. As he looks into the boy's eyes, he sees a single tear run down his face. Within seconds, more tears begin to flow, Tom's chest is soon covered with Andrew's tears.

"Do you want me to leave?" Andrew asks.

He is too afraid to look up. Tom can see the fear expand over Andrew's face. He is so young, so beautiful. Tom feels anger move through his body. Not toward Andrew, but for him. Now there is a virus running through this boy, invading him. Tom holds Andrew's head down on his chest as the boy weeps.

"That's the last thing I want you to do."

Andrew feels safe for a moment. A slight sense of relief comes over him, but it is short lived. He had been so scared since getting the news. Andrew was not sure how he would tell his johns or even if he should. They knew sex was a risk and now he knows that more than ever. Was it really his responsibility to tell these men, who were paying him for sex, or was it their responsibility to protect themselves? Would they stop wanting to see him? Some were married with families. What would he do for money? How would he live? This news has completely screwed up his plans. What will he do now, he wonders?

"How long do you think you've been positive?'

"I'm not sure."

"Well, I don't care, Andrew. I still want you."

"How can you want me now that you know?"

"I'm in love with you. There I said it. I'm a fifty-nine year old man in love with a kid. God help me."

That was the second time in Tom's life that he ever spoke, "God help me."

"You say that now, Tom, but in the morning you may feel different."

"No, I won't, and if you stick around until then you will find that out."

"Are you crazy, Tom? What if I've infected you? I told you we should use condoms," Andrew states in his defense.

At first, Andrew's news ran a panic through Tom. He wondered if he might be positive soon. After all, he had been inside Andrew without a condom on several occasions. Inside of him raw. Not for long, but inside him all the same. There could have been blood from Andrew's rectum on his penis and it could have gotten into his urethra. He had taken Andrew's cum in his mouth and fed it back to him. What if he had a tear in his mouth? The old deep-seated underlying fear in all HIV negative men, wondering when it will be their turn to get the news, boils up. It soon settles when he realizes he has lived in fear all his adult life about AIDS, and at fifty-nine he is not going to worry about it anymore. It may be the only good thing about being fifty-nine, he thinks. Now that he is faced with the possibility of being exposed, he does not care. Like he declared to Andrew, Tom still wanted him. He knew he was not the one who infected him. As he had told him as well, he got his test result. Any residual fears he had, soon subsided. He was too old to worry about himself. All he cared about was the moment at hand. Tom was unconcerned about his own future. Andrew is his only concern now. Nothing else matters.

"Look Andrew, I'll be sixty in a few months," Tom says as he looks down. "God! I never thought I would hear myself saying that. SIXTY FOR CRYING OUT LOUD! FUCKING SIXTY! My life has been full. And God knows I've had my share of men. I should be the one that is positive, not you."

"What are you saying, Tom?"

"I'm saying that this is more to me than a money arrangement. I care about you. I want you. You know that," Tom confesses.

"I don't know what to think now. I was planning on giving this up at some point, going back to school and being something. Being something more than a whore. Now, I'm not sure," Andrew says full of regret.

Tom raises his head to look at Andrew.

"You're not a whore. You're my beautiful boy. I will make everything right," Tom says.

They kissed. Andrew feels grateful. Grateful Tom has not kicked him out of bed like he had feared all his johns would. Grateful Tom did not run to the shower to scrub himself down, as he had done upon returning home from the doctor's office. He stripped his body of its clothing trying to look through his skin; wondering if the virus was spreading throughout his body at that very moment; wondering how fast it would spread before it consumed him. Andrew thought about slitting his wrists to drain the virus out of him. He stood in the hot shower until the water ran cold, hoping it would cleanse him, and maybe wash away the virus before it had a chance to take hold. He knew it was too late, but he had to try. He felt soiled. Andrew cleaned his body until the bar of soap was all used up and his skin was red and raw from the abrasion of the bath sponge. He had to do something, but all he could do was stand in the shower and cry.

They were both vulnerable now. Andrew with the knowledge that he tested positive for the HIV virus, and Tom knowing he still wanted Andrew regardless. They both lay on the bed, side by side, Tom on his back as Andrew turns over on his stomach, his head facing away from Tom.

"Look at me, Andrew."

Slowly he turns his head. His eyes are red as are Tom's. There is nothing but quiet in the room until the sound of more police sirens makes its way up from the avenue below through the open balcony doors. They go as quickly as they came. Andrew opens his mouth to speak, but quickly closes it, unsure of what he was going to say. Tom turns on his side, placing his hand on Andrew's back. His skin is so beautiful, so soft to the touch, he thinks.

"I'm in love with you," Tom says again, but this time in a whisper.

Andrew does not speak.

"I know there is no future in it, but still the same, I love you. I'm an old fool."

"A fool, yes, but old, no," Andrew offers to ease Tom.

"Oh, yes, I'm old by today's standards. Just look at the cover of every gay rag in this town. You don't see men my age, or even close to it, on them. And you are young. I've spent my adult life chasing youth as it was being eaten up by my body."

"No, stop saying that."

"It's going to be okay, Andrew. I'll see that it's going to be okay."

As time moves forward on the face of the clock sitting on the side table, Andrew and Tom continue to lie quietly on the bed, each with different thoughts running wild in their heads. Realizations were forming in Tom's brain like loose puzzle pieces locking together to give a full picture, that for years had been waiting to be connected.

There was so much truth to those words spoken by Tom. He had done just that — chased youth, hoping he could replenish his own. In return, Tom filled them with his manhood, becoming their lover, father and keeper. He washed his body with what amounted to countless buckets of the cum from young men. His tongue licked their skin, his mouth sucked their cocks dry and his dick probed to take their innocence. He was a scavenger of youth, like an arrogant king from a lost land, who made a ritual of the drinking of cum of virgin men as a source of strength and vitality. He mixed his blood with theirs and managed to stay negative. He preferred the ones from small towns, who came to the big city with wide eyes and virgin holes. Tom was an addict. Not of drugs or alcohol, but of young men. Now he was tired of the chase, and for what time was left, he wanted to spend it with Andrew. Tom was beginning to realize it was a losing battle. He lost count of the number of guys he fucked, thousands perhaps. Every name in the book had opened their legs wide for him. But no matter how many he had done, he was still getting older by the day.

Tom's past was catching up with him. Trey was so much like Andrew at that age. They could have been brothers. What if he had stayed with Trey? The idea popped into Tom's head, getting tangled up with the strands and strands of other thoughts. He often thought of him while in the heat of passion with other guys. There was a warmth and comfort surrounding Trey, which was lacking with most the others. With Andrew there beside him, Tom remembered the countless occasions he had called Trey in the late hours after having sex, especially in the early days after they broke up. He would slip out of bed to the library, after getting an overwhelming desire to hear his voice.

"Are you alone?" Tom would ask, in a low whisper.

"Oh, it's you," Trey answered, not saying if someone was over or not.

"I just wanted to hear your voice, Trey."

And that would be the extent of the conversation. Trey would fall back asleep thinking of his past love, as Tom went back to the youth in his bed. Tom is feeling the desire to call Trey now.

Trey had been Tom's only real relationship. Everyone after Trey barely lasted a few months at best. Now he is on the edge of sixty, in bed with a twenty-three-year old boy. The recurring thought, maybe he should have stayed with Trey, comes again.

After all these years, and even if Trey would take Tom back, he felt there was nothing to offer him. At thirty-nine, Trey was still young, still very handsome with the body of a twenty-something-year-old. They both joked about getting back together if neither one managed to settle down with a partner, but Trey had a boyfriend now; and, like all addicts, Tom knew it would just get harder and harder. The temptations would be too great, and the desires to be back with Trey would be overshadowed by his panic that time was slipping away. Inevitably, Tom's need for replenishment would only be found in the youth of many — many boyish faced lovers.

A Turning Point

The cooler climate only lasted a few days. The last weeks of summer returned for an unwelcome visit, and with them, the dreaded heat. Fall would have to wait a little longer.

Andrew stopped returning the calls from his regular johns. He was confused to the point of being tormented, and did not want to face any of them, much less tell them about his situation. Surprisingly, to him, it was an easy decision to make. Andrew never wanted to be a prostitute, thinking all along that it was just an acting game he would end after getting his first big break. When he moved to the city, he would have never thought he would be in the situation he finds himself in now. He imagined a much better scenario, finding himself on Broadway with his name on the marquee, perhaps not headlining, but on the marquee all the same. Instead, he managed to fool himself, as he did his parents back home in Michigan. During phone conversations with them, Andrew went on about how he was doing some small bit theater shows. He even lied about doing a few more commercials just so they would not worry about him. Perhaps it was just wishful thinking on his part, or he truly was a good actor, good enough to fool even himself. Like an actor, he embellished his lines of lies, even going so far as telling them he just finished one for Old Navy and it would be airing soon.

Andrew finds himself at a crossroads of a dreadfully busy intersection. Until he can sort out things in his mind, he needs Tom. They both seem to be standing in the middle of the road looking to see what direction the traffic is headed.

Tom is delighted to find out Andrew has stopped prostituting. He went as far as asking him to move in full time. But for the boy, it is still too soon. Even though he cares for Tom, he is still one of his johns, his only one left. But for the month following the news of his exposure, Andrew practically spent every day and night at the penthouse. Peggy knows something is up, but does not know what the situation is. She continues with her duties and even takes pleasure in looking after them both.

Andrew decides to take a trip to Michigan to visit his parents for a weekend at the end of the month. Upon his return to the city, he breaks the news to Tom.

"I'm moving back home."

"Why, Andrew?"

"I have to make something of my life now that I know. I can't stay in this city anymore."

"But I'll be lost without you, Andrew."

"We can stay in touch, Tom."

"That's not enough for me."

"It'll have to be. I have to do this. I told my parents everything, and they want me to come home and start over."

"Andrew. Please don't go."

"I have to, Tom. I just have to."

"I can give you anything you want. Just name it. Anything. Tell me what you want me to do."

"Can you take this virus out of my body?"

"I would if I could, Andrew. I would take it from you and put it in my body if I could."

"I know you would. But I still have to go. I have to go home and pull my life together."

"Andrew. NO."

"Tom, you have to let me go."

Later that afternoon, Andrew goes back to his apartment to begin packing. He is going back to Michigan the following weekend for two weeks. His parents want him to see their family doctor and talk with a psychiatrist. After that, he will return to the city for a week before the movers come to empty his apartment. His parents have swiftly arranged everything.

In distress, Tom calls Trey in Atlanta.

"I don't know what to tell you, Tom."

"Yeah. It was quite a shock."

"Tom, I don't mean to be insensitive, but he's a prostitute. You can't depend on him. "

"He was, Trey. He was a prostitute."

"Are you still paying him?"

"Not like before. I have not paid him anything this past month except to cover his expenses. And he has not asked me for any money."

"Okay. Let me ask you something."

"Yeah?"

"I know how you are, Tom. Now that Andrew is positive, are you being safe?"

"Yes, of course."

"Tom, are you sure?"

"Yes, Trey. You don't need to worry."

"Well, I guess that is something at least. So what are you going to do?" Trey asks.

"He wants to move home, back to Michigan. What can I do?"

"I guess there's really not a lot, Tom."

"Yeah, but that would just kill me."

"Maybe it will be for the best, Tom."

"No, it won't. I'll not be able to handle it."

"Yes, you will. You'll be fine. When is he planning on leaving?"

"In about a month," Tom answers in distress.

"Why don't you come down to Atlanta and stay with Kyle and me for a while. We'd love to have you."

"Thanks, Trey. Maybe. I'll see and let you know."

Tomorrow Is Another Day

The night had been washed by a rain that started falling earlier in the previous evening. Like infinite tears of relief to answered prayers, it quietly cascaded down from the heavens onto a grateful earth, which for almost a month, had laid under a torrid sun-soaked sky, thirsting like a virgin to receive its source of life. Gently the rain finally came, washing the tall buildings of New York City, and away the sins of many, many days.

With daybreak, temporarily void of heat, a faint light rises from the east seeping through the moist city like an endless gush of honeyed baby's breath leaving an early fog engulfing Central Park. From far above, the city seems to be caught in a black and white still life. The view from the penthouse makes the treetops in the park appear to be sitting on large white cotton balls.

Tom sits in silhouette as the sluggish light creeps through the partially opened slats of the heavy shutters hanging in the narrow Palladian window. A hushed stream of light torpidly enters the exposed arch at the top. Just missing his head, it spills onto the floor not far from his feet. In the quiet light of morning, tiny dust particles stir in the air around him as if dancing to some touching music composed by the sweetness of his soul. The tall window and high ceiling make him appear small and insignificant. With a soul still young, but with a body feeling old, Tom sits so very still in the light that is slowly inching its way inward from the outside, illuminating the darkness left from the night before. The only movement in the room is that of the air, the particles of dancing dust, and the inching of light, all of which he is unaware, as his mind is rethinking a life of some fifty-nine years.

The dancing dust particles are being serenaded by a song Tom mumbles — a song he has recited in jumbled words throughout the night, accompanied by the falling rain. A melody he has heard Peggy sing time and time again, telling of a story of lost little children and of angels dancing in the rain. He is surprised that he even remembers some of the words, never having sung the song before. If you listen intently, you can hear the song he tries to sing:

Little lost child, little lost child listen to the rain.

Each drop dancing in the air.

They are angels' tears filling the sky.

Little lost child, little lost child won't you dance in the rain.

Sing your prayers, sing your prayers to the angels

and all your troubles will go away.

Peggy had always told Tom that everyone is surrounded by angels that hover above their hearts. They listen to our deepest prayers and carry our voice to God. Perhaps Tom is trying to talk to God as he sits rigid in a beautifully constructed side chair, a few tattered strings of cloth hanging from its cushion. From there he has not moved as the night has come and gone, this time, his conscious mind unaware of the movement of time or the changing of light to darkness as he waits for his prayers to be answered.

Since Andrew left, the night has become his only time of true solitude as he waits for his return. When the outside light reaches through the window and touches the door of the attic, the day will come and take his seclusion, leaving him to face another day without him and another day of regret. As the light fills the grayness of his space, he cannot hide from the movement of time, which has increasingly become more of an enemy than a friend.

There is no color in the room as he sits in the still life with New York City filling the backdrop, sitting among lose photographs pulled from a well-worn leather album. Some are scattered on the rumpled bedcover of an Empire daybed relegated to the attic some years ago. His chair is pulled close to it. There are pictures of years of realities, but few of the dreams come true. Collectively, they comprise an open book where he has no choice except to reread the lines upon lines of his life until now. These scattered images serve as a small archive, freezing time: pictures appearing to be of carefree children, a young Tom and Nancy playing on blankets, surrounded by images of people standing alone and in groups; pictures of their older brother Nathan and their parents; and scores of young men Tom has known. There are smiling faces in some; in others, they are not so joyous.

He is a young man in many and in his mind he wonders where the years and dreams have gone. Somehow it is apparent to him that the pictures are really not of him anymore. He is saddened to realize how the photographs have not told the true story behind the faces caught for a brief second by the camera; Tom wonders how to tell the truth behind those faces the camera was unable to reveal. In the event he is able to tell, his mind wonders, who would care to listen?

As in many of the very pictures he has been studying for the past hours, color has long since left his life. The years, too, have left him behind as he sits and waits for another day to come and go again. It is a waiting game Tom plays, waiting for the day that he will no longer have to remember what he has tried so hard to forget. In the trunk where he retrieved the photo album, he finds a broken old gold watch forgotten about years ago. Its discovery triggers his memory of a face of a man, the sound of his soft but valiant voice speaking in the background.

◊

Smoke fills the room, trapped in stale air of an unventilated bar. Images of scantily clothed young men flash on TV monitors tucked in the corners. A young man stares into the eyes of strangers looking for something to connect with.

His hands rest on the cool counter of the bar as he occasionally sips from the bottle of beer in front of him. He nervously plays with the thin gold face of his watch, checking the time. Tom is that young man, sitting at the bar. The voice in the background is that of a much older man. He is looking, too. Looking to find a connection to his past in the present that he has found himself in, a present that can never be his.

The old man sits alone at the other end of the bar from Tom. They are surrounded by muffled voices and occasional outbursts of laughter from groups of men scattered in little huddles throughout the dimly lit gay establishment. Tom can feel the man's eyes on him, like he is looking deep underneath his skin. The old man strains them as he looks for a part of himself lost over the years, looking for a glimpse of what he used to be. He looks through years of age, layers upon layers of it, hoping to remember what it feels like to be the young guy sitting at the other end of the bar. Wondering what it feels like to be Tom.

Tom takes a gulp of his beer as he looks at the man from the corner of his eye. For some reason, he is afraid of the old man, but is relieved he is not him. He hears the man speak something, but is unable to quite make it out. Tom can feel his eyes on him again. The man shakes his head and repeats his words, and again Tom cannot decipher what he is saying. He tries to ignore him, but the old man is persistent. He speaks again, something like, "Too old for this." The old man lays down a handful of crinkled dollar bills on the bar before clumsily getting up. He struggles over to where Tom is sitting.

"I said, never get old, young man. Never get old."

He pats Tom on the shoulder and looks into his eyes like he is pilfering for his soul. Tom tries to look away, but he cannot. The man stands there for what seems like an eternity, but it is in reality only a matter of seconds, and walks toward the front door.

"Look at that old cocksucker," someone in a nearby gaggle

rags the man as he leaves.

Tom hopes the old man did not hear the comment and takes another swallow of beer.

◊

The dust continues to stir in the light now fading. His silhouette moves as the day migrates into another night, and the memories of the old man race in the back of his mind. Tom is now that old man.

Day by day, with the realization that Andrew is moving away, Tom is becoming a recluse. He has not seen Andrew for almost two weeks. They have talked online and on the phone, but Andrew refuses to stay in New York. Tom keeps telling himself that the boy will not move — that Andrew will change his mind at the last minute and stay. Peggy does not ask where the boy is. She can tell by the agony on Tom's face that something bad has happened. As the days turn into a week and more, Tom has not set foot out onto the city streets, preferring to stay locked up in the sky with little desire to venture out. Peggy and the Internet have become his only connection to the world.

"Are you going out today, Mr. Tom?" Peggy asks, already knowing the answer.

Maybe later."

"Thank God for the passing rains. He has answered our prayers. The heat was getting unbearable, but you wouldn't know, locked up in here like you have been. The sun is breaking through the clouds. It's going to be a beautiful fall day. Even the birds are flying in the sky again. They are like little angels watching over us. Lord knows it has been too hot for their little feathers. That heat would have surely melted them off. You're like a vampire locked up in this museum," she rambles.

Tom says nothing. He feels he has nothing to be grateful for.

"It's not healthy, Mr. Tom. You need some fresh air."

Peggy is becoming more and more concerned about her employer's state of mind. She finds herself constantly checking on him, tiptoeing around the penthouse to see if he is okay. Even though Tom is ten years older, it is a motherly concern. She still sees the boy in him, and having never married and being childless, taking care of Tom is the next best thing to motherhood. He has a way of pulling out the motherly instinct in the women in his life, all the women, except in his mother. Peggy turns to her religion and prays Tom will come around. She prays for the boy as well, sensing he is the reason Tom has come to such a state. Peggy would welcome him back if that would make Tom happy again.

Oh, the boy, Peggy tells herself, things have not been the same since he has stopped coming around. Her concern has prompted a decision to call someone. Who, she wonders. Tom will not like it, but she knows she must. She ponders for several days while watching Tom become more and more removed from life, spending hours shut up in the attic. Perhaps she should try to get ahold of Nancy, but believes she is in Paris with some new poet. Perhaps, more likely, she will call Trey.

Yes, I must call Trey, she tells herself. Peggy gives it another day to see if Tom snaps out of this funk. But she knows not to wait much longer because over the last week or so, Tom has been sleeping later and later into the day, not getting up until past noon. She has noticed he is drinking more and more, finding empty bottles of vodka in the trash.

Now another day comes.

It is almost one p. m. on Thursday. Peggy gives three quick knocks on the bedroom door.

"Are you up, Mr. Tom?"

There is no response. She tries again with a single knock.

"Mr. Tom?"

Again nothing. Clinching her teeth, Peggy quietly turns the knob on the bedroom door. She is relieved there is no noise as it opens. The room is totally dark. The draperies are closed tight, keeping out the day. Peggy is careful not to allow too much of the hall light to enter with her. Once in, she pushes the door almost closed while adjusting her eyes as she looks in the direction of the bed. The room smells like liquor. The air is cold as Peggy wraps the pale blue sweater Tom gave her for Christmas last year around her torso to contain her warmth. Cautiously, she makes her way toward the lump in the bed. She looks to see if there is any movement. As Peggy gets closer, she is consoled to hear erratic breathing coming from under the covers.

Suddenly, she gasps. Peggy quickly covers her mouth, startled by Tom letting out a grumble in his sleep, as if in discomfort. All she can see is the top of his head, hair sticking out in all directions. The rest of him is covered up like a boy hiding from monsters in the night. She notices the empty cocktail glass on the bedside table next to a bottle of Dalmane sleeping pills, and another of Valium for anxiety she refilled for him three days ago. She decides to leave him in peace as she quietly turns on her heels, slowly exiting the dark of Tom's room. Her concern grows stronger. Especially with the increased drinking and the sleeping pills he has been taking like candy.

I have to do something for him, she thinks while walking down the long wide hall. One of her hands anxiously rides her hip, while the other comforts her forehead like it hurts from thought. Once in the kitchen, Peggy removes the freshly washed frying pan from the sink, returning it to the large overhead copper pot rack. She opens a cabinet for a glass to get herself water from the tap. It is cool and refreshing as it moves down her throat, dislodging the lump of worry that has been hanging there since the morning. She bows her head to say a small prayer before picking up the phone to call Trey. She knows Tom will be mad if he finds out, but she knows she has to do something.

The phone feels heavy in her hand. She punches the numbers and raises it to her ear. She can feel the worry collecting in her throat again while waiting for someone to answer at the other end. Peggy counts the rings in her head until she is relieved to hear Trey's voice.

"Hello."

"Mr. Trey, it's Peggy."

"Is something wrong?"

"Mr. Tom hasn't left the house for days and days," Peggy whispers nervously into the phone, as if not wanting Tom to walk in on the conversation.

"You know he gets in those moods," Trey replies.

"I know, but he's really acting strange. And I haven't seen any signs of the boy either."

"You mean Andrew?"

"Yes. The boy."

"What happened?

"I don't know. He hasn't been coming around."

"Did Tom tell you that Andrew was moving back to Michigan?" Trey asks.

"No, he didn't say a word about it."

"Exactly how has Tom been acting, Peggy?"

"He keeps to himself and spends a lot of time in the attic, and doesn't even work out in that gym he spent all that money on."

"Yeah, that's not like Tom to not work out."

"And he has not been eating right, just living off those nasty protein shakes."

"I see."

"I think you need to call him or something, the man is talking to himself."

"Peggy, what do you mean talking to himself?"

"Just that. He sounds like he is talking and singing to himself. He shuts up when I walk in the room."

"I'll call him Peggy. Thanks for letting me know."

"He's sleeping now. Can you call later?"

"Yes, I will, Peggy. Take care of yourself."

"Oh, Mr. Trey."

"Yes, Peggy."

"Don't tell him I called. He would be mad if he knew."

"I won't, don't worry."

"God bless you Mr. Trey."

Peggy looks over her shoulder before returning the phone to its cradle. She feels a slight sense of relief as she returns to fixing Tom's dinner, which she will leave to warm in the oven.

At seven in the evening, Peggy checks on him one more time before retreating to her apartment to dress for Bible study. If he needs her after that, Tom can call the service line in her room, or get her on her cell.

Peggy finds the door halfway open. The room is still dark, except for the hall light spilling in. He is sitting in a wingback chair by the window. She stands at the open door and watches him for a moment before speaking. Tom is still dressed in his pj's as he seems to be looking off into space. She can tell he does not notice her presence.

"Mr. Tom," she announces herself.

There is still silence as he sits rigid like a statue. Peggy calls out to him again.

"Mr. Tom, you all right? I have your dinner in the oven. You hungry? You must be hungry."

"Thanks, I will eat in a bit."

"I can bring you a tray if you'd like."

"No, really, I will be fine."

"Okay then, I have Bible study tonight."

"You run along," Tom insists.

Peggy changes and gathers her black tote before rushing out. The penthouse is totally silent except for the low hum coming from the dishwasher in the kitchen, which she started earlier.

The doorman greets her good evening, as she exits the building onto Park Avenue. She could have caught a cab, but welcomes the ten block walk to the church. Her mind is still concerned with Tom and wondering if Trey's call will help bring him around. Peggy walks faster than normal, disturbing an odd number of pigeons on the sidewalk pecking at their dinner of a discarded pretzel; most of its cheese spread has been licked off by the previous owner. Suddenly they fly up around her, only quickening her pace. She covers her head with the Bible in her hand. Peggy is going to Bible study to pray for Tom.

◊

Friday morning, Peggy can tell Tom has been up and about. There is a glass of half-consumed orange juice on the counter, the container sitting next to it. She also notices he has eaten part of the dinner she left in the oven the night before. A plate of partially-eaten roast beef, new potatoes, and snow peas is in the kitchen sink. It seems like a waste to her, but she knows Tom does not like leftovers.

Peggy finds Tom sitting at the desk as she carries in two dozen white roses she ordered yesterday from the florist, and which were delivered earlier in the morning. They are Tom's favorite, which she has beautifully arranged in a large crystal vase. A slight smile appears on his face as he watches her place them on the library table.

"For me?" Tom asks.

"Well, you paid for them," Peggy jokes, glad to see a smile on his face, even if it is a poor excuse for one.

"That was so sweet of you," he says with light sarcasm.

"I know," Peggy responds.

Tom smiles a little bigger this time.

"Are you up for breakfast?" she asks.

"No, it's getting late for that. How about something in a few hours for lunch."

"What's your pleasure?"

"Just surprise me."

Peggy leaves the room. Tom gets up from his chair and walks over to the roses. He leans into them to take a deep breath, holding in the delicate aroma as long as he can before releasing it. As he is about to take another inhale, the phone rings. It is Trey.

"Hey Tom. Tried to call you last night."

"Guess I didn't hear it ring."

"You okay? Haven't heard from you in awhile," Trey asks.

"I'm fine."

"You sure?" Trey questions again.

"Oh, of course."

"So, what has been going on, Tom?"

"Nothing, Trey."

"What about Andrew? What's the latest?"

"We've talked a few times. He'll be back in the city in a few days," Tom answers.

"Is he still moving?"

"I hope not," Tom answers.

"Well, if you need to talk, call me," Trey says with concern.

"I will. Thanks."

"Okay, I can tell you are in one of your moods. Call me later."

"Thanks, Trey. Be good."

Almost to the minute, two hours later, Peggy taps on the open door with her foot.

"Look at what I have made you," Peggy says boldly, as she shuffles her way into the room carrying a dinner tray.

Tom looks up at her from the sofa and then back at the book opened in his lap. It is obvious to Peggy that he has not taken his morning bath, and it is already past noon. His stubble is grey, contrasting with his dyed hair. Usually, Tom would make it a point to shave every day of the week, even on weekends, to keep the age off his face.

"You must eat something, I've made your favorite lunch," Peggy insists, as she parades the tray — with large pieces of grilled chicken on top of dry coleslaw and a generous helping of fat-free ranch dressing on the side, accompanied by a nice tall glass of peach iced tea — in front of him.

"It looks very nice. I will eat it in a while."

"You had no breakfast, Mr. Tom. You're going to starve yourself, and I don't feel appreciated when you don't eat my good cooking."

"I appreciate you and your good cooking, too," Tom responds. "Why do you think I keep you around? It's certainly not for your looks."

"Well, most men find me very appetizing."

"I'm sure. But you're not my type," he forces a jest.

"Honey, I know your type," Peggy comes right back at him.

She sits the tray on the coffee table and stands there looking at Tom with her hands on her hips.

"What am I going to do with you, Mr. Tom?" Peggy says in a huff before leaving him to his solitude.

The Calm Before the Storm

Tom takes another drink from his glass before setting it down on the counter. Outside, twenty floors below, the city is alive with excitement. Andrew has been back for a week, and has spent most of that time with Tom. He came out of his depression as soon as the boy returned. Things seem to be normal again, or as normal as can be expected. Tomorrow night, Andrew will be leaving for Michigan again, this time for good, but they have not discussed the topic. He has been at the apartment most of the day with the movers and is expected back at the penthouse later in the evening.

The sound of running water brings a calm feeling over Tom. His robe is loosely wrapped around him as he watches the steady stream fill the black marble tub. A thick haze of steam begins to swell in the air. Tom leans over to dip his hand in, seemingly unconcerned with getting his sleeve wet, testing to see if the water is at the right temperature, not too terribly hot and not lukewarm either. Somewhere in-between is how Tom likes it.

He reaches for a bottle sitting on a shelf above the tub. Tom removes its cap before bringing the bottle to his nose. He takes a deep breath allowing the cedar wood aroma to fill his lungs. Tom holds the scent in as long as he can before slowly exhaling. He pours a good part of the blue bottle's contents into the water. He reaches for another container filled with juniper from the same shelf, and repeats the smelling and pouring ritual. The copious oil dives into the water. It floats back up in many pearl-like spheres of varying sizes to the surface.

Tom begins stirring the cedar wood and juniper oil into the warm wet. Oh, how he loves his daily baths. They are usually his way of greeting the morning, washing away any leftover emotional stresses while cleansing the mind as well as the body in preparation for the day ahead. Normally, Peggy would start his bath shortly after serving breakfast, but it is now long since morning.

Madame Butterfly is turning in the CD player. One of Tom's favorites, it is a tragic opera. Cio-Cio-San, known as Butterfly, is a fifteen-year-old geisha who falls in love with an American lieutenant, Pinkerton, who has taken her as his "port wife." He is recalled home soon after their marriage and she waits faithfully for his return.

What is left of daylight is being squeezed out of Manhattan. The city lights are beginning to blink on in an orchestration oblivious to its residents. The penthouse is dim, but within minutes, the timers throughout will start turning on the lights and a soft glow will fill Tom's haven in the sky.

By the clock on the counter it is eight-sixteen p. m. Tom picks up the phone, almost lovingly holding it in his hand as he watches the water circulate in the bath. He can smell the earth calling to him as the cedar wood and juniper permeates the air. Its aroma is enabling and strengthening, giving Tom an inner peace. He pushes the eleven numbers that will ring Andrew. Patiently Tom waits for the beep before speaking.

"Hey, it's me. Just wondering if the movers are done. What time can you make it back over? Call me. Peggy has fixed us up some goodies to eat."

Tom places the phone down next to the tub before untying his silk robe. It drifts to the marble floor, falling like feathers, slow and quiet. Tom walks over to the full length mirror, taking his drink with him, and stands in front of it looking at his reflection. From his eyes, he looks old and tired. Used. His vision is unclear without glasses.

"So this is what sixty looks like, well almost," he thinks to himself. "How did you get here so soon? So this is sixty. I don't want to be sixty."

At three-fifteen a. m., in approximately seven hours, Tom will turn sixty. He takes another gulp of his drink before taking the dozen or so steps back to the tub. He sits the vodka down by the phone. The water is still running; within seconds, if not attended to, it will spill over onto the floor. Tom turns off the faucets before gingerly stepping into the water. Noiselessly, it begins to surround his body like a warm hug, sucking him down. Slowly he eases lower, and lower, while holding on to the sides of the massive tub until he is covered up to his neck. He lets out a sigh of relief, partly due to the comfort he feels from the warm water, but more so glad the pain in his joints has subsided.

Some of the water spills out, running down the marble sides making numerous puddles on the floor. The music of the opera continues to play, filling the bedroom suite as it does every corner of the penthouse. Tom rests in the tub alone with his thoughts, and his waiting as he listens to the music. He knows the story of the opera well. He is waiting as is Butterfly, who is waiting for Lt. Pinkerton to return. Tom is waiting for the phone to ring, waiting to hear Andrew's voice on the other end. In the meantime, he has a lot to think about.

This would be the night. There is no changing his mind. Tom is scared, but sure of himself. There is no other choice to be made. He has to do it and there is no need to wait any longer. What is the point of waiting? Would days, weeks or even months make a difference? No, he thinks. He has to do it now before any more time passes. Now, before any more age grows on his body. Everything was well planned. Tom is ready to exit his mortal existence before any more time has a chance to take away what youthful appearance his doctors managed to pull, nip, tuck or reshape back into place.

He knew there would come a time when even all the best plastic surgeons would not be able to keep defying nature's plan. In his mind, it was time to put a stop to the ticking of the clock. He will leave this earth the way he wants. He will leave in Andrew's arms, in the arms of sweet youth.

Tom cannot imagine life after Andrew moves back to Michigan. He has had weeks to think about it. Weeks of it swarming around in his mind like he has a head full of killer bees. Night and day for weeks, they have gone around and around — the killer bees — in his head. The thought is too much to bear; the impending loneliness takes the very breath from his lungs. He knows what it feels like, the loneliness, and he does not want to be left with it, or with the bees.

Anytime now, Andrew will call and they will set a time to meet. Tom will kiss him the very minute he walks in the door. He will wrap his arms around Andrew, holding him as close as humanly possible without crushing the boy's ribs. He will fix him a drink and they will talk about nothing and everything until the hours grow late. Tom will fill his eyes with Andrew's beauty, savoring it, while giving thanks to God for bringing such grace into the world. They will have sex. Yes. They will make love one last time. Andrew will spend the night, and it will be Tom's last.

A million years could have passed as far as Tom is concerned, as he soaks in the cedar wood and juniper-laced water. As it begins to chill, he turns the hot faucet handle with his big toe to ease out a slow steady stream of heat. There is no reason to rush to do anything now. Everything has been done. Tom rereads the list in his mind, making sure he has made his wishes clear. Yesterday, he met with his attorneys to sign his Last Will and Testament. In his mind everything is final. Everything is done.

He will not allow himself to become anguished. Andrew will return his call. To calm himself, Tom concentrates on the music, humming parts of the opera with his eyes closed as thoughts of Andrew fill his head. Tom thinks of how sweet the boy's lips are, remembering how agreeable and sensuous they feel. Oh, how he wants to taste them again. He is reminded of the many baths they had taken together in this very tub. So many hours together on top of Manhattan, Tom holding Andrew in the warm water as he repeatedly kissed the back of the boy's neck. A smile grows on Tom's face.

An hour passes before the phone rings. Excitedly, Tom reaches for it.

"Hello," Tom greets, as he clears his throat.

"It's me," Andrew announces.

"How are you?" Tom asks.

"Okay, but tired. How about yourself?"

"I'll be fine when I see you. Are the movers done?"

"Yes. How soon do you want me there?" questions Andrew.

"As soon as you can."

"See you in forty-five."

"It's a date."

Tom continues to hold the phone to his ear after he hears the click at the other end. His eyes close and he takes a deep breath.

This is it, he thinks to himself. This is it. Andrew really is leaving. The movers are taking his things out of the city. They are taking them back to Michigan.

Tom remains in the tub for another twenty minutes. It will take Andrew that long to get across town, he knows he will not be early. The clock in the living room rings out. Reluctantly, Tom grabs hold of the sides of the tub to push himself up. The water begins to slide off his body. There is an obvious change in the temperature. He is now cold and wants to slide back down into the warmth where he felt comfortable and peaceful. It is tempting, but time is of the essence now. He has to make himself ready for Andrew and the hours that lay ahead. In those precious minutes collecting into hours, Tom has to make peace with himself. He has to make himself ready to leave this world, the one hidden away in the sky above Manhattan. A part of him wants to wait and delay his plans. Over the last few weeks, Tom has questioned his beliefs about a life after death. Did he really believe that God existed? It was a roller coaster of emotions. Up until now, there were only a few times he had given it much thought.

Tom reaches for the large plush towel. Like a sponge, it soaks up the remaining water from his skin as he moves it over his body. He redirects his thoughts to Andrew, who has been his religion from the night they met. How he wants him. Until recently, his youth has been a blanket of comfort to him over the past many months. Nothing else seems to matter, or make sense.

Tom walks to the vanity as he wraps the towel around his waist. A picture of Andrew, one taken while they were in Miami, sits under the mirror next to the others in a gold frame. Tom still finds it uncanny how much Andrew and Trey resemble each another. Sometimes in his dreams, when he was able to embrace sleep, Tom often got the two confused. One moment he would be making love to Andrew, and the next time he looked into his face, he would see Trey. All his dreams were like that.

In another recurring one, Tom would relive an actual train ride from Rome to Florence that he and Trey took almost twenty years ago. In the dream, they were running to catch the train as the conductor yelled out, "all aboard." The dark morning hour had not yet been broken by the new day's light. They hurried aboard as the large steel wheels began to slowly roll the train out of the station. Tom and Trey were sitting across from each other in the private compartment. In his dream, Tom falls asleep; when he wakes up, Andrew is sitting in Trey's place.

Last Written Words

There are several unopened birthday cards and two packages sitting on the long entry table; they were delivered by the doorman in the late afternoon. Peggy is putting the finishing touches on a surprise carrot cake — Tom's favorite —for his birthday tomorrow. There are no party plans as far as she is aware. Tom told her, as he has for the last decade, he did not want to make a big deal out of it this year. The last surprise birthday party he had was the last year Tom and Trey were together.

Peggy secures the cake in a large opaque Tupperware container and hides it on the lower shelf of the refrigerator, pushing it to the rear, in hopes he will not discover it. She has already prepared the appetizers and put them out on the terrace with the wine for later that night as he requested earlier. Peggy is glad Tom seems to be coming out of yet another slump. Soon it will be time for her to leave for the Sunday evening service at the church. After finishing up a few chores, she will check in on Tom before heading out.

She finds him squeaky clean, wrapped up tightly in his bathrobe standing in the living room, looking at a large nine-by-twelve-foot abstract painting hanging over the huge fireplace, which Trey had done years ago. It is titled "Wrestling of the Soul." The swirling colors are rich and dark, inciting passion and mystery in the mind of the observer.

"You need anything, Mr. Tom? I'm heading out in a few."

"Off to church are you?"

"You're welcome to come."

"Think I'll pass. But you can say a prayer for me, Peggy."

"I always do. I always do."

"Thanks."

Tom walks over to her.

"Everything looks great. Thanks. I won't need anything else tonight, Peggy. You do a great job of looking after me," he says.

"Well, someone has to," she jests.

Tom reaches out to give Peggy a hug. The gesture surprises her. Tom is usually not that affectionate, but she savors the moment. Their embrace is tender, but brief. Peggy looks into his eyes.

"Are you feeling okay?" she asks.

"Just fine."

"Well then, what's with the hug?"

"Just wanted to hug you. Now go along."

Peggy hugs him back before turning away. She takes a few steps, then turns around to address Tom again.

"God loves you and so do I."

Tom swallows and looks away for a second.

"Me, too."

He hears the front door close behind Peggy. Tom returns his attention to the painting. After a few minutes, he heads for the library. Tom takes a seat at his desk. He begins typing on the computer.

Trey,

Hey, buddy. Yeah, I know what you are thinking. How could I do this? Well, not sure if I can explain it so you would or could understand. Maybe one day you will know what I'm going through, but I hope not. Now you have to carry on. I have left it all to you except for a few million. Make sure you are sitting down when they turn everything over to you. You might get a head rush. I know you never were into the drug scene, but I could just bet it is going to be something like a pretty big coke high for you. This one will just last longer and it won't kill you. You have been a great friend. Thanks. Thanks for everything. And thanks for loving me.

There are a few things I want you to take care of after you get over being angry at me for doing this. I have left some money to Lee Ann and the boys she and George adopted. I want to make sure they get a good college education. Tell her I said goodbye. I have left everything in the hands of my attorneys. Give a few dollars to whatever charities you think could use it. I will leave that up to you. Make sure my ass is cremated like we had talked about before. You know Nancy would have me put in the family crypt to decay with dear old Mom and Dad for eternity. God knows I could not get along with that man in life and I do not plan on trying in death. It is all in my will. And there are a few other things my attorneys will inform you about. After you meet with them you will know what I mean. Keep what they tell you in complete confidence. You can decide what to do with the rest of my ashes. Just don't leave me around on some book shelf or mantle. So, my dear loving friend, I am counting on you to see all my wishes are honored.

One more thing. Look in my phone log for Andrew Moore. Give him a call and tell him I'm sorry and I appreciate him seeing me out of this world. Let him know my attorneys will be sending him some money.

A lot has changed since you left me in that hotel room with those two guys. I should have wised up, but I didn't. I was a jerk. Sorry. You saw something good in me that I could never see.

Now, don't get all strange on me. Remember, I always said I just came to dance. This dance is over for me and I don't feel like hanging around for the last song. It's time to leave this dance floor before they turn on the lights. You know how I cannot handle those bright lights. At least not at four in the morning.

Man, those were some great times — you and I on the dance floor in the Atlanta days. I was so proud to be seen with you. No one can beat those old Donna Summer songs. Remember that song, "You Will Carry On." Think of me if you ever hear it again. It's me talking to you. You have to carry on for me. I wonder what happened to that DJ, Bobby something or another, we always went to dance to his spins at Backstreet. Anyway, time to go.

Love always and forever,

Tom

He hits the print key and takes a deep breath. Tom writes Trey's name on a white linen envelope; his hand is unsteady. Tom pulls the letter from the printer and folds it twice before sealing it inside. As a last gesture, he presses it to his chest, then lays it down on the desk where he knows it will be found. Tom also types a short note to Nancy and one to Peggy, leaving them under the one to Trey. He wants to write one to Andrew, but does not know what to say. He will be sure to tell him how he feels again tonight.

Tom looks at the clock on the desk. Andrew will be arriving soon. It is time to get dressed for his date.

The Last Kiss

He glances at the clock and then stares at his reflection in the mirror. Tom looks good, he thinks, but of course he is not thinking straight. He has not been in weeks. He would not know if he was looking good or not. But in truth, he is. Tom is dressed in gray slacks and a black pullover V-neck shirt with a slight collar that lies flat. He runs the pearl-handled comb through his hair one more time to keep his boyish cowlick in check before setting it back down on the countertop. Within minutes, Andrew should be arriving.

Oh, one more thing, Tom reminds himself. He walks into the bedroom and over to the box on the bedside table to get a blue pill. Tom puts it in the pocket of his slacks for later.

He makes his way out to the balcony and gazes over the city

for a minute or two. It is one of the best postcard views to be seen. Tom ambles to the table and pours himself a glass of wine in a sparkling crystal flute reflecting the shimmering light from the candles. Everything looks good, he thinks: the food, the wine, the candles and the view. All that is missing to make the picture complete is the presence of a beautiful young man named Andrew. So, he takes a seat and waits. Tom sips his wine and watches the lights in the surrounding buildings trickle out into the darkening skyline. The air is cool again as he sits back while listening to his opera and the bustle of the city rising up around him.

It is not long before he hears Andrew's footsteps approaching. Tom gets up from his chair and turns around to see his desire walking toward him.

"You made it," Tom says.

"Yes. What a day."

"I'm sure it has been. Let me pour you a glass of wine."

"That would be nice. I could use it."

Tom fills Andrew a glass and hands it to him.

"Let's make a toast," Tom says.

"Sure."

"To you, Andrew, and to the life that is before you."

Andrew lifts his glass, as does Tom, without responding. He is unsure of the future.

They spend the next hour side by side on the balcony watching the night take hold of the city. There is little dialogue. They both have a lot pressing on their minds. Tom is drinking most of the wine, well into the second bottle, while Andrew nibbles on the food. From any other viewpoint, they appear to be a loving spring-fall couple. Perhaps it is the quiet that makes them appear as such as they sit in silhouettes. Andrew gets up from his chair and walks over to the railing. While his back is turned, Tom uses the opportunity to take the pill hiding in his pocket.

He walks over and stands by Andrew. The boy looks at him and then directs his eyes back out over the city. Tom places his hand on top of Andrew's, which is resting on the railing.

"It's a beautiful night," Tom says.

They continue to stand there for the next twenty minutes as the night surrounds them.

He turns Andrew around so his back is to the city. His body is outlined by millions of lights. Slowly he unbuttons Andrew's shirt and slides it down around his shoulders until it partly hangs from the waist of his jeans. The boy watches the flames of the candles on the table dance. Tom leans in to kiss Andrew's chest, and continues until he reaches his belly button, his hands sliding down his back as he goes.

His kisses are measured, supple and tender. Tom is on his knees now; his exhilaration for the boy overrides the pain in his joints in getting there. Andrew eases out of his flip-flops, as Tom unsnaps the jeans before pulling them to the balcony floor. As usual, the boy is not wearing underwear. Tom presses his face into Andrew's crotch and takes a deep breath of pleasure. Andrew sidesteps out of the jeans. Tom confidently holds onto his butt as he takes the boy's penis in his mouth. Andrew pacifies Tom's head loosely in his hands as he sucks.

The music from Madame Butterfly, set on repeat, spills out

of the balcony speakers into the night. Lieutenant Pinkerton has learned of Butterfly's devotion and is ashamed to face her.

Tom's mouth envelops Andrew's penis. It tastes like no other. It's pre-cum is syrupy as it oozes out. Tom drinks it up like fine liquor. He continues to suck and suck, his head moving back and forth, back and forth as Andrew's butt cheeks moon New York City. His back is arched. He moves his hands to the railing, spreading them widely to hold on for dear life. Andrew's eyes open as he views the city upside down. It is making him light-headed. Voraciously, Tom's sucking continues.

"You're going to make me come," Andrew calls out.

Tom comes up for air. He looks up at Andrew, whose eyes are closed now. Tom turns the boy back around to face the city again. Now Andrew stands before New York City naked. He opens his eyes to the spectacular view before him. To Tom, the boy and the view are equally as magnificent. They are both full of life and beauty; and both have the ability to bring pleasure and pain.

Tom buries his head in his ass. Andrew leans further over the edge, his legs spread wide as his hands regain a tight hold on the railing so as not to go plunging over. Tom pushes his tongue in deeper and deeper. The wind is rushing through Andrew's hair; his entire body is covered in goose bumps.

Tom reaches for a hold on the railing to pull himself to his feet. He then wraps his arms tightly around the boy.

"Let's go into the bedroom," he says.

Andrew follows without saying a word. He sits on the edge of the bed watching Tom shed his clothes. He looks tired to Andrew, who is unaware of the many sleepless nights Tom has endured in his absence. The boy is touched by the heartfelt E-mail Tom sent while he was in Michigan. He is not heartless. Andrew knows his leaving is hard on Tom, but he feels he has no choice. His dreams have been shattered, and he wants to go back home, at least until he can come to terms with his unsure future.

As Tom stands in front of him naked, the boy moves to the center of the bed and lies on his back, his head propped on a large pillow. He spreads his legs so Tom can see the pink of his ass. He knows what Tom wants. Within seconds, Tom is on top of him, kissing Andrew as he runs his hands all over his body. Pensively, he kisses him, the saliva from both their mouths glazing over their faces. Seconds and minutes pass, turning into an hour of kissing and fondling. Their lips are red and chapped. Tom rises on his knees and pulls Andrew by the thighs closer to him. He rubs his penis against Andrew's. All he is thinking about is the moment at hand with his desire in his arms. He leans in, kissing Andrew deeply again before speaking.

"I want you. You have no idea of how much I want you."

"I do," Andrew acknowledges.

"Then let me have you. Give me a night to remember."

"I will for tonight," he answers.

"Then that will have to do," Tom resigns.

Tom reaches in the drawer for the lube. Frantically he squirts a large glop in his hand and shares it with his penis and Andrew's ass. With great care, he slides his middle finger in the boy's hole, moving it in and out over and over again, each time deeper and deeper, steering his finger in a circular motion. It is warm and consoling and hot, all at the same time. Andrew lets out a quiet

269

whimper. After a few minutes, Tom removes his finger. He lays over him. Andrew wraps his legs up around his waist, locking them at the ankles. Tom begins to rock his body over Andrew's, his penis searching for the boy's hole. Finally, it finds it and begins to enter.

"But Tom," Andrew speaks out.

"It's okay. I know what I'm doing."

"Tom."

"Sh."

Andrew does not say another word. He concedes. Tom enters him all the way, pausing for a moment to saver the ecstasy before moving his dick out and back in in a slow methodical rhythm. He kisses the boy again and again, sometimes sweetly like in their foreplay, then savagely without any restraint. He begins to pound Andrew harder and harder with a fierce untamable passion, so much so that the boy cannot keep his ankles locked. Andrew takes it with no opposition, seemingly wanting more. The sheets soak up their sweat. Now holding them at his ankles, Tom spreads Andrew's legs as wide as he can without snapping them like a wishbone. The massive bed hits against the wall so hard and often that the bedposts knock holes in the sheetrock.

Tom is lost in the vision under him. His pounding slows and then feverishly speeds up again. Fast, slow, fast, slow, then fast again. Tom's focus moves from Andrew's eyes to his mouth to his chest, then to his rock-hard penis repeatedly slapping against his stomach. He is taking in all of the boy as he pushes his dick deeper and deeper into him. Tom once again wraps Andrew's legs around his waist and continues to pound him while firmly taking hold his ass cheeks in his hands. The boy manages to lock his ankles again as he holds on to the bedpost with one hand and masturbates with the other. The sheetrock continues to take a beating.

"Oh, I'm, I'm going to come any second," Andrew calls out.

Tom slows his movement and watches the boy shoot his ample load on his stomach and chest. His dick still inside of Andrew, Tom leans over to lick up some of the boy's cum. He then brings it to Andrew's mouth and feeds it to him. Tom scoops up the rest in his hand. He pulls out of Andrew long enough to rub it on this penis and then slides back inside. Tom begins fucking the boy with his own cum as they resume kissing, the full sweet flavor of Andrew in their mouths. Harder and harder Tom plows into him until he lets out a loud moan. His cum, mixed with the boy's, floods into Andrew as his movement jerks and then slows to a sluggish pace until he stops. Exhausted, they both lay motionless, Tom on top of Andrew, his penis still inside unwilling to exit. Neither one has noticed the blood stain on the sheets.

After a few minutes of repose, Tom pulls out. He kisses his desire sweetly on the lips. Andrew curls on his side; Tom wraps his arms around the boy. He finds a strange comfort in knowing that he has filled Andrew and mixed his cum with his.

"I have to be up before noon," Andrew says. "Have to do a few things before my flight back to Michigan tomorrow evening."

With those words, Tom is brought back to a heartbreaking reality.

"Yeah, I know," he says with great regret and misery. "Just go to sleep. You need your rest for tomorrow."

Andrew soon falls asleep, and for an hour, time is lost. Those reminding words reiterate to Tom the boy will be leaving. They hang in the air above the bed, and as Tom rereads them over and over in his head, his soul dies a little more each time. From the very second the words left Andrew's lips, the desire for life began to flee Tom's body. But he has been dying for weeks. Minute by minute, hour by hour, day by day. Dying. Tom holds the boy tighter now, feeling his skin pressing against his. He wants to lock Andrew up in the penthouse, perhaps in the attic with all his other memories and keep him for himself and no one else. But Tom knows he can never have him. He is leaving. Tom knows what he must do. He kisses the back of his neck. Andrew kicks his feet like he is running in a dream. Tom lies frozen, the boy in his arms, until his kicking stops.

Quietly, he gets up from the bed. He looks at Andrew still lying on his side before walking out of the bedroom and down the hall toward the bar. He has not bothered to put on his robe. The opera continues to serenade the night. Butterfly has waited for three years for Pinkerton's return. She is overjoyed until she finds out he has taken an American wife.

Tom pours vodka in a tall glass. He takes a gigantic swallow and fills the glass once more. He carries it and the bottle back to the bedroom, stops to look at Andrew once more before making his way to the bath. He gently kicks the door closed with his foot. Tom sits the glass and bottle on the counter before reaching in a cabinet for a full prescription of Dalmane and another of Valium. He spills them both out in his palm before discarding the containers in the sink. They roll around sporadically before stopping side by side on the drain.

Tom looks at the handful of pills. In all his planning, until now, he has not thought about what effect this action will have on Andrew. For a moment, he thinks it is a cruel thing to do. But Tom thinks the boy's leaving is even crueler. Again, he is not thinking clearly. He does not want to hurt Andrew, but he does not want to be without him either. Tom thinks about putting the pills back in their containers and waiting until Andrew leaves. That thought — until Andrew leaves — brings a painful image to his mind. He knows the very minute the boy walks out of the door of the penthouse, for what he believes will be the last time, Tom will feel horrible pain and anguish, and an immeasurable amount of loss. Andrew is young, he tells himself, he will get over it somehow, but Tom will never get over him.

He does not hesitate between swallows. To do so would encourage failure in his plan. With several large gulps, they are gone. He finishes what is left in the glass and fills it again. Tom picks up the picture of Trey one last time. He studies it like he has on many occasions before. Tom mumbles something inaudible if anyone has been listening, and sets it back down next to the one of Andrew. He finishes the third glass of liquor before returning to the bedroom, and to his beloved.

Andrew has not stirred from his position. Tom stands over the bed and watches the boy sleep before easing in next to him. Andrew's sleep continues undisturbed. Tom is beginning to feel drowsy, his head starts to spin. He moves in closer until his chest is pressed to Andrew's back as if trying to melt into him. Tom pulls the sheet up to their waists. He places his left arm just above Andrew's head so his hand can touch the boy's hair. He wraps his right arm around Andrew, resting his hand on the boy's smooth stomach. Tom kisses the back of his neck one last time. His lips remain there as his eyelids become heavy and close. Their nude bodies lay side by side. Butterfly sings "Little idol of my heart," as a farewell to her son after reading the inscription on her father's knife: Death with honor is better than life with dishonor. For Tom, death is better than life without Andrew. Cio-Cio-San stabs herself. Tom becomes unconscious as the opera plays on into what is left of the night.

Saying Goodbye to Love

They hold everything — every hope, dream and anticipation, every violation, disappointment, or lost moment. They are the connection to the soul, bringing the world into our deepest parts. From them flow the tears that cleanse our spirits when factors in life, or people have soiled that innermost part of our being. Like rain, they wash away the pollution, the dirt and grime that blur our vision. They filter the world around us, while they lead us forward or backwards in a quest for the answers to the questions that fall upon us from the first time our eyes open, as each one of us enters the world. Hopefully, in doing so, we can better see what life brings to us.

But, sometimes, what they see is not always what is really there. Usually, our fears only allow our eyes to scan the surface, therefore hindering us from looking deeper into the outer layer of skin, and further through muscle and bone. In reality, what needs to be seen is not that easily reflected in the retinas of our eyes. Because of such limitations caused by fear, they miss the truth of what has happened. Instead, our eyes only see half-truths and pictures only partly in focus. It is the images on the other side of fuzzy, which need to be seen. Only from there, can we know the story of which the complete in-focus picture has to tell.

The eyes are like the lens of a camera, feeding the mind with moving pictures of life. As we sleep, it reviews those clips, mixing past events with our emotions. It is there, in the deepest part of the mind, we sometimes are able to see and understand what has happened.

This was not the first time Trey suspected Kyle had cheated or been less than faithful. Despite those speculations, there was no doubt in his mind that Kyle loved him. But love is different to different people. After his experiences with Tom, Trey was not sure gay men, or even men in general, were capable of being monogamous. He had seen the desires for others in Tom's, and now in Kyle's eyes, and he had felt it in his own heart.

They had been at a bar celebrating Troy's, a friend of Kyle's, thirtieth birthday. The evening had been full of the usual jokes about passing over that invisible line into thirty. Twenty-nine was the last holdout of youth and now Troy had crossed over. Physically he was desirable by most standards. Like Kyle, he was a Bostonian transplant. Oddly enough, Kyle and Troy dated briefly a few years before Trey came into the picture. There was still an obvious attraction between the two. They hugged and flirted all through the evening's celebration. The more they drank, the more the flirting and hugging continued. Soon, both

Kyle and Troy were hanging on to a still-sober Trey.

"What do you think about Troy?" Kyle asks, whispering in his ear.

"He seems like a nice guy."

"Well, he thinks I'm the luckiest man in the world to have you as my boyfriend."

"Oh, he does. I like him even better now," Trey responds.

"Yeah, he does."

"Well, what do you think about that?"

"I know I'm lucky to have you, baby," Kyle answers.

"Sweet."

"He wants you, baby," Kyle reveals.

"Who wants me?"

"Troy does."

"But I'm yours."

"I know, but it's his big THREE-O."

"He'll survive," Trey laughs.

Troy moves his arm lower around Trey's waist until it rests on the top of his ass.

"Man, you could hold a cocktail on that ass of yours, Trey," he comments.

Trey laughs again.

"I think you should give him a big birthday present and fuck him and me together," Kyle suggests out of nowhere.

"You what!"

"Think you should fuck Troy and me tonight."

"You're drunk, baby. Think we need to go home and put your ass to bed."

"Good. You, me, and Troy."

"No, just you and me. Say good night," Trey instructs, as he leads a staggering Kyle out of the bar.

Trey could not help but wonder if it was the alcohol talking, or real desires that were deeply-seated in Kyle. Everyone has fantasies, but would Kyle's, as Tom's obsession had, Trey wondered, get in the way of his own personal quest for true love?

Trey had seen what he believed to be true love between his parents, but even they had to pay a price for it.

"You have your mother's eyes," Trey's father would always say.

She was seriously injured after her car went out of control and slid off the road in a summer storm just days after his twelfth birthday. It was a Monday. Trey came home from school to discover his father standing in the doorway of the trailer. It was unusual to find him waiting. Normally, he would still have been at work and hours away from returning home from the factory. Now, nothing would ever be normal again. For some reason, that day has been preserved in a little boy's mind. Every detail, cataloged as if it happened yesterday, leaving him able to recall it as if it had been recorded on a DVD — one Trey could pull out of its plexi container and insert into the player.

That was twenty-seven years ago. But time had not made much of a difference; Trey still remembered the day his world changed.

He could still pull the DVD out and insert it in the player of his mind. After a few seconds of snow, the screen clears and the day is relived.

◊

At the time, they lived in a smaller trailer community closer to town, not moving to Hidden Woods until a year later. The sky hung low, just above the treetops, leaving a hazy white glow, partially obscured by the hood of the yellow parka that fell over his forehead until it touched the tips of his long eyelashes. Trey's bright eyes peer out into a world that brings a steady gentle rain from the sky, filling the space between where his father stands and the muddy trail Trey stops to make the turn up the path to the trailer.

Up to a few weeks before, his mother had made it a practice to wait for him at the bus stop, until he pleaded he was old enough to walk from where the bus dropped him off by himself. He excitedly explained he was a big boy and did not want the other kids to make fun of him because his mother waited at the bus stop. She conceded. Instead, she stood at the edge of the dirt walk, lined with weeds leading up to the trailer, until the school bus was in sight. When she saw him step off, she quickly retreated to the front door to wait.

The evening of the first day she permitted him to make the journey alone, Trey ran up to his father upon his arrival home from work to proclaim, "Daddy, Daddy, I'm a big boy now." But this day, she would not be peering up the street; Trey would be making that walk alone without her loving eyes to watch.

A clean smell brought by the rain permeates the atmosphere. The storm passed, leaving sporadic showers. Puddles of water fill in the low spots of the path, and as little boys do, Trey manages to step in each one, making the small irregular shaped pools splash out onto the already soaked grass. His father meets him halfway, and for a moment, the world stands silent, except for the sound of rain. Towering over him, the rain continues to cascade around them collecting in his father's graying black hair. It was a cool summer rain; if not for the day's event, it would be a welcome drizzle that felt fresh on the skin. The kind of rain one did not mind because the southern sun had beaten down on the earth for weeks killing the grass and everything green while leaving cracks in the dirt. If it had just come a week earlier, the grass would have been saved. But, it was too late. In vain, the ground under the dead grass sucks down the water, past the dried-up roots, pulling the wetness deeper and deeper into the earth.

With dark deep-set eyes, his father peers into Trey's as if he is looking for something he misplaced. He is looking at the face of his wife. Trey instinctively knows there is something wrong, as his grandmother stands quietly in the open doorway, her eyes looking past him.

"Son, go with your granny. She has something for you at her house," Trey remembers his father instructing.

"But where's Mother?" Trey quizzes, as he looks around his father's tall frame at his grandmother.

His father looks at her, motioning with his head to take him.

"Just run along, Son, go with your granny."

From an early age, Trey knew what love looked, smelled and even tasted like. A stranger could have seen how apparent it was in their eyes, the eyes of his parents. Even as poor as they were, they had a way of looking at each other that made everyone else feel insignificant. Upon entering a room, everyone else faded into the walls and floor. God had given them the gift of beauty. Not just the kind of beauty which one acknowledges upon first glance, but also the kind that grabs you deep in the heart; for some with admiration, while others experienced the hot stinging sense of jealousy that it is not their beauty — neither obtained through nature or conquered by love, they would never in a lifetime understand or experience that kind of beauty.

If they had not been so poor and isolated from the rest of the world, Trey's parents might have been movie stars, a dream of his mother's. She met Trey's father, Frank Bishop, two months before her seventeenth birthday. He was eighteen. A month later, she was carrying Trey, their love child in her belly.

Perhaps as others around them, Trey, too, felt some jealousy at a distance. Not for their God-given beauty, but for the love which seeded from it and consumed them. It made him an outsider. Although a part of them by blood, Trey never felt he was allowed to enter that sacred realm that housed their existence.

As a child, Trey can remember gazing for hours into the mirror with amazed eyes, searching for parts of them in his face and body. He, too, like all the rest, was taken by their exceptional beauty. Trey had to find assurance that at least some part of it had been passed on to him. In all his childhood years of looking for their likeness in his being, Trey never looked for what was different in him, or removed from them. Even if he had noticed a difference, any difference, he would have cursed it, only wishing to be more like his parents. What brought about such an obsession, Trey would only come to understand many years later.

He watched them from the corner of a room, or from the swing in the back yard sitting quietly, an audience for them, like someone sitting in a theater watching a performance. Trey could have been anyone, observing their interactions with one another, understanding they were the only two people on stage. He faded into the background like the rest, unseen except for a dark silhouette among many. If it were not for his granny, Trey would have most likely starved to death or have been left behind in a restaurant or department store like a misplaced handbag or package.

It is not that his parents didn't love him; they just loved each other more. Trey was a product of that love, but never felt to be cherished as greatly. Perhaps it made him love them more. He had to earn what love he could from them, but it was more like Trey was stealing it; devising cleaver ways to take it without their knowledge, so that they might step out of their private world for a moment to acknowledge his existence and his relationship to them.

With beauty, there always comes a price. For Mary Sue, it was Frank's jealousy. He was paranoid, believing every man in the trailer park wanted to sleep with her. On several occasions, Frank punched a guy square in the face for eyeing Mary Sue when they had been out at the local dive bar. The more he drank the worse his jealousy became. At the height of his anger, he almost beat one man to death.

Trey grew tall like Frank, and slim like Mary Sue. It would take him years to fill out into his father's muscular frame; Frank was a weekend body builder of sorts, which was one of the reasons Mary Sue loved him. She would hang off his larger-than-life muscular arms that were bigger than an average man's thighs. He posed for her, flexing his biceps, making them round like grapefruits.

Trey's hair naturally parted above his left eye, just as Frank's. Instead of his father's straight black hair, Trey acquired his mother's brown wavy locks. His eyes were identical to hers. His mother often told him that one could see the sea in them — a blue-green drifting sea. Trey had her lips, round and plump with slight pouting corners. He had his father's coloring, dark as opposed to his mother's ivory skin. But that is all they gave him, pieces and parts of their physical beauty. Perhaps to them, that was enough. They just assumed because Trey was a part of them that he required nothing else.

Trey's mother barely survived the car wreck after three months in the hospital. Besides the numerous internal injuries, her face was disfigured, requiring many operations over the next several years to restore it to some resemblance of what it once was. Regardless, Frank still loved her and managed to see the same beautiful face as before. Trey felt further isolation as his mother required even more attention from his father while she was in the long recovery. He deeply wanted to find the love he felt he had been denied. Trey searched for it in Tom, and in Kyle. He never realized it had always been there, in both of them, as it had been in his parents. They had not intentionally denied him love; it was just the circumstances that surrounded their lives that seemed to keep it from him. Trey was finding out that love means different things to different people, and it is shown in different ways. He might possibly have to adjust his understanding or look in other avenues for the kind of love he desired.

In The Blink of an Eye

A new day inches through the city. Pigeons gather on the marble table and balcony floor outside Tom's bedroom. They frantically peck at a tray left out from the night before consisting of partially eaten fruit, hardened sliced French bread and what is left of a wedge of cheese. Two empty bottles of pricey wine rattle on the table from the pecking of the pigeons. A single white dove perches on the iron railing looking out over Manhattan, seemingly uninterested in the pigeons or the leftover feast, but more engrossed in witnessing the beginning of a new day as a magnificent sunrise awakens New York City.

Andrew opens his eyes as the light moves into the room. It warms his face. He runs his hands over his head, like a comb, to bring some order to his hair. Andrew looks over his shoulder to see Tom's head smothered in a pillow.

"Hey, baby, you awake?" Andrew asks.

No answer.

"Hey, wake up birthday boy. I'm starved. You think Peggy can make me some of those peach pancakes this morning? I could eat a whole stack."

Still no response.

Andrew rolls over in bed as he lifts Tom's arm from around his waist. He places his lips to Tom's ear.

"Hey, sleepy head, you awake?" he asks again, while gently shaking him at the shoulder.

Still, no answer. He continues to shake Tom as he rolls him onto his back.

Suddenly, Andrew jumps to the floor. A loud scream races through the penthouse after Andrew's hand hits the intercom button by the bed; his voice erupts through the speakers.

"Peggy! Peggy! You there? There's something wrong with Tom."

She is busy in the kitchen. Startled by Andrew's voice blasting out of seemingly nowhere, Peggy drops the coffee filter filled with freshly ground beans on the floor. She races out of the kitchen and down the hall in the direction of Tom's bedroom suite. Peggy hesitates at the closed door for the blink of an eye.

"Oh my God! Tom. Tom, you okay?" Andrew screams out.

With that, Peggy bursts through the door to see Tom and the boy naked. Andrew is standing by the edge of the bed shaking Tom's lifeless body, whose lips are covered in white dried foam.

286

His body is sallow. Even the color of Andrew's face has turned waxy white from shock.

Peggy hurries to the bed.

"Boy, put your clothes on," she instructs, while pulling the covers over Tom's private parts.

She leans over, placing her head on Tom's chest. Her ear struggles to hear a faint heartbeat. Andrew's body is shaking as he puts on his jeans and shirt.

"What's wrong with him?" he frantically asks.

"Not sure. But I think it's best you go home, son," Peggy says, as she reaches for the phone by the bed to dial 911.

"I'll take care of him. Now go, before the ambulance gets here, and there are questions to answer."

Andrew pauses for a moment at the doorway. His eyes are full of fear.

"Go boy. It'll be okay. God will make everything okay."

He races toward the front door, faltering at first before reaching for the knob. Many questions appear in Andrew's mind. Why is he running? Maybe he should go back to help Peggy with Tom, but she told him to leave. What if he is dead? Maybe the police will find out he is a prostitute and arrest him.

Reluctantly he opens the door and walks down the wide vestibule to the elevator. It stops on the next floor where a short elderly white-haired woman carrying a small white fluffy dog with two pink bows clipped behind each ear steps in. She also has a larger pink bow on the back of her head. It would be funny, if it were another day or any other elevator ride. The dog barks at

Andrew. He does not know the breed.

"Sh, sh," the women says, as she covers the dog's snout with her hand.

It tries to bark again, but she is successful in keeping the dog quiet.

The woman gives Andrew a standoffish smile before darting her eyes forward. He can tell she is scrutinizing him from the corner of her eye, looking him up and down. He wonders if she knows he is a prostitute. She does. The woman knows he is coming from the penthouse. She has ridden down the elevator with many other boys over the years.

As they reach the lobby, the ambulance has arrived at the exclusive address. A crowd quickly begins to gather in front of the building wondering who is in distress. The white-haired woman lingers to see what all the commotion is about, as her fluffy white dog barks out of control. A dazed Andrew makes his way to the street. His head hurts possibly from the wine the night before. His heart races from the adrenalin rushing through him. He crosses his arms close to his body, while shoving his hands deep in his armpits. Andrew leans against the side of the building in an attempt to regain his sanity and try to calm down. Sliding his back along the outside of the building, Andrew eases a few feet further away from the commotion. He can hear the assembly of New Yorkers as they bombard the doorman with questions: Who is it? What happened? Did someone die?

The wait seems like hours before two paramedics roll Tom out on a stretcher with an oxygen mask covering his face as a faithful Peggy holds his hand. Andrew continues to watch as they put Tom inside. Peggy sees him at a distance, but does not

288

acknowledge him. The driver helps her up after the stretcher and closes the door. The sirens echo between the tall buildings as the red and blue lights of the ambulance disappear in front of the paused traffic.

Andrew now holds his head in his hands as he looks at the cracks in sidewalk. The onlookers disperse and he is left standing alone.

Of Good Conscience

Trey walks with the crowd looking for a good venue to watch the parade as the June sun burns off the muggy haze that started the morning. Forgoing the sidewalk, he maneuvers his way through hundreds and hundreds of people spilling out on the street, celebrating their freedom to be who and what they are in this life. Familiar faces spark memories in his mind of past years. Some look good, seemingly unaffected by the wear of years, while others are showing the truth of time's passing. Trey wonders how he looks to them, as brief hellos and nods are exchanged. He keeps a fast pace, only stopping for a second to chat before hastily moving on, as if not wanting to give anyone ample time to examine the years crossing on his face.

"Trey," someone calls out from the crowd behind him.

He turns around to see who it is. A balding guy in his mid forties, dressed in cut-off shorts with tattered edges and a one-size-too-small white tank top, approaches. He is sporting multiple strands of beads in rainbow colors around his neck and several temporary Equal Rights tattoos on both shoulders. He is with a group of five guys all wearing similar drag.

"Hey, bud, long time no see."

"Allen, is that you?" Trey asks.

"In the flesh."

"Wow, it has been a while," Trey comments.

"Sorry to hear about your friend Tom. Steve told me."

"Thanks, Allen."

"So, bud, haven't seen you around much," Allen says.

"Yeah, been keeping to myself a lot."

"Steve tells me you're having some big memorial party at the Abbey for Tom next weekend."

"Yes. I hope you'll come."

"Is it okay? I mean, I didn't really know the guy," Allen asks.

"Of course it is. Everyone is invited. Bring your friends."

"Okay, thanks," Allen says.

"The more the merrier," Trey says with a smile.

"Okay. See you there."

"You bet. Have fun, Allen," Trey says, as he hurries off through the crowd.

"Who's that hot number?" one of Allen's friends asks, as he slides his sunglasses down his nose to get a better look at Trey's ass as he leaves.

"He's way out of your league," Allen says with a laugh.

"And yours too," his friend comments, as he shoots Allen the finger.

"So, did I hear something about a party next weekend?" another friend asks.

◊

Tom has been dead for almost eight months and Kyle moved out of the house back in November. It was too much for Trey to lose Tom and the trust of Kyle — too much disappointment from the two people he cared about the most. Trey shut everything out. He spent the fall and winter in a self-imposed isolation locked up in his studio, painting. He spent hours, days, weeks and months watching paint dry on his canvases. It was not until spring that he started to feel anything again, then the feelings came slow.

There were still some loose ends with Tom's estate. Nathan tried to stir up some trouble about the money Tom left him. But Tom's attorneys had no problem crushing his opposition. Nathan tucked his tail between his legs and walked away. Nancy bought a summer home in the South of France, and from her last phone conversation with Trey, was filling her time with a young French poet named Pierre. So much like Tom, Trey thought, as she went on and on about her new conquest. He was happy that Nancy was getting on with her life and he knows she will somehow handle her young "boy toys" better than Tom handled his. Peggy moved back to Birmingham, where she bought a house in Hampton

Heights and opened a bakery in the Highland Village area with the money Tom left her. She still went to Bible studies without fail. Lee Ann, George, and the boys are still in Chattanooga, settling back into their quiet lives. Lee Ann could not be happier. After all, it is the life she always wanted. Some dreams do come true.

Trey did get in contact with Andrew as Tom had requested in his letter. After the paramedics took Tom away, he went back to his empty apartment and sat in the middle of the floor crying until he had to catch a cab to the airport. Andrew called Tom's mobile the next day, but that was a call never returned.

Tom's attorneys transferred a nice sum of money into Andrew's account insuring he will never have to turn tricks again, making Tom his last john. Andrew stayed with his parents through the winter and moved to California the following spring. He is in grad school now, adjusting to the life changes that resulted in his two years in New York City. He had no idea that Tom took an overdose. Trey decided to take Nancy's lead as she had done with the obituary and keep him in the dark, telling Andrew instead that Tom had a stroke. He thought, under the circumstances, there was no point in Andrew knowing the sad truth.

The penthouse sits unoccupied, filled with all the beautiful things covered in large white sheets. Tom willed it to both Nancy and Trey, perhaps in hopes that they would come to New York to visit his spirit, which surely walks the halls and stands on the balconies looking out over New York City just at the hour the night comes to engulf the day. Surely, when it comes, Tom's spirit without a doubt lies on the bed and watches the wind make the sheer draperies dance into the room again and again. They have not yet decided what to do with it.

Now, another summer has made its way on the calendar again, and Trey is beginning to feel the effects of time. Suddenly, he is forty. He looks back over the past years since he moved to Atlanta. The two men in his life are gone and he is feeling the void. When he thinks of his relationship with Tom, he remembers great innocence lost to passion riding on submission. Tom had been in total control until Trey walked out of that hotel suite in Miami. With Kyle it was different. As Tom saw the innocence in Trey at nineteen, Trey wanted to see the same in Kyle when they first met. They both were passionate and loving relationships, but flawed.

Trey's nighttime dreams are filled with haunting memories of Tom. They are much like that old photo album Tom kept in the attic of the penthouse. His dreams are like a slide show of images and moments lived, of deep passion and desire experienced, and ultimately the fear of never finding true passion again. Kyle has been in contact, realizing he has lost someone special and now wants him back, but it has been a slow healing for Trey. When he wakes in a cold sweat in the middle of the night — his head trying to shake those images and moments loose — Trey wonders if he will ever settle down in a strong relationship; if he will ever be able to trust someone again; or if he will ever meet a mate that will result in something that will last more than a few years.

Atlanta Gay Pride puts the choices right out on the streets. Many take note of Trey while attempting to catch his eye or yell out some remark like, "hot man," to get his attention, but he is too busy trying to find a place to stop and just watch. He removes his Braves baseball cap long enough to run his hand through his hair before readjusting it on his head. Trey wonders if among all these men there is someone for him. Just one. He only wants one.

Perhaps the choices are too many, he thinks, or it is just easier to go from encounter to encounter. He knows that sounds too much like Tom. But he also knows he is different and does not want more on his plate than his stomach can digest. Tom was the one with the voracious appetite for men. Trey's appetite is for true love. One true love. One man to hold and never let go of. One man to grow old with if the powers that be allow.

Now, surrounded by so many men at this celebration of Gay Pride, he wonders if he will have sex this weekend. How many guys will approach him with a smile? How many more empty moments after the act of sex will he have to endure while the stranger hurriedly puts back on his clothes and heads for the door. Trey thinks about the two sex partners since November that resulted in emptiness, but it was too lonely in the house without Kyle, and the knowledge that Tom was gone was still raw. The Internet makes it too easy to hook up on a lonely night, too easy to find sex, mistaking it for comfort, where you are left with regret the next morning.

Like Alif's and so many of the others' who fed Tom's obsession, Trey's looks were almost a curse. Maybe that is why he is still alone, single and forty, he wonders. It took him some years, but Trey realizes now just how good-looking he is. How much longer will he look good? How many more cute young men will soil the sheets of his bed before it is over? Time now seems to be traveling fast. God, Trey continues to think, I am sounding just like Tom. He wants to find the love he believes his parents had, but without the jealousy. But time seems to be running out.

He misses Kyle. He wants to be walking with him in the middle of the gay mayhem. Trey misses the feel of Kyle's hand in his. He remembers their first walk through Piedmont Park together and how Kyle kept reaching for Trey's hand. It was uncomfortable for Trey to hold hands with another man in public, even in Midtown Atlanta, in the gayest park in the city. It was not that he did not want to hold Kyle's hand; rather he just wanted to avoid a possible confrontation with any straight people in the park and spoil the day. Now he found himself longing for that very day, longing to have Kyle's hand in his and to hell with anyone who might object.

After Trey started dating Kyle, and once he believed it was more than physical, he felt a sense of hope and relief again. Yes, they were both beautiful, yes the sex was incredible, but it was the "after" that he wanted. The way he felt after the sex; the holding and cuddling, and the sweet talk. They appeared comfortable together. The kind of comfort where dirty socks and morning breath, although avoided, were not a concern. Now they had been at odds for eight months. Kyle wanted to come back, and Trey was not sure if he could trust another man again. It was a roller coaster of emotions for Trey. He wonders if Kyle is somewhere in the crowd, and what will he say if their paths cross today?

After watching part of the parade, Trey makes his way into Outwrite Bookstore & Coffeehouse on the corner of 10th and Piedmont Avenue. The storefront is wrapped in rainbow banners. It is as crammed as a popular gay bar on a Saturday night. The only difference is there is a better selection of reading material. A large crowd is standing at the coffee bar, while others mingle around the shelves of books filled with places to go, personal stories of coming out, and picture books with buff men filling their pages, among many, many others.

Trey finds an open spot at the bar and orders a Diet Coke. It is not long before he is cruised by a young boy. He is afraid to guess his age. Trey takes his drink over to a small bistro table by the window that has just become free. The boy follows and stands within arm's reach by a table with a sign that reads, "New Releases." Trey can tell the boy is getting frustrated that he has not acknowledged him, but he has to give the boy credit for his doggedness.

Trey notices the fresh-face boy pick up one of the books. He begins hurriedly flipping through it, looking at the pages fly by and then back up at Trey. Trey cannot help but smile. That is so me twenty years ago: nervous, curious, and frustrated, Trey thinks.

"So, does that look like a good read?" Trey speaks up.

"Excuse me?" the boy asks nervously.

"The book you have. Does it look like it's any good?" Trey clarifies.

"Might be," the boy answers.

"You putting on your gay pride today?" Trey asks.

"Yeah, I guess."

"You from around here?"

"No, Macon."

Oh, you poor kid, Trey thinks to himself. He remembers what it is like to be gay and from a small southern town.

"So, just down the road."

"Yeah. I drove up early this morning."

Trey is relived that the kid at least has a driver's license.

"How often do you get to Atlanta?"

"This is my second time."

"I'm Trey. What's your name?"

"Toby."

"You're welcome to sit with me and watch all this craziness going on outside," Trey offers.

Toby puts the book he was uninterested in down and takes the empty chair at the table. Trey looks up toward the ceiling, but he is looking beyond. Man, he thinks, I am sure you have your hand in this, referring to Tom in heaven or that gay Mecca that all homosexual men go to after they die. Trey is sure it looks a lot like Miami Beach, but a million times bigger and flashier.

He wonders what to say or do next, now that he has this very young, very cute guy following him around the bookstore on a busy Sunday afternoon in the middle of Atlanta Gay Pride weekend. With all the men in the park, and on the streets of Midtown, this is what is chasing after him, he thinks and then smiles.

"You have a nice smile," Toby says.

"Thanks. So, how old are you?"

The boy looks away before speaking, "I'm nineteen."

He is lying.

"Do you have any idea how old I am?" Trey asks.

"I really didn't think about it," he replies.

"Really?" Trey responds.

"Yeah, you're very handsome."

"Well thanks, bud. There is no question that you're way pass cute."

The boy smiles, showing off his deep dimples, having the same result as turning on a light in a dark room. His face, framed with jet black hair, lights up and his blue eyes shine like diamonds.

"So you want to go somewhere?" Toby asks.

Trey almost chokes on his Diet Coke as it goes down the wrong way.

"Yeah," he replies, "in about five years."

"What, you don't like what you see?" Toby questions.

"Oh, yeah. I like, but I'm not sure how I'll like myself in the morning," Trey says.

"You want to find out?" Toby nervously asks.

"Man, you've got a lot of talk there, bud."

Trey is flattered, but really does not want the conversation to go any further. Yeah, he thinks, the boy is very cute, but he is young. He thinks again that Tom must be loving every minute of this as he watches from Miami Heaven.

"I think I'm going to see what's going on in the park now that the parade is over," Trey says.

"Cool. I'll go with you. You mind?"

Trey thinks for a second. "Guess not."

He knows that the boy is bound to get into trouble if he walks around alone. He is concerned for him.

Toby follows Trey around the park for the remainder of the

day like a lost puppy. In a way Trey is glad the boy is tagging along with him. It keeps them both out of trouble. The sun is beginning to go down. Local politicians — who have been trading promises for votes in an upcoming election — are making way for the yearly drag extravaganza starting on the stage set up in the clearing. Toby has never seen a drag queen until earlier that day in the parade. They take a spot on the hill overlooking the stage and a huge crowd of celebrators.

The boy has been growing on Trey all afternoon and he cannot help but wonder what his life is going to be like. As they sit back and watch the show, Trey's thoughts continue on the boy's future, wondering if Toby will leave his small town as he did, and come to Atlanta or some other big city where gays can live in some kind of freedom. Trey knows the gay world is just beginning to open up for this newbie.

Two hours later, the drag show comes to a finale with an amazing array of scantily dress divas that could be any straight man's fantasy or nightmare, as fireworks light up the dark sky over Piedmont Park.

"Wow," Toby calls out in amazement.

"Pretty cool," Trey comments.

"Yeah, only thought they did fireworks for the Fourth of July."

"Just think of it as your coming out party," Trey tells the boy.

"I like the sound of that."

"Yeah, me too," Trey says.

"Well, bud, it's getting late. Don't you need to be heading

back to Macon?"

"Yeah, but I would rather go home with you," Toby says.

"Aren't your parents expecting you home?"

"I live with my aunt. She's pretty cool."

Trey knows there is a story there, but does not want to know it right now.

"Is that so?"

"Yeah. I really don't want to drive back this late."

"Okay, bud. I have a spare bedroom you can use."

"Thanks."

Buffy and Sam greet them at the front door. They thoroughly sniff Toby to see if he is friend or foe. Their wagging tails show approval.

"Nice place," Toby says.

"Thanks. You hungry? Want something to eat?"

"Yeah, what you got?"

"I'm sure we can find something."

The dogs follow them into the kitchen, hoping to get a treat. Trey lets them out the back door on his way to the refrigerator.

"How about a turkey sandwich and a glass of milk?" Trey offers.

"How about a beer?" Toby interjects.

"How old did you say you were?"

"Oh, yeah. Guess you aren't going to let me slide on that."

"You're right about that."

Toby gobbles down the sandwich and swallows two glasses of milk like he has not eaten in days. Trey opts for a protein shake instead.

"Okay, bud. Time for bed. Let me show you your room for the night."

"Can I sleep with you Trey?"

"Don't think that's a good idea."

"Why not?" the boy asks.

"Have you even had sex yet?"

"Well, yeah. I sucked this guy off in school.

"That's it?"

"He sucked me, too."

"And have you been fucked yet?"

"No. But, I want you to."

"I'm not breaking in any virgins tonight. Okay. Now get cleaned up and get yourself in the bed."

Even though Trey is tempted, he restrains himself. The boy is beautiful and willing, but he knows he will hate himself in the morning. He also does not believe Toby is of age and still thinks he might be younger than what he told him earlier; but he knows it is hard to tell these days. So there is a legal issue too. Toby followed him over to the house in a new Lexus, so Trey at least knows he has to be sixteen and comes from an upper class family. The Bibb county tags confirm he is telling the truth about being from Macon. Trey also knows most privileged kids have more opportunity to see the world, and as a result, grow up even faster. Kids grow up so much faster than when he was young.

Trey wanted to ask him more about his background and if indeed he did really live with an aunt, and if so, what was the story there, but it was late and Trey did not want to stretch the evening out any longer.

"I think you should be nice and comfortable in here. There is a bath through that door with fresh towels. If you need anything else, just let me know."

"It's great. Thanks."

"Good night."

"Night, Trey."

Trey lets Sam and Buffy back in. They immediately head for the bedroom; Trey follows them as they make a comfortable spot in their overstuffed doggy bed in the corner. He brushes his teeth and showers before turning in after the long day at the park.

Trey lies naked in bed thinking about the boy. He grabs hold of the base of his cock. It is hard and thick with pre-cum oozing from its head dripping onto his stomach. He is thinking about Kyle as well, wondering if he is alone or with someone tonight.

Sometimes he thinks he was too hard on Kyle, fully aware there is a lot of pressure on young gay men living in a community consumed with sex. But there had been more to the story than first told, about what happened between his lover and Kim and Eric that Sunday night Trey was out of town.

After a run-in Trey had with the forty-something overgrown party boys, and more repeated arguments with Trey, Kyle finally confessed that they had made it as far as the bedroom. He was pretty drunk, as he had originally stated. He finally came to his senses, but by then, Kim was giving him a blow job and Eric was

304

fondling his ass. Kyle felt excitement, but was soon overcome with guilt and panic when he caught a glimpse of a picture of him and Trey on the bedside table. It was enough to momentarily sober him up and remind him what was at stake. Kyle then told them to leave before passing out on the bed.

When he woke up the next morning, he did not remember what had transpired the night before until later in the day. As he told Trey, he knew it was not worth throwing away what he had built with him. With the truth squeezed out by Kyle's guilt, and with Tom's death, everything for Trey ballooned out of control until it popped, and the ugliness went everywhere. Trey needed time.

One thing is for sure, after a few broken bones and some much bruised egos, Kim and Eric will think twice before invading the sanctity of another relationship. Trey made sure of that.

Maybe in the middle of the night Kyle will miss him, Trey thinks, and the phone will ring in the blackness as it has on many nights with Kyle at the other end. Trey would just let it ring until the voicemail picked it up. This time, if it does, maybe he will answer it and find it in himself to forgive. He tries to think of other things, but his mind keeps flip-flopping between Toby in the room down the hallway and Kyle. They are both reminders of what it is like to be young and beautiful with the world at your fingertips.

The fights with Kyle left a lingering sour taste in his mouth, but the nights without him were mounting and getting harder and harder to deal with. Trey wanted to call, but resisted. Kyle was still young, he told himself, but he still missed being with him. So much so that at times, it was hard to get out of bed in the mornings, hard to shower and shave because of missing him so much. With all the money Tom had left Trey, he could very well stay in bed all day and not face any of the disappointments, or make any decisions. Kyle is just a guy, Trey has been trying to convince himself again and again over the past months, there are so many out there like him. Or are there? Trey wonders why he is still so caught up in him, and if his pride will give in to forgiveness.

An hour passes, finally his eyes are getting heavier by the minute and he feels sleep approaching. Trey's body jerks twice. He is in the first stages of slumber.

Buffy lets out a low growl as she perks up her head.

"Sh, sh," whispers a voice entering the room.

It is Toby tiptoeing his way in, trying not to wake Trey, easing toward the bed where he stands with a full-on erection. He listens to see if his host has fallen asleep. Toby is reassured by Trey's heavy long breaths. Gradually, he slithers off his stark white briefs and lets them fall to the floor. The moonlight seeping through the window casts its light onto his young perfect body as he continues to stand looking at Trey; the bed sheet is pulled up to his crotch, but Toby can clearly see what is underneath. Daringly, he takes a deep inhalation and slips into bed next to his crush.

"Who's that?" Trey calls out, still partly asleep.

Toby says nothing. He just scoots in closer until his back meets Trey's chest. Instantly, Trey's erection returns. He puts his arms around the boy and pulls him ever closer. Toby feels so good. It is too late to say no, or tell him to go back to the guest room. The boy can feel Trey's penis pushing against his ass. His butt squirms against it.

"Just try and sleep," Trey says softly.

"But I can't. You have me all excited."

"And I'm not?" Trey jests in a sleepy voice.

Morning is still hours away; Trey has been unable to sleep with Toby wrapped in his arms. It is all too tempting: the sweet smell of freshly washed smooth skin; areolas red like cherries; young wanting eyes staring at him; Toby's ass round and full rubbing against his crotch.

All day Trey had looked into the clear wide blue eyes of youth and now he is holding him in his arms. He wants to slide down and eat the boy's ass, and what a sweet beautiful one it is, he thinks. Trey knows how warm his ass must be and how much he wants to fuck him. Man, he wants to this very moment. He wants to take the boy's virginity. Toby will do anything to get laid by me, Trey thinks, anything. It would be better for the boy if he does, Trey thinks more. Better me than some asshole stranger who will use him and then cut him loose. At least Trey believes he will be loving and understanding, treating the boy well and not fuck him like he is just a hole to fill. He will give the boy total pleasure, so he will remember his first experience with a smile and satisfaction.

A cloud of guilt storms up. His stomach begins to ache with fear as queasiness runs through him like greasy food. Trey is confused and excited. It would be fine if he could get Kyle out of his head. He tries not to think about him, tries not to see him in his mind as he looks at the back of Toby's head. Trey thinks he should be happy to have this boy in his bed and it should make things easier, but nothing has been easier since Tom died or Kyle moved out.

He pretends to sleep, taking in deep breaths, letting them out little by little. He opens his eyes and looks again at the back of Toby's head. Trey feels the texture of his hair with his eyes. His nose can still detect a scent of the shampoo Toby used in the shower a few hours ago, the same that Kyle always used. It is vanilla — sweet and gentle like the boy. Trey can tell he is still awake and wonders if Toby thinks he is sleeping. He wants Toby. Trey wants to roll him on his stomach and slide his dick into that sweet round ass, but he wants Kyle more. Toby rubs his ass against Trey's passion.

God, what am I doing with this kid, he thinks? He is just a kid. Sixteen, seventeen, eighteen, nineteen years old, whatever! I could be his father.

With that unwelcoming realization, Trey loses his erection. The blood leaves his penis and he feels a sense of relief. Annoyingly, the clock ticks on the bedside table spilling time into the room. Trey wants to reach out and grab it. He wants to throw it across the room to make it stop ticking. Instead, he lies there listening, wondering and waiting.

A new day comes. Trey wakes with the boy facing him with large blue eyes looking into his sleepy ones. He has morning wood as does Trey. Nothing has changed since the night before. Now it is even harder to resist youth calling to him. It is lying next to him in the bed again, as it was the night before, waiting for him to take pleasure in it. The boy is waiting, offering his body to Trey. He reaches out to touch Trey's face. Toby runs his hand over the stubble of his beard. It will be another few years, Trey thinks, before the boy will have to shave. He grabs his hand and brings it to his lips. Trey warmly kisses the center of his palm.

"You're amazingly beautiful," Trey says.

"Then take me. Have all you want of me," the boy replies.

"I think you've read too many romance novels," Trey says almost in jest.

"Not a one," the boy answers. "But I watch *Queer As Folk.*"

Trey rolls his eyes. He runs his hand through Toby's generous head of hair. The boy moves down on the bed. Trey turns his head to look out the window. Suddenly, Toby is sucking his dick. Trey closes his eyes.

"Stop. Stop, Toby." Trey says in a murmur.

Toby keeps sucking. It feels so good to Trey. The boy's beautiful full lips run up and down his penis as his hands reach up to rub the light hair on Trey's chest. He pulls at the boy's head to make him stop, but Toby resists. He does not want to stop his sucking. Trey forcefully removes his cock from the boy's mouth and pulls him up to eye level.

"Do you know what you're doing?"

"Am I not doing this right?" Toby questions.

Oh, yes, Trey thinks to himself. He is doing it right and he is also thinking how much he wants him to continue.

"Do you know anything about sexually transmitted diseases or AIDS?" Trey asks.

"A little. Do you have something?"

"You should have asked me before you started. But, no I'm

clean and negative."

"So, what's the problem?"

"The problem is that I care about someone else. The problem is that I want you. I want to fuck you like crazy."

"Cool."

"No, it's not cool."

"If you're worried about me clinging to you all the time, it won't happen. I'm not planning on moving in with you or anything."

Trey laughs. He needs to laugh.

"Is this what you want?" Trey asks with an air of concern, his hand guarding his hard cock.

"Yes, give it to me. I've wanted to feel you inside of me from the minute I saw you walk into the bookstore," Toby answers with assurance.

"You just think you want that."

Trey is getting mad at himself. He wants to repetitively hit his head against the wall until all the mess and confusion in it concerning Tom and Kyle fall out on the floor. Damn it, he thinks, FUCK the kid. He wants you to FUCK him. SHIT, FUCK the boy and get it over with. You are not a FUCKING SAINT. FUCK him.

"Look kid. You're hot. I'm going to write down some web sites for you to check out. Okay. One is AID Atlanta and the other is YOUTHPRIDE. Promise me you will check them out. I'm going to give you my number. Call me when you get back to Macon. We can talk on the phone. Call collect if you have to. But promise me, you will not have sex with anyone until you look at these sites and find out about AIDS and STD's."

"So, you don't want to fuck me?"

"Yes, I want to, but I'm not. At least not today."

Trey leans over and opens the top drawer of the bedside table. He pulls out a pen and notepad and writes down the information.

"Lets get cleaned up and I'll buy you some breakfast. I'm sure you have to get back to Macon."

"Okay, I guess," Toby says.

Trey has one more thing to do. He will take the boy to eat and get him on his way. He has to finish up the plans for the memorial party for Tom and a last good-bye.

The Last Dance

The mid-afternoon sun cautiously slides through the weathered round stained-glass window, which surprisingly remains intact after years of neglect. In spite of the time of day, this former place of worship is strangely dim. In reality it is still a church, but without a minister or a congregation to fill the pews, which have been long-since removed. Even in the absence of bright light, Trey can see where they had once been bolted to the wooden floor. Like a little boy, he looks up over his shoulder, studying the illuminated image of Jesus and a lamb. The outside light carries the images in a cylinder, like a kaleidoscope, to the floor. Dust moves in the confined light. For a moment it reminds Trey of the large jigsaw puzzles he put together in his childhood. He feels like a lamb wandering in an open field: lost, confused and lonely.

Almost twenty years have passed since he met Tom in a bar, just minutes away from the building in which he is now standing.

Trey stops in the weak reflection the stained glass mirrors on the floor. Faint colors of red, blue and yellow cross over his face. He is carrying a small leather box with some of Tom's ashes. For a moment he feels spiritual, a sense of peace moves through him. This is Tom's day, Trey thinks to himself. As soon as the boys arrive, Tom will make an appearance. How could he miss the last dance? Trey smiles for a moment seeing Tom in his prime in his mind's eye. He flashes back to their first meeting at The Cove. He knows Tom will make one more appearance on the dance floor, then, he will go to his rest. This is the last tribute to his once lover and friend, one last night of dancing in a sea of men.

Since their first meeting, Trey has seen a lot of changes. He has transformed from a beautiful slim boy, full of innocence — considered chicken — maturing into an extremely handsome and older muscular man. Over time he has become a younger version of his first lover.

Trey's memories of Tom and their first intimate moments flood his head. For the first time in a long while, Trey feels nineteen again. It seems like just a few years ago, not nearly two decades. God, he thinks to himself, as Tom had so many times, where have the years gone? At that moment, Trey wants them back. He wants the floor of the church to open up so they can rise from the ashes. He wonders what it would take to get them back.

Trey closes his eyes, still feeling the light moving over his face from the colored glass. The damp air of the Abbey moistens his skin. A chill runs through him like the first time you step out into summer rain from shelter. His eyes flood with tears. Everything is catching up with him — Tom's suicide, the fights with Kyle, and the realization that time is always moving forward. The clock is still ticking, its hands moving in a continuous circle like the earth around the sun. He wants to make the clock's hand move in reverse and the earth in reverse as well. If that was possible, then perhaps he could go back and change things for everyone. Trey could make Tom only love him and save them both from the desire to be forever young. They could grow old together, and even with Tom being older than Trey, he would still stay with him. He would still welcome Tom into his body like he had before.

But what about Kyle, he thought? What would become of him if Trey had never met him? His life would be different as well, maybe better or worse. Trey hoped for the better. He had to focus his thoughts on Tom now. After all, it was his day, his special memorial, so different from the one Nancy put on. This will be the one that Tom would have wanted.

What if things had been different? What if they had stayed together? What if Tom had not been so obsessed with growing older? As the thoughts grow in his head, Trey's heart begins to pound, pushing the blood through his body like hot lava spewing from an erupting volcano. If Tom could come back, would he want things to be different, too?

His heart continues to pound faster and faster until it almost feels it is going to race to an abrupt stop at any second. The sound of an express train echoes in his ears. The echoes grow louder and louder, the train moves faster and faster out of control, close to jumping the tracks. Trey's heart now feels it will flip over in his chest. Suddenly, it seems time is indeed moving in reverse.

A cloud in the sky covers the sun cutting off the light shinning though the stained glass. The colors from the image of Jesus and the lamb disappear from the floor and retreat from Trey's face. Minutes later, the cloud moves on and the light once again travels through the stained-glass. The colors return to his face and spill the image of Jesus and the lamb onto the floor once again.

Trey's body drops to the floor in a seated position, his lungs gasp for air. In a second they fill to capacity. He begins to breathe at a slower pace as he looks toward the source of light. Trey closes his eyes; he sees an image of Tom. He lies down on his back. His whole body is covered in color. Like the light sliding through the stained glass above him, Trey can almost feel Tom sliding gently inside of his young flesh as if he were nineteen again. He can smell Tom's scent, and remember how strong and heavy he felt on top of his youth.

Trey's legs open wide to welcome in all that Tom has to give him; all the power and strength thrusting inside of his virgin flesh. His lips are over-powered by Tom's with each passionate kiss; his lover's tongue reaching, as if searching to taste Trey's soul.

Now, he is holding the ashes of a man he has never stopped loving in his arms. A man who took his youth and opened up the world to Trey. He continues to lie on the floor. His eyes remain closed. Trey's body is wet with sweat as he holds the box so tightly to his chest that it makes an imprint in his flesh. In those moments, it seems time has come and gone, and gone back again. Tom has come to this holy place to be with Trey one more time. He feels Tom's spirit wash over him like warm rain, then move in him to touch Trey's very core.

It has been years since a prayer was sent to God inside these stone walls. Now, one has been answered. Trey returns to his feet. The empty shell of the church amplifies the sounds of his footsteps as he walks across the floor of the still sanctuary. In a few hours the Abbey will be filled with men; many unknowingly will come to celebrate the life of Tom. They are coming to a tea dance, and as long as the DJ is good, the liquor flowing and the drugs plentiful, they will dance and party. It is how Trey wants to say good-bye. He will celebrate Tom's life as the dance music fills the rafters where the echoes of angelic choirs from around the world once raised their voices to praise the Lord.

Trey wishes Tom had not decided to exit the dance floor by filling his gut with pills and booze. The loss saddens him still, and will forever leave a void. The dance floor is for everyone, young and old, he thinks. The music is awash, covering all those who come to dance. For the time they are here to worship the music, they become all the same as it permeates their bodies, reaching deep into their souls. Trey wants to believe that life is a symphony of songs, each one to be cherished from year to year and decade to decade until death.

He makes his way to the electrical box. At the flip of a switch the huge dusty chandeliers explode with flickering lights. Within the hour, the crew will come to set up for the party. On this eve there will be a different congregation. Hundreds of worshipers, their shirts off with high spirits and eyes wide, will each claim a spot and fill this now-quiet holy place. The bare bodies and pounding music will melt together in celebration of life, as the music plays well into the early morning of another day.

Trey makes several steps up to the altar to an ornate podium high above the hall. Once it served as a platform, where the gospel was spoken to God-fearing men, women and children. Now it stands silent, as it has been for years. He sets the box inside it for later.

◊

A line began to form outside the Abbey doors at seven p. m. Thirty minutes later it wraps around the block. Trey bought a full page ad in both of the popular Atlanta gay magazines to announce the tea dance in honor of Tom. The ad stated it was a free event, requesting donations to benefit the local gay youth group. Tom was buying the drinks.

The event organizers Trey hired totally transformed the place in a matter of hours. At least a hundred disco balls hang from the rafters, seemingly endlessly spinning in the air. Red, purple, blue, gold and white lights reflect off the tiny square mirrors showering the Abbey in a continuous rain of prismatic color. Four temporary stages are erected on the sanctuary floor for very buff young strippers. Go-Go boys hired by Trey will assume the position high atop those erected platforms, and they will dance to entertain the departing spirit of Tom, as well as the massive crowd of drooling men.

At midnight the Abbey is packed. It is like no other party this town has seen in a long while; the boys are pouring in by the truckloads. It seems like the party will never end. Trey has offered to make a hefty donation to the local fire department to keep the fire marshal happy. By a stroke of luck, Trey managed to locate Bobby, the DJ from the old Backstreet days. He had not been on the scene for several years, but Trey has brought him out of retirement for the night.

Trey feels he has come full circle in some respects after so many years. Now he is back dancing in a sea of men as the music rings out. Part of what is left of the physical Tom is in a box inside the podium. For a few moments, Trey has forgotten this is a memorial. He scrolls back through the years as he sees his reflection in the eyes of the men surrounding him on the floor. He feels free again, the freedom of youth rises in his blood. For a brief period of time, he feels the past years have never happened. They are discarded on the other side of the big old arched wooden doors of the Abbey with the rest of reality. With them is Tom's suicide and Kyle's indiscretions, and every disappointment and unfulfilled dream. They are outside those doors along with every moment of heartache and all the feelings of loss.

Inside, Trey wants to never leave again, like he did night after night when he first found a place on the dance floor. He never wants to walk out those doors into a world he cannot understand. He feels safe as he dances to the music and with the strangers.

Like Tom, he knows the lights will eventually come on at some point. It is something he knows he cannot control, but for now, he closes his eyes and he dances as his body is rubbed and bumped by the other dancers. Trey still carries the reality of the past somewhere in the back of his mind. Unable to totally block it out along with the memories of Tom and Kyle, Trey wants to believe that Tom's spirit is dancing with everyone, that somehow in death, Tom has shed his aging body and is now reborn. He wonders if Kyle will show up.

Trey stops dancing and makes his way toward the podium to retrieve Tom's ashes. In all these years, nothing has really changed, he thinks, as he climbs the stairs to the balcony. At the top, he stands at the railing overlooking all the shirtless bodies.

Some guys are leaning over the balcony waving glow sticks – well, maybe those are somewhat new, he thinks — to the music, while others are making out and who knows what in the darkened corners. He looks at his watch, straining to see the time. It is almost three-twelve a. m. If it were eight months and sixteen days earlier, it would have been Tom's sixtieth birthday. He checks his watch again, hoping Bobby will remember to play the song he requested at exactly three-fifteen.

All of a sudden, the music slows as does the flashing lights. Bobby remembered. The most important song of the night — at least for Trey — begins to play: Donna Summer's *Carry On*. A bolt of arousing approval moves through the crowd. Trey holds the box close to his chest as he watches the men dancing below. A few more seconds into the song, he slowly opens it; then, as if in slow motion, with arm extended over the multitude, Trey sets Tom's ashes free over the sea of men. Tears fill his eyes as they snow down on the crowd. One starry-eyed young gorgeous blond looks up at the falling ash, watching it float down. He opens his mouth wide in amazement. Tom has come home.

Trey feels a hand on his shoulder. He turns around. It is Kyle. The DJ begins to mix in *Last Dance*.

Author's Note

Some have made it this far. They have ridden the hands of time finding themselves decades older. Was it a matter of luck, or precaution or both? I am not sure of the right answer, or even if one exists. Perhaps it is a game of balance, crossing the tightrope of life from birth to death. For some reason, or many, those reading these words have remained, their lungs still drawing breath and hearts beating, pushing blood through their bodies. A good number of friends were taken too early, mostly by AIDS, while others fell victim to drugs, overdosing in dark rooms. Some drank themselves to death and others died by their own hands. Many died still young on the inside, young in years, but old and frail on the outside with young eyes looking out of old tired bodies. As all of us still here, they were searching for something, and when some had lost hope in ever finding it, they just gave up, without really knowing they had given in and fallen off the rope of life that ties all of us together.

Life does goes on, as they say. Time moves forward as the years collect under our belts and on our chins. Unwelcome by most, its first undetectable approach slowly covers once-smooth young flesh, the layering years of lies and truths eventually turning it hard and coarse. Skin that was formerly soft to the touch and with a satisfying taste takes on a different texture and flavor. With such transformations come realizations not easily swallowed.

There is no stopping the cycle. At moments, I am unsure I am happy to have remained. A part of me thinks those passed have left me behind, while they have gone on to a better place. As for me, I have seen lots of change in my life's search and I do not believe I have found what I am searching for. Perhaps that is why I am still here standing at the midpoint of life. What is in the past is frozen behind me, as it should be, and what waits ahead, I can still call the future. Hope tells me there is something good waiting as another day awakens the dark sky and I slowly slip from the comfort of down and damask sheets. Onward I go into another day of life. It has come fast, this midpoint. Faster than I imagined it would. Maybe faster than it should have. But none-the less, it is here.

In my early years, I had always been told to cherish my youth — how fast it slips through your hands — by one older person or another. Live your life while you are young so there are few, if any, regrets in old age. Of course, those were just words then, and I was much younger than those sharing with me their secrets of life. Even still, I knew this day would come. It is something to be grateful for, even in the youth-oriented society in which we live.

So many others — too many — who started out with me, did not make it to this point of life. It is for their sake that I must embrace this midpoint and cherish it for them. If given a choice, surely they would have wanted to be here with me; and, of course, I wish they were here to cross over this tightrope into the rest of our lives. It would be a greater journey savored with the like of my contemporaries still here with me. Their names are still in my address book as if their information was recently entered. Page after page of names and addresses, phone numbers with notes of birthdays jotted to the side, listed among those still living. Only, their numbers have been reissued to others, their address now belong to different people. But there, undisturbed, they are still in that address book on my desk, seemingly just a phone call away.

Funny, or maybe not, when I was in my early twenties, it seemed that the late-forties would be a lifetime away. Now they have come and are knocking loudly on my door. I must greet them as if a cherished friend is standing in their place waiting to be welcomed inside.

Years from now, if you see an older man dancing in the center of the floor, just throw him a smile and keep dancing. He may appear to be dancing alone, but that is far from the visual reality. This stranger will be dancing with all his buddies passed, dancing for them.

DJ, spin the music, everybody dance.

Acknowledgments

No one gets through this life alone. Whoever first stated that, and many reading this, know what I am referring to. As many of us have experienced, life can be full of struggles and roadblocks. I have always believed in the goodness of people and held the conviction we are on this earth to help one another, and that the light of love and compassion will keep the darkness away.

Personally there have been people and events that have caused me at times to lose faith. Some have made my journey extremely harder, whereupon I found myself at the lowest of possible places in a dark hole that seemed too impervious to climb out, and close to giving up on life. With each grasp on every rung of that invisible ladder back to the top and toward the light of day, I was able to get a little closer to overcoming great disappointment and loss, and once again find the way to believe in myself and in the dreams I have always carried in my heart. As a result, I was able to see the truth of what transpired and come to understand that there is truly a fine line between love and hate, and I have been reminded that what may seem as good on the outside is not always the case on the inside. I have learned two things: love is better, even if it appears one-sided, and love lingers long after the hate has been absorbed by the soul.

Because of this knowledge, there are several people I wish to thank for their support. Mace P., for his constant unwavering love. Mary S., for always showing up in my life at the right time. Will R., for your love and allowing me to see that you never know what good things await around the corner. Michael E., for your help, support and love. Don S., for your steadfast and valued friendship. Patricia C., for your struggles through a painful past. I hope you will persevere and make peace with it. Wil I., for always making me feel like I have a friend and dropping everything to come to my aid when I was falling apart. Alva L., because people like you do not come along often in life, and your father for making you the man you are today. Pat W., for listening when you knew all along I was talking in circles. Brian M., for the sun that shines every time you smile. Dr. P., because of your capacity for caring. My mother, because regardless of what the years have laid between us, you will always be my source of life. Margaret M., for your invaluable help on my first book. Megan S., for swimming through a sea of semicolons. Ed P., for bringing the cavalry. Philip R., for Outwrite Bookstore and Coffeehouse, the heartbeat of the Atlanta gay community. Also, Jeff J., Elaine E., Dr. Neil K., Cheryl H., Tony M., "the pretty one," Bill A., Nipper J., Joe W., and Jenna T.

I am grateful to all of you for believing in my abilities and helping me to believe in myself. Each one of you have played a part in making this book a reality. I have been blessed with loving friends. To all, you have my heartfelt gratitude.

A special thank you to my readers who had such wonderful things to say about my first book. You are one of the reasons I keep writing.

Printed in the United States
33822LVS00007B/40-45